"Who do you think you are?" Clair raged,

clinging to the rage like a lifeline. "Let go of me! Who do you think *I* am?"

With passion clouding his brain, Jake's temper flared. "I thought you were a woman who wants to get naked as much as I do."

Desire disappeared faster than gold in a mining camp. "You arrogant bastard! Get away from me! *Stay* far away from me!" She pulled free of him.

He looked momentarily taken aback, his eyes wide with suppressed passion. "Woman, you can curse me all you want, but I know what was happening here. You want me as much as I want you."

Without thinking, Clair reached back and swung at him, but he caught her hand, trapping it in his larger one. Black eyes locked with blue, and then he released her.

"Stay away from me!" she flung at him, and with a flounce of black cotton, she spun on her heel and stormed up the stairs.

Dear Reader,

Known for her moving and dramatic Westerns, award-winning author Susan Amarillas's new book, *Wild Card,* is the story of a lady gambler who is hiding in a remote Wyoming town, terrified that the local sheriff will discover she's wanted for murder in Texas. Susan's last two books have won her 5★ ratings from *Affaire de Coeur,* which has described her as "...well on her way to becoming the queen of the frontier romance." Don't miss your chance to read her new story.

Talented newcomer Lyn Stone is back with her second book, *The Arrangement,* a unique and touching story about a young female gossip columnist who sets out to expose a notorious composer and winds up first agreeing to marry him, *then* falling in love with him. Kit Gardner's *The Untamed Heart,* a Western with a twist, has a refined English hero who happens to be an earl, and a feisty, ranch hand heroine who can do anything a man can do, only better.

This month also brings us a new concept for Harlequin Historicals, our first in-line short-story collection, *The Knights of Christmas.* Three of our award-winning authors, Suzanne Barclay, Margaret Moore and Deborah Simmons, have joined forces to create a Medieval Christmas anthology that is sure to spread cheer all year long.

Whatever your tastes in reading, we hope you enjoy all four books, available wherever Harlequin Historicals are sold.

Sincerely,

Tracy Farrell
Senior Editor

Please address questions and book requests to:
Harlequin Reader Service
U.S.: 3010 Walden Ave., P.O. Box 1325, Buffalo, NY 14269
Canadian: P.O. Box 609, Fort Erie, Ont. L2A 5X3

SUSAN AMARILLAS

WILD CARD

Harlequin Books

TORONTO • NEW YORK • LONDON
AMSTERDAM • PARIS • SYDNEY • HAMBURG
STOCKHOLM • ATHENS • TOKYO • MILAN
MADRID • WARSAW • BUDAPEST • AUCKLAND

ISBN 0-373-28988-X

WILD CARD

This edition published by arrangement with Harlequin Books S.A.

® and TM are trademarks of the publisher. Trademarks indicated with ® are registered in the United States Patent and Trademark Office, the Canadian Trade Marks Office and in other countries.

Printed in U.S.A.

Books by Susan Amarillas

Harlequin Historicals

Snow Angel #165
Silver and Steel #233
Scanlin's Law #283
Wyoming Renegade #351
Wild Card #388

SUSAN AMARILLAS

was born and raised in Maryland and moved to California when she married. She quickly discovered her love of the high desert country—she says it was as if she were "coming home." When she's not writing, she and her husband love to travel the back roads of the West, visiting ghost towns and little museums, and always coming home with an armload of books. She enjoys hearing from readers. You may write to her at the address below.

Susan Amarillas
P.O. Box 951056
Mission Hills, CA 91395

To my editor, Margaret Marbury, for her skill, her patience and her encouragement. Thanks, Margaret. You're simply the best.

Prologue

Texas 1879

The gun fell from her hand....

The sheriff's body slipped silently to the floor....

Heart racing, Clair watched as the crimson stain on the man's shirt grew steadily larger. With every frantic beat of her heart she backed away, one faltering step after another. This couldn't be happening. It couldn't. Her mind denied the reality of the gruesome scene.

Panic overcame all other thought.

Run!

She flung open the door and slammed full force into the chest of Buck Hilliard, deputy sheriff. He grabbed her hard, his fingers digging painfully into her shoulders through the torn cotton of her dress, his steely gaze focused on the body beside the bed.

"You bitch," he snarled. "You've killed him."

"I didn't," she managed to say, though it was obvious to anyone, including her, that was exactly what she had done. Dimly she realized all sound in the saloon below had stopped.

"Hey," a man's voice called up. "Who's shootin' up there?"

She met the deputy's icy blue eyes and she knew she was doomed. Every muscle in her body tensed wire tight. Blood pounded in her neck and her temples. He had her. Trial, jail...and worse.

Terror merged with a lifetime of self-preservation. "Let me go!" she ordered, struggling as she did.

He was still staring at the body when, without a word, he did just that. He let her go. She didn't wait to ask questions. She shouldered past him and raced full-out toward the rear door, her red satin skirt hitched up around her knees.

Behind her, she heard the men clamoring up the stairs, their voices raised in question, heard the creak of door hinges as someone upstairs probably looked out. The sound of another shot increased her panic.

She glanced back quickly and didn't see anyone. The deputy was gone—inside the room, most likely, she thought in the fleeting instant before she yanked open the back door.

Down the outside stairs she sprinted, taking them two at a time, the weathered wood creaking and flexing under each urgent step.

Run!

Escape was her only choice. They'd never believe *her*. Not her, not when their sheriff was dead on the floor of her room.

Down the dark alley between the buildings she fled, careful to keep in the shadows.

She lost her balance in the soft earth. Her hand

slammed against the wood siding of the wall and she got a palmful of splinters for her effort.

"Where is she?" a man's angry voice shouted from the doorway above.

There was no turning back now, no time for explanations.

"Find her!" came another's voice. "She's killed the sheriff."

Like the answer to an unspoken prayer, she spotted several horses tied to a hitching rail in the street. Wild-eyed, her body shaking with fear, she plunged out into the open street.

"There she is!" a man yelled, and she turned in time to see him pointing at her from his place near the saloon doors. Lamplight shone through the windows and landed in a yellow-white square in the center of the street.

She darted through the light—no sense pretending they didn't know where she was. Her only hope now was that damned horse.

She grabbed a fistful of mane and rein and somehow managed to swing up into the saddle.

Angry men surrounded her, pulling at her, grabbing her.

"Get away from me!" she screamed, slapping, pushing anything she could think of.

The horse twisted and whirled like the beginning of a tornado. Clair hung on for her life.

"Murderer!" a man shouted, leaping up to clutch her arm, his fingers clamping on to her wrist.

She kicked him in the chest with her foot. Stunned, he fell back, landing in the dirt. At the same instant she drove her heels rib-cracking hard into the horse's sides.

The animal reared up, screaming its protest—and hers, it seemed. Men scrambled clear of the flying hooves.

She spotted the opening and raced through and into the night.

Chapter One

Wyoming 1879

It was hard to say anything good about Broken Spur. Of course the same was true for most of the cattle towns west of the Mississippi, and in the three months since she'd fled from Texas Clair felt as though she'd seen every single one of them.

But this was a first time for her in Wyoming. As for Broken Spur, it was a quarter mile of dirt street as bumpy as the bark on a cedar tree, if there'd been any cedar trees, which there weren't. There were no trees at all, not as far as anyone could see, and that was clear to hell and gone, it seemed.

Tired, back aching, Clair squinted up at the late-afternoon sun and, shielding her eyes, couldn't help thinking that a little shade would be nice right about now. That sun was darned hot on this navy blue dress of hers. Little beads of perspiration formed on her back and trickled down her spine inside her corset in an annoying itch she couldn't scratch. And she wondered for about the millionth time in her life what fiendish mind had devised this instrument of female torture.

The stage driver handed over her carpetbag. "Thanks," she said with a smile. "Are there any saloons in town?"

The husky driver gave her a wide-eyed look of astonishment. "Ma'am?" he muttered, snatching off his hat to wipe perspiration from his forehead with a red bandanna. "Excuse me. Did you say saloons?"

Absently she brushed at the dust coating the front of her dress. "Yes. Are there any?"

He slapped his hat back on his head, tugging on the brim as he did. "Well, yes, ma'am there's two. The...ah, Lazy Dog over there—" he pointed across the street and south "—and the Scarlet Lady two doors down the other way on this side."

A mischievous little smile pulled at the corners of her mouth. "Thanks," she replied without further explanation. She couldn't help chuckling. She always took a little perverse pleasure in making men wonder what she was about.

She hefted her one and only carpetbag and started off down the sun-bleached pine of the sidewalk, taking care not to catch her foot or hem on the uneven boards. Her heels made a steady clip-clop as she went.

She passed several people, women mostly, and she smiled. "Afternoon." She kept walking, glancing in store windows as she did, checking her appearance in the reflection there. Not bad, she thought, adjusting her hat a little more to the left, brushing at her skirt front again. It was a miracle she looked decent, considering she'd been bouncing around on that stage for the better part of three days now.

She was tired and dirty and would have sold her soul for a hot bath and a soft bed. But business first.

She passed Nelson's Grocery, with a sign in the window proclaiming a sale on yard goods, then angled across the street in front of Nellie's Restaurant. The smell of freshly baked apple pie made her stomach growl, reminding her she hadn't eaten since breakfast.

Lunch later, she promised herself, glancing over her shoulder at the restaurant as though to cement the pledge in her mind. A couple of cowboys rattled past in a buckboard loaded with crates; they tipped their hats and she nodded her response.

The Lazy Dog was the last building on this end of the street, and she paused outside to give the place a quick once-over. It was large, square and reasonably well cared for. A one-story false-front with an alley separating it from the other buildings. The name of the establishment was emblazoned in a curve of faded red letters on the front window. Being cautious, she looked in through the glass trying to get a feel for the place, trying to make sure if there was anyone in there she wanted to...avoid.

Pushing open the doors, she walked inside and got the usual double take from the three cowboys seated at a table near the end of the bar. The man behind the bar had a scowl cold enough to freeze milk. She didn't speak to anyone, just scanned the room.

The floor was bare. That was good; she always hated sawdust clinging to her skirt. The place looked pretty quiet, but it was only afternoon—around three, she thought—and saloons didn't really come alive until after sundown when the men finished working.

A mahogany bar took up the length of one wall,

and six—no, eight—tables were scattered around the room. The wallpaper was so faded the dark flowers dissolved into the cream-colored background. A half dozen stuffed animal heads decorated the walls—elk mostly, and one antelope. Over the bar there was a painting of a well-endowed nude.

The air smelled stale and acrid from too much tobacco and whiskey and sweat.

The barkeep was a slick-haired little guy who was staring at her with all the fierceness of a bulldog. He toyed with his flimsy excuse for a mustache that appeared to have enough wax to make a candle jealous. She took an instant dislike to the man.

Arms braced on the bar's surface, he leaned forward, his white shirtsleeves pulling tight against his wrists. "Lady, if you're on one of them temperance crusades you can save your trouble and just move on," he told her in a voice that rubbed on her nerves. "This here is a saloon, not a sideshow. So just turn your behind around and sashay right on out of here."

The three cowboys lounged back in their chairs, laughing.

"Come on, lady," the barman prompted. He made a shooing gesture with his hand. "Or do I have to come around this bar and move you out?"

Clair hesitated for a full five seconds. His type always rankled her and she was tempted to tell him just what she thought of him. But she didn't. She didn't want any trouble. She didn't want to attract any…unpleasant attention to herself, all things considered. So she bit back her deliciously sharp retort and merely said, "Too bad, mister. It's your loss."

Turning on her heel, she strode out the door, which

she slammed just as hard as she could. Hey, she had to do something with that temper of hers, didn't she?

Outside, the sun was high overhead. A pair of blackbirds perched on a hitching rail squawked but didn't move as she went past. She skirted a supply wagon parked in front of Hansen's Hardware and cut across the street, the dirt marble-hard against her shoes.

A breeze tugged at her upswept hair and she had to fuss with pushing a stray lock back under the rim of her hat.

On down Front Street she continued purposefully toward the opposite end of town and the only other saloon Broken Spur had to offer. This one was two stories and shared a common wall with Brownell's Feed and Grain, and it sure looked the worse for wear. The outside was raw wood, weathered and cracked from too much sun and too little paint. The one large window hadn't been washed since Noah was a boy, judging by the dirt and mud splattered there.

Over the doorway someone had nailed up a hand-made sign proclaiming this to be the Scarlet Lady Saloon. Scarlet Lady, huh? Sounded good to her.

Feeling a little more confident, she pushed open the door and went inside. It took a couple of seconds and a little blinking for her eyes to adjust to the darkness.

The place was pretty much the same layout as the first, though this one was more rectangular than square. The bar ran the length of the left side of the room and the walls had the added elegance, if you could call it that, of wainscot halfway up—though it was anyone's guess what kind of wood it was, it was so black with dirt and stains.

The nose-stinging scent of unemptied spittoons permeated the air, and dust motes drifted in the sunlight that managed to filter inside.

A dozen tables were mismatched with an equally odd assortment of chairs. The floor hadn't seen the business end of a mop in a week of Sundays. A big yellow dog, with a tail as long as a whip, was licking up beer from under one of the chairs.

With a heft of the carpetbag, which was getting heavier by the minute, she walked over to the bar, careful to keep her distance from those spittoons, and tried not to look at the paintings of nudes on the wall.

"Afternoon," she said to the rotund man who was eyeing her suspiciously.

"Lady, you sure you're in the right place? This ain't no tea parlor." His Adam's apple bobbed up and down as he spoke. His black vest tugged dangerously at the buttons holding it closed over his bulging stomach.

"I'm sure." Well, at least he was being civil—sort of. Better than the other place. She was hopeful.

She let the carpetbag drop to the floor with a thud, glad to put the thing down for a while. She flexed her fingers to work out the cramps.

"You ain't temperance, is you?" the man prompted.

"No. Not temperance."

He seemed to think on it for a moment, then shrugged. "Okay, girlie. It's up to you." He wiped at a spot in front of her on the bar. "What can I do for you?"

"I think it's more what I can do for you."

Clair turned around and surveyed the room again. It was dark, dingy, with paint peeling from the ceiling over near the front doors. Common sense said she should swallow her pride and go back to the other place—at least there were customers there. This place was clearly the poorest of the two, the underdog.

Ah, well, now, she always did have a weakness for underdogs. Probably because she'd always been one herself. Besides, she thought with a ghost of a smile, how could she walk away from a place called the Scarlet Lady?

Instead, she said, "Business slow?"

The man stopped his cleaning. "A little. You gonna order, or what?"

Clair had worked in saloons a long time and she knew her way around men—most of the time. Taking her hat off, she slid the long hat pin through the blue satin, then put it lightly on the bar in front of her. "What do you do for entertainment around here?"

"Huh?" He raked her with an explicit gaze. "Why, honey," he said in a voice rich with innuendo, "you don't look the type. You lookin' for a job...girlie?" His mouth quirked up in a lecherous excuse for a smile that revealed a broken front tooth.

Clair didn't falter. She was in her element. She did, however, put him straight. "I don't do *that* kind of work."

His smile disappeared faster than the setting sun. "What kind, then?" He went back to rubbing that same spot on the bar. "I don't need no one to clean and—"

"That point is debatable, but if you'd like to increase your business I suggest having someone to play cards."

If thoughts were sounds she would have sworn she heard the wheels turning; she half expected to see steam coming out of his ears. "Cards?" he muttered, rubbing his beard-stubbled double chins.

She knew the instant the whole picture came together in his mind. His eyes widened and he regarded her with new interest. "You?" Incredulity was obvious in his baritone voice.

"Me." Without hesitation, she produced a deck of cards from her drawstring reticule and thumbed the ends, making a fluttering sound like a stick on the spokes of a wagon wheel.

"I like a game of cards as much as any man, girlie, but…"

Crossing to a table, Clair dragged out a chair and sat down. "You name it and I can play it." She gestured for him to join her and he obliged. "Five-card all right with you?"

"Huh, yeah, sure."

She dealt and he watched like a man trying to keep track of the pea under the walnut shells.

They played six hands.

She won six hands.

He frowned. "You think you're pretty slick, don't you?"

"I think I'm good, if that's what you mean."

Clearly he wasn't a man who liked to be bested. "Hold on there." He retrieved a fresh deck from a drawer behind the bar and slit the seal with his dirty thumbnail. "Let's try that again…with *my* deck."

"Okay," she agreed. "You deal this time." She wanted him to know that she was good, not a cheat.

Up till now there'd been no money wagered. Clair was merely demonstrating, proving her ability to do what she said she could do. Men liked the notion of taking on a woman. They got all loud and know-it-all and took for granted that they could win.

Mostly, Clair was lucky. Though ever since Texas, well, her luck had taken a turn for the worse. Now, there was an understatement if ever she'd heard one. Ever since Texas her luck had been harder to find than an ace high straight. All of which was why her bankroll consisted of exactly fifty-seven dollars. Not a lot when you have to be your own banker.

"One dollar," the man said, tossing the money on the table.

"Look, we don't have to—"

"One dollar. Put up or shut up."

Reluctantly, Clair matched his bet.

Six more hands and she was up by eight dollars, which was a lot of money; it was a week's room rent and a couple of dinners.

Could it be? Was her luck changing? Something was happening. She glanced appreciatively around the worn-out saloon once more. Maybe it was one Scarlet Lady to another, this change in her luck. Whatever it was, she wasn't going to question it, just enjoy it.

When he started to deal another round, she stopped him with a touch on his sleeve. "So how about it?"

The barkeep lounged back, folding his hands over his barrel chest like a man in a coffin. He looked at the cards that he'd been dealing and the money still on the table. His gaze rose. "You been gambling long?"

"Long enough," she told him, not willing to give him her personal history, not after Texas. Absently she shuffled the cards, feeling more at home with them in her hands.

He cocked his head to one side. "I don't want no trouble. Women and saloons—"

"There won't be any trouble. Just more business...which it looks as though you could use." She lounged back, the chair creaking as she did.

"I suppose." He let out a long, slow, thoughtful breath. "I ain't bankrolling you. You understand that?"

"I'll play for myself. Whatever I make I keep. You get the extra business at the bar. Having me here won't cost you anything."

"When do you want to start?"

"Tonight."

He gave a sharp nod. "Okay."

"Okay." She beamed and shook his paw of a hand. "My name's Clair."

"Bill Mullen."

"Nice to meet you, Bill. You are the owner, right?"

"Yeah." He stood and started for the bar.

She picked up the money. "Is there a boarding-house?"

"Addie Hocksettler's. Middle of the street, blue clapboard. Sign's in front," he added.

"By the Lazy Dog, right?"

He glanced back over his shoulder. "You know Slocum?"

She frowned. "Who?"

"Slocum. Beady-eyed little runt. Owns the saloon."

"We've met."

His expression turned dark. "Say...did he send you here? 'Cause if he did—"

"No one sends me anywhere." She cut across his

words. "I met a man—I guess it was him—a while ago. We *didn't* hit it off."

Mullen made a derisive sound in the back of his throat. "Man's been trying to run me outta here for—" He broke off, as though thinking better of what he was saying. Not that she cared about his troubles—she had more than enough of her own. All she wanted was a place to do her work for a few nights, maybe a week, if business was good. She put her hat on, adjusting the pin in her upswept hair. "I take it you and Slocum aren't friends."

Mullen circled behind the bar. "One of these days I'm gonna..." He looked at her directly, straightening as he did. "You said tonight."

"I'll be here." She picked up her carpetbag.

"I'll tell the boys when they come in," he called to her as she headed for the door. "And I'll be wanting to get them eight dollars back."

"You're welcome to try," she said as she stepped outside, a smile on her lips.

Thank you, Scarlet Lady.

By seven she was comfortably seated at the table nearest the window and in plain view through both the window and the propped-open front doors. The place was empty, but it was the first of the month and payday. The cowboys from the local ranches should be coming into town—at least, that's what Bill had told her when she'd returned from getting settled in her room at the boardinghouse.

She'd pressed the creases out of her working dress—burgundy satin, black lace trim, cut low enough in front to be, what was the French—oh, yes, risqué. Part of the image, she confirmed, fluffing the lace.

She wore no jewelry—didn't have any to wear, having lost it and everything else when she'd fled an angry mob.

"Get her!"

"Murderer!"

Clair blinked hard against the sudden terrifying words and forced herself to focus on the reality of the present. She was here, a long way from Texas, a long way from that grim night.

You can't change the past.

That was for sure. Besides, things had taken a turn for the better. Why, she hadn't been in this town but a few hours and already she had a place to work and was up eight dollars.

Not bad. Not bad at all. Seven of those newly won dollars had gone toward a week's rent at the boardinghouse, so her bankroll was untouched—an important factor for her these days.

"Feels like rain." Bill's gruff voice broke into her musings. "I'm getting mighty tired of rain. You know, it never rains in California in the summer and there's places there where it never snows. Ain't that something?"

"So I've heard." She glanced up to see him standing at the doorway, peering out at the darkening sky. "I guess this means it'll be a slow night."

Bill only shrugged in answer.

"Maybe the rain will hold off," she said hopefully. Rain meant muddy roads, which meant that cowboys couldn't get to town. All she needed was a couple of good days. She wasn't asking for much, no million-dollar bets, just enough to get her to the next town and the one after that and the one after that....

Shaking her head to dispel her dismal thought, she dealt the cards out on the table, her fingers brushing over the gouged surface as she did.

Bill wandered over, his boots thudding on the floor. "Solitaire?"

"Keeps my fingers nimble."

With a nod, Bill went to light the three kerosene lamps suspended from the ceiling down the center of the room. The metal shades clinked against the glass as he worked.

Red six on the black seven...

She glanced hopefully toward the street, scanning the sky beyond. The air felt damp and heavy, quiet, as though in anticipation of something. An involuntary shiver shimmied over her skin and she tensed against the feeling. This was silly. *She* was being silly. Still, the feeling of eerie foreboding lingered just a minute longer.

Black eight on the red nine...

You're just jumpy, tired, is all.

Yes, sure, that was all.

Red queen on the black king...

As she played the cards, her nerves calmed. Cards and saloons. It seemed as though she'd spent most of her life sitting in a saloon somewhere playing cards and waiting; waiting for that big hand, waiting for enough money to buy her own place, waiting to settle down.

Settle down, now where had that come from?

Probably being on the run, that's where.

Why was it a person always wanted the one thing they couldn't have? Sometimes, late at night, she'd lie awake feeling alone, wondering about the future. Times like that she would have liked to have someone to turn to, someone to lean on.

It'll take more than luck for that to happen.

Red two on the black three...

Yes, she knew about luck and the lack of it. Clair was a realist and she had absolutely no illusions about who she was or what she did for a living. She crossed her legs, and the satin of her dress rustled as she adjusted the skirt under the confines of the table.

There were those, she knew, who objected to gambling and drinking and other vices mostly attributed to men. She understood it was easier to blame the temptation—namely her—than the man. But men had been drinking and gambling long before she was born, and they'd probably be doing the same long after she was dead and buried.

If she'd had more choices maybe she'd have done something else, something more...respectable. But there weren't a lot of choices for women, not poor women, anyway, and Clair Travers had been born dirt-poor in New Orleans. She'd never known her father, and her mother—a good woman—had taken in laundry to try to make ends meet. Clair had seen her mother age ten years for every one on the calendar. She was old by thirty and dead by thirty-seven, and at fourteen Clair had been left alone to fend for herself or starve.

So *she'd* done laundry and cleaned houses. She'd gotten barely enough to live on, and more than a tolerable amount of groping from the "gentlemen" of the house for all her trouble.

Well, she wasn't going to end up like her mother, and when that temper of hers had made her dump a pan of scrub water on a certain banker, she'd quit or been fired, depending on whose version you believed. Out of work, with no references, those few choices of hers had disappeared like snow in July.

She'd begged, borrowed and even stolen food when she'd had no other choice. It was something she wasn't proud of but, dammit, she was nothing if not a survivor. She'd slept in stables and alleys and abandoned buildings, always looking for that better way— always refusing to sell her body as so many women did in desperation. After a year, she'd begun to think there was no hope, that she, like her mother, was doomed to a life of subsistence, only to die early and probably be glad for going.

Then one day she'd seen the boys shooting dice on the dock. Intrigued, she'd stood by and watched. It was a simple game and she'd caught on quickly enough. Like a true gambler, she'd wagered her last three cents on a throw of the dice and won. Another throw and another win. Two more and she was up twenty-five cents and grinning ear-to-ear.

She was a natural, they'd told her. After that she was there on that dock every day. It didn't take her long to figure out that the boys came around because they were intrigued playing against a scrap of a girl who always seemed to win. It got to be like a badge of honor with them, trying to beat her.

But luckily for her, they couldn't—not most of the time, at least—so they'd challenged her to other games: poker, monte and faro. She learned fast, got cheated a few times in the beginning, but only a few. She'd learned to defend herself. Yes, Clair had learned to fight and to win, to do whatever it took to stay alive.

By the time she was seventeen, she was playing poker in a local saloon and making a living—not a great living, but she was off the streets and had three meals a day.

Over the past eight years she'd played in saloons and gambling halls all over the West. She played poker and she played fair. Oh, not that she couldn't have cheated—she could. But she didn't need to. She was that good. Even if she hadn't been as good as she was, well, there was a thing called ethics.

Yes, the lady gambler had ethics. She might have had to fight and scratch for everything she got, but she was no liar and no cheat—a matter of pride.

Black nine on the red ten...

Two cowboys wandered in. They stopped dead in their tracks and stared at her as though she were a three-legged heifer.

A nervous flutter moved through her stomach. These days, strangers always gave her an anxious moment until she realized she didn't know them—that they weren't the law. "Good evening, gentlemen." Pulling the cards into a neat stack, she smiled sweetly. "You gentlemen play poker?"

What do you know, they did. So did about a dozen more who filled the Scarlet Lady that night. The rain held off and business was good. She was winning. For the first time in months, she was winning. A smile threatened, but she held it back, afraid of jinxing her new found luck.

She just dealt the cards, made small talk and collected her money. Cowboys stayed a few hands, then left. Bill strolled by every so often, paused to watch a hand or two, then ambled away. She figured he was checking on her, and that was fine. She didn't mind.

Occasionally she'd see him at the bar, talking, taking a drink or two with the customers.

"That's it for me, ma'am," a young cowboy said. Scraping the remains of his money into his hand, he left.

Bill surprised her when he plopped down in the vacated chair. "Uh, Bill, shouldn't you be watching the bar?"

"Bar's fine," he replied, his bushy brows drawn down almost to one. Before Clair could argue the point, he banged a handful of money on the table— a mix of coins and notes—and an open bottle of whiskey, one-third empty. Judging by his red-eyed appearance, she knew exactly where that missing liquor had gone.

Seeing Bill at the table got everyone's attention. Men who'd been at the bar and other tables moved in. The four other men seated at Clair's table scooted forward, eyes wide, giving everyone a closer view of what was about to happen—whatever that was.

Clair coughed slightly as a puff of smoke circled her head like a gray cloud. The pungent scent of several unwashed bodies permeated her nostrils. Apparently some of these boys didn't adhere to the notion of a weekly bath.

Bill spoke up, his deep voice loud enough for all to hear. "I been watching you all night and I figure I can beat you now." His chin came up in a defiant gesture that got him several pats on the back from those who'd lost a little money over the past few hours.

Clair studied him through narrowed eyes. Under any other circumstances she wouldn't refuse a man so intent on playing, but this was Bill, the owner. It didn't take a genius to figure out that losing to a woman gambler would make him angry, *had* made him angry. If he got his tail in a knot, he'd be bound to send her packing just to save face. He might even call the law, claim he was cheated or such. No, this definitely wasn't a good idea.

"Bill," she began in what she hoped was a sweet, soothing voice, "I'd rather not play against you."

Bill obviously got the wrong impression. His grin got Cheshire-cat big and there was another chorus of encouragement from those gathered. Damn, this wasn't working.

"I got you scared, huh?" Bill announced triumphantly to her and those backing him up. He dropped a fresh deck of cards on the table in front of him and took a swig of that whiskey straight out of the bottle. "You ain't gettin' outta here without me winnin' back some o' that money you owe me." He slit the seal and pulled out the cards with a flourish. A quick shuffle and he removed the jokers from the deck.

"You tell her, Bill," one cowboy said.

"You can win," another added.

There was a general egging-on all around.

Now, Clair didn't mind a little heckling, didn't mind the men watching, but she did object to the implication that she owed him money. "I won that money fair, Bill. I don't *owe* you anything." Clair shoved back her chair, moving about an inch before she rammed into a lanky cowboy who was intent on leaning over her shoulder.

"Do you mind?" she prompted, assuming he'd step back. He didn't. She felt cornered, trapped, and the first stirrings of unease swirled in her stomach like storm clouds.

"Come on. Come on," Bill was demanding. "You ain't backin' out." He took another long swig of whiskey from the bottle and put it down with a thud. Liquor trickled out of the corners of his mouth and he wiped his face with the back of his hand.

Muscles clenched along Clair's bare shoulders. "I'm tired, Bill. How about later? Tomorrow night?" She tried to stand, pushing harder against her chair with the backs of her legs, and this time managing enough room to rise. She reached for her money. "I was just thinking about calling it a night when—"

"Oh, no, you don't, woman." Bill grabbed her hand to stop her, his rough fingers clamping tight around her wrist. Fear exploded in her and she jerked free.

"Don't!" she flared. "I don't like to be touched."

Bill rose out of his chair to mirror her stance. "You ain't gettin' outta here without dealing them cards."

Bill was staring at her, and so were eight or ten cowboys—she was in no mood to count Stetsons. Their expressions ranged from daring to smug confidence.

Damn. This wasn't good. Why the devil wouldn't the man take no for an answer? By tomorrow he'd be sober, and grateful she'd refused to play him. Sagging down in the chair, she tried again. "Look, Bill, what say we do this tomorrow when you're…more yourself."

He sat down, his eyes never leaving hers. "Nope," he said, punctuating his refusal by slamming his hand, hard, on the tabletop. Money sprang upward like Mexican jumping beans. "What's the matter? Afraid?" He earned himself another round of encouragement and back slapping.

She was trapped. If she did this, she'd be out of a job. If she didn't, she'd be branded as unfair or worse by those watching and her chance of playing cards in this town would be over before she got started.

This wasn't fair, not when her luck had just changed. A quick look around at the faces all staring at her told her she didn't have a choice.

"Okay." She relented, adjusting her skirt, the light catching on the satin and making it dance in shades of fiery red. "Two hands." She figured she'd try to placate him. Absently she traced a long, curving gouge in the tabletop.

"Five," Bill countered, his mouth pulled down in a grim expression that said he was determined.

Clair straightened. Her gaze flicked from one intent face to another, then back to Bill. "What is this, an auction? Two hands and then I'm done for the night." She wanted out, and she figured a couple of hands wouldn't get her into too much trouble.

"Five." Bill's tone was adamant.

Apprehension circled in Clair's brain. "Five," she reluctantly agreed. If she could keep the bets small, they could get this over with quickly. "Win or lose, that's all. *Right, Bill?*"

Bill's brown eyes widened with excitement. "Five." His head bobbed up and down like a pump handle and he was already reaching for the deck of cards. "Five."

"Show her, Bill," a wide-faced cowboy in a black Stetson prodded.

Thanks a lot, she thought but didn't say. She didn't object to Bill dealing—in fact, she preferred it. There'd be no arguments later about her cheating.

She beat him three out of four, and she guessed she

was up about twenty dollars, though she never counted her money at the table.

He kept looking around at all those frowning male companions, the ones he'd been so arrogant in front of, the ones who were never going to let him live this down. Never mind that most of them had also lost at least a few dollars to Clair—at least they'd been smart enough not to make a public spectacle of the losing.

"All right, Bill, last hand—*right?*" It was an order, not a question. She shifted in the chair, the wood rough against her bare skin above her dress. That acid in her stomach was swirling with tornado force. One more hand and she was out of this. Twenty dollars didn't seem so bad—surely he'd understand tomorrow.

Yes he might, but she knew these men wouldn't. Bill would be the talk of the town for months, and not pleasant talk, either.

He dealt the cards, five to each of them. Clair took a quick peek, careful not to reveal them to the onlookers, then put them facedown on the table again, her fingers lightly resting on the stiff paper.

Bill took a long gulp of whiskey, his Adam's apple moving up and down in his throat with each swallow, then slammed the bottle down with a bang on the table. "Bet fifty."

If the man had said "Bet a thousand" she couldn't have been any more surprised. "Five-dollar limit," she told him emphatically. She was so close to getting out of this reasonably unscathed.

"My saloon. My rules," he countered. "Fifty."

Those ogling cowboys all got openmouthed quiet. They crowded the table as though Bill was serving a free lunch and they didn't want to miss their share.

They pressed in so tightly she was actually bent forward, a belt buckle cutting into the base of her neck.

"Hey! Watch it!" she snapped, twisting and pushing the man back with the flat of her hand against his chest.

"Sorry," he, at least, had the good grace to mutter, though if he moved it was so fractional she could hardly tell.

Shaking her head, she turned and counted out the fifty dollars, which was a hell of a wager in any man's game.

"Cards?" Bill barked, the deck dwarfed in his big, clumsy hands.

Clair kept her gaze focused on his face. "I'll play these."

He hesitated the barest fraction of a second, his whiskey-hazed eyes honing in on hers. She never flinched, never looked away.

Finally he said, "I'll get one." He slapped the card down on the others with a force that threatened to tear the paper. Cautiously, like a man looking under a rock for a rattler, he picked up the cards and fanned them out. She knew the instant he got to that draw card. Something—excitement—flashed in his eyes. She had seen it often enough in men's faces.

So, she thought, he'd drawn whatever card it was he was wishing for. She figured he either had a straight, probably jack high, or four of a kind—couldn't be higher than tens.

He straightened in the chair and squared his shoulders beneath his stained white shirt. "A hundred."

"A hundred! Are you crazy?" She eyed that nearly empty bottle of whiskey. He was drunk as hell, that was for sure. "Now look, I—"

"What's the matter? Ain't up for a *real* game?" he mocked, and several cowboys laughed. The man was practically preening, he was so damned pleased with himself.

A leather-faced cowboy spoke up. "That's it, Bill. You've got her on the run now." There was more backslapping and grinning.

But Bill's smile melted faster than ice in summer when he looked down at his money. It was obvious he didn't have anywhere near a hundred dollars— thank goodness.

"You seem to be a little light there," she observed, thinking a hundred would clean her out if she lost.

Bill took another slug of liquid courage and said, "I'll just git the damned money." He lurched to his feet, swayed and grabbed the shoulder of a plaid-shirted man for support. "Watch my cards," he commanded, and several men nodded with all the solemnity of being asked to guard the bank vault.

Clair watched Bill make his way to the bar. She had to give the man credit—he walked as straight a line as any man in the place, a hell of a thing considering the amount of whiskey he'd consumed.

She looked around, her eyes stinging from the smoke-filled room. "Look, Bill, we could—"

"Never mind," he pronounced. "I'll git the money."

What could she do? She shook her head and waited while he banged around behind the bar. Maybe he wouldn't find the money. There hadn't been that much business tonight and—

"This'll do it!" he exclaimed, returning to the table.

So much for playing out a lucky streak.

"Okay." He plunked a piece of paper down with the flat of his hand. "This 'ere is the deed to the Scarlet Lady. I'm puttin' her up for the...money."

For about five seconds you could have heard a pin drop in the place. Clair didn't believe her ears.

"I don't want your saloon," she told him.

"She's worth a hundred," he countered in a tone that brooked no challenge.

"I'm sure she is, but—"

Then everyone started talking at once.

"You can take her, Bill."

"Wait till word gets out."

"Wait till Slocum hears."

Clair didn't care about Slocum or male pride or anything else. Things kept going from bad to worse. Where was all that luck she'd been so sure of only a few hours ago? All she wanted was to sit here and play a few friendly hands of poker. This wasn't fair. "I *don't* want your saloon."

Bill drained the last of the whiskey from the bottle and put it slowly but firmly down on the table. "If you can't match the bet, then what are you, scared?"

The cowboys fell silent.

That temper of hers was getting the best of her. She figured she'd done about all anyone could do to be fair, more than fair. Her conscience was clear.

"Have it your way." She counted out a hundred— all the money she had on the table plus an emergency gold piece she kept sewn in the lining of her reticule.

Bill grinned Christmas-morning big. He put down the cards one at a time as though to savor the victory. "Straight, jack high," he announced to everyone at once. There were gasps from those present, smiles on most of the faces as all eyes turned to her.

Clair looked at him directly and said, "Four aces."

Chapter Two

Rain came down harder than a springtime waterfall. It poured off the brim of Jake's hat and ran in rivulets down his tan slicker, soaking the black wool of his trousers where it was exposed below the hem. It seeped through every opening around his collar and cuffs and generally annoyed the hell out of him.

Overhead the sky was gunshot gray; ominous clouds were snagged on the tops of the mountains and showed no sign of easing away. The rain beat down the buffalo grass and made puddles in the loamy soil.

Jake shifted in the saddle and tucked the last of his breakfast into his mouth. Breakfast—cold jerky and no coffee. No way in hell could he build a fire in this downpour.

"Looks like we're in for a long one, Tramp," he said to his gelding as they trudged steadily through the storm. He was headed northwest.

Lightning flashed across the sky, arcing like a long, bony finger pointing the way. Thunder crashed. The packhorse neighed and balked at the sound, pulling the rope Jake had tied to the saddle horn tight against his leg.

"Hey," he snarled, grabbing the lead and yanking on it where it cut into his thigh. He turned and glared at the horse and the grim cargo that was strapped to the animal's back. There, wrapped in canvas, was the body of the man he'd sought, the man he'd killed. Ben Allshards.

Jake had been out here alone for the better part of a week chasing Allshards and the man's partner. He'd followed them from one hole to another, always a half day behind them, always pushing to catch up. He'd finally closed in at Jensen's, a soddy saloon on what was commonly called the outlaw trail. But Allshards had spotted Jake, and he and his partner had slipped out the back door. To make matters worse, they'd split up.

Jake had had to make a choice. Too bad for Allshards—he'd won the toss.

The wind picked up, sending the rain swirling in odd directions, water pelting Jake on the side of his face. He flipped up his collar and turned his head away. "Damn."

For two more days and nights Jake had followed wherever Allshards had led. With no sleep, and eating in the saddle, Jake had nearly run old Tramp into the ground, a dangerous thing to do in this unforgiving country. But he'd be damned if he'd give up.

Allshards had broken the law. No one broke the law in Jake McConnell's territory and got away with it. First and last, Jake was a lawman, second-generation lawman. He believed in justice and fair play, and mostly he believed in the law. Rules to live by or, in an outlaw's case, rules to die by.

Late yesterday he'd cornered Allshards in a canyon near Angel's Peak, a strange outcrop of rocks that shot up a hundred feet out of the prairie floor like some misplaced giant spike. Allshards must have figured he could hole up in the small cave at the base. Maybe he figured Jake would get tired, what with the rain and all, and pack it in. Hell, the man had said as much in a little shouting match they'd had along about sundown yesterday.

Now, Jake might be a by-the-book lawman, but nobody ever said he wasn't fair.

He'd tried to get the man to surrender, had talked to him for quite a while on the subject, but Allshards hadn't been buying. He'd probably known he was facing a rope for killing that bank teller.

Right after the sun went down, the outlaw had made a break for it and Jake, left with no choice, had done the job the good people of Carbon County paid him a hundred and fifty a month for.

Grim faced, he glanced back at the tarp-covered body once more, the feet bobbing up and down with each slogging step of the horse. Hell of a way for a man to finish his life, he thought with a touch of sadness for the man, and perhaps for himself.

He dragged in a long, slow breath, the slightest hint of sage tangy on the air, and let it out slowly, feeling the tension ease in his shoulders and gut. Adjusting the reins in his hand, he glanced upward and got a faceful of rain for the effort.

Disgusted, he scanned the treeless horizon. Even the usually ever-present antelope were nowhere in sight. That town had to be close. He stood in the stirrups, the stiff leather groaning in response.

Where the hell was Broken Spur?

A quick look out the front window at the sky confirmed Clair's concerns. The rain that had started during the night showed no sign of letting up. Water cascaded off the porch roof. Water pooled in the street. Water dripped from the leak in the ceiling near the end of the bar, plick-plopping into a metal bucket in a way that was beginning to irritate her nerves.

As of ten-thirty yesterday, Clair Travers was the proud owner—a laughable overstatement—of this ramshackle saloon: peeling wallpaper, faded mirror, mismatched tables and all.

Business was bad. Heck, there was no business. Bill, with all his belongings in a small trunk, had left on yesterday's morning stage. She'd tried to talk to him, tried to give him back the Scarlet Lady. What the devil did she want with the a saloon?

But Bill had had other ideas. It seemed he'd been thinking about California for quite a while, thinking about those summers without rain and winters without snow. Mostly, he'd been thinking about a certain woman who had a small apple orchard near the base of the sierra. He just hadn't wanted to sell out to Slocum.

No, he didn't hold any hard feelings, he'd told her in a tone that lacked sincerity. She was sure there was a certain amount of deflated male pride involved in his willingness to leave.

His parting remark, as he'd stepped up into the stage had been, "This town is too small for two saloons."

"Well, great, but what am I going to do with it, then?"

"That's your problem," he'd said, and the stage had pulled out.

So here she was, alone in an empty saloon.

That drip had turned to a thready stream. Terrific. She went to get a larger bucket from the storage closet she'd discovered near the back. Bill had stashed everything in there, from food to mops.

As she substituted one bucket for the other, she had to shake her head in wonder—maybe it was disgust. Both, probably.

She needed to own a saloon about as much as she needed an anvil chained to her leg. She hefted the rain bucket to the back door and tossed the water into the mud behind the building. Kicking the door closed, she turned.

You aren't staying.

No. Of course she wasn't. She was wanted by the law, for heaven's sake.

Her mind flashed on a man's leering features, his hands pawing at her body as his mouth covered...

She jumped as though she'd been struck. Heart pounding in her chest, she sucked in a couple of deep breaths.

Abruptly she tossed the empty bucket down with a ringing thud and, needing to move, strode across the room, ten long strides from front to back. She pulled open the front doors and stood there, watching the rain splash and puddle in the street. The chilly air penetrated the worn yellow cotton of her shirtwaist, and she rubbed her upper arms. After a minute or so, she felt calmer and stepped back, looking at the room.

It's yours, lock, stock and leak.

This was something, wasn't it? A ghost of a smile teased her lips. She'd never owned anything before— nothing more than the clothes on her back, anyway, and a few pieces of jewelry.

"Umm." She made a thoughtful sound in the back of her throat. "My saloon."

Intrigued with the notion, she strolled around the room, sort of checking things over—not that she was staying, mind you, but just...checking. There were twelve tables and an odd assortment of chairs, all in need of a coat of paint. How much was paint these days, anyway?

That wallpaper was a disgrace even for a saloon—red roses on a background that had probably been white at some time in the ancient past. Now it was closer to brown, dark brown.

The place did have possibilities though. She'd start by doing a thorough cleaning, take down the wallpaper and see—

You aren't staying.

Well, she hedged, there's staying and then there's staying. She sure wasn't going anywhere in this rain. Why, she doubted the stages were running today. The mud was probably up to the wheel hubs by now.

She toyed with a stray lock of hair that had come loose from the pins, twisting the blond strand around her index finger, thinking.

An old adage about a moving target being harder to hit or, in this case, harder to find, floated through her brain. Move on. It was the wisest thing to do. It was the only thing to do, but...

As she ran her hand along the top of her bar, her fingers glided over the rough surface and her eyes skimmed the floor, badly gouged from too many pairs of spurs. Floors could be sanded, bars could be painted, and walls...

Her saloon.

The words, the reality settled softly, warmly in the

pit of her stomach; she felt like a child with an unexpected present.

Broken Spur was remote, she reasoned. The likelihood of running into someone from Texas was next to none. She'd been on the run three months and she hadn't seen any posters—not once. Maybe they weren't looking for her.

Phrases like ''starting over'' and ''second chance'' flitted through her mind. Logic struggled with a lifetime of longing.

Her luck had changed here. The Fates wouldn't hand her this dream, this wish, if she wasn't meant to have it. Broken down as it was, it was hers and…and, dammit, she was keeping the Scarlet Lady.

Decision made, exhilaration soared in her. Breathless, eyes shining, heart racing, she was actually grinning when a sudden gust of wind banged the front door open; hinges squeaked as the door slammed against the wall, then bounced back. Cold air poured into the room like a ghostly presence, carrying with it an eerie foreboding that sent her euphoria fleeing. The fright was so real, so intense, it took her a couple of seconds to shake it off.

''This is silly,'' she said out loud as though to dispel any demons that might have floated in with that rainy mist. Forcing her smile back in place, she strode across the room to close the door, her black skirt flouncing with each long step.

That was when she saw him.

A moving shadow against a menacing gray sky, he was all but obscured by the rain. A shiver moved through her. Instinctively, she hugged herself in a protective gesture, though why, she wasn't quite sure.

The street was a lake, ankle-deep in water and mud.

The horse and rider didn't seem to notice. The sorrel moved slowly up the street, lifting his legs free of the quagmire one at a time. As though heedless of the rain, the rider never hurried the animal or the packhorse he led.

Sidestepping, she edged over to the window as she paralleled his progress.

She could make out his tan slicker, the bottom third stained brown with splattered mud. Water ran off his black hat, front and back, the brim sagging. He was tall, she could tell that much, and he moved with the horse in the way of a man who spent a lot of time in the saddle.

So what brought a man out in this miserable weather? she mused and almost instantly she spotted the answer. That packhorse he was leading wasn't carrying supplies—it was carrying a body, slung face-down over the saddle, the boots protruding from the end of a dark brown tarp used as a shroud.

Clair went very still.

"Bounty hunter." She said the words on a funereally-quiet whisper as though to say them too loud would confirm her fear, as though he would hear her and know she was there, watching.

Self-preservation made her take an instinctive step back, then another and another, until the rounded edge of the bar pushed hard into her back, the corset stays digging painfully into her flesh.

"He's come" was all she managed before she spun on her heel and started for the back door, only to come up short.

Dread snaked coldly and relentlessly up her spine as she stared at the door that represented escape—but escape to where? She didn't own a horse or a wagon of any kind. There were no stages until day after tomorrow, assuming the stages got through. In the meantime, where could she go?

Trapped!

Calm. Stay calm.

She repeated the words like a litany until the panic eased and her heart rate slowed to a manageable level. She glanced over her shoulder toward the window and the man still visible through the glass. Her gaze flicked from him to the back door then to the man again. If he came in here, she could... What?

So he's a bounty hunter. So what? There could be a hundred reasons he was here. Broken Spur was the only town around for at least fifty miles. The storm could have driven him in.

Through the rain haze she saw him again. He was here to get out of the storm and collect his bounty, his...blood money. He'd be gone soon, tonight, tomorrow at the latest. She'd seen his type more than once. His type liked noise and women and wild times, none of which he'd find around here. Confidence built on reason.

He'd get his money and go and she'd never even see him again. Again? Why, she never had to see him at all, she realized with a start.

Cautiously, almost on tiptoe, she moved toward the front doors and pushed them closed, pulling down the shades and praying she didn't attract his attention.

Her breathing came in shallow, rapid gasps as, eyes fixed on the man, she reached for the lock. Her fingers brushed against the cold metal, feeling the hole where the key should have been. Nothing.

No! There had to be a key. Where the hell was the

key? Everything would be all right if she could just lock the damn door.

Gritting her teeth in frustration, she grabbed up the closest chair and wedged it under the rusty knob, but the knob was too low and the chair too tall and it only slid to the floor like some drunken cowboy.

Think. She shoved the hair back from her face. Hitching up her skirt, she tore around behind the bar. Paper. She needed paper, something to write on. Frantically she scanned every surface, every nook and cranny.

Spotting a pasteboard box buried under the weight of empty whiskey bottles, she dumped out the bottles in a wild tumble of glass that shattered on the floor.

Her fingers slipped on the slick paper surface as she tugged, muscles straining, and finally ripped off the top flap.

Okay, now pen, pencil, something. She yanked open drawers, one after another, her hand groping in the dark confines until blessedly her fingers closed around a pencil.

Quickly she scrawled a word and raced back to the door, sliding the sign in front of the shades.

Closed.

With a sigh, she turned and sagged against the door frame, her trembling hands sandwiched between the smooth wood and the cotton of her skirt.

Closed. It was so simple. She was safe.

Jake was never so glad to see any place as he was to see Broken Spur.

Muscles in his legs, stiff with cold, complained as he swung down from the saddle and stepped in mud that oozed up around his boots like quicksand.

Looping the reins of both animals over the gnarled hitching post, he grabbed his gear, saddlebags and rifles and strode the three long steps to the marshal's office.

"Damn, it's cold," he grumbled by way of a greeting as he stepped inside. As he shook his hat and himself like a hound, water sprayed against the wood walls and dripped on the pine flooring, making tiny circles in the dirt.

"Thanks a lot, Jake," Woodrow Murphy said, looking up from his place behind the desk. "And here I just cleaned."

"Oh, yeah, I can see you've been hard at work." Amusement danced in Jake's jet black eyes as he scanned the ten-by-twelve unpainted room, glancing at a pair of barrel-backed chairs and an oak desk that looked scarred enough to have been through a couple of wars. Every flat surface was stacked with papers, and Jake figured Woodrow hadn't filed a thing since he'd taken this job three years ago.

"Why, I have been cleaning," Woodrow retorted, his expression remorseful enough to make a parson smile. "You shoulda been here last month."

Jake chuckled. "Woodrow, it's good to see you again, old timer. It's been too long."

Woodrow grinned like a kid on the last day of school and came around the desk, his hand extended as he walked. "You, too, Jake. What's it been—six months now? Seven?"

"I couldn't say." Jake shrugged out of his slicker and the black wool jacket he wore underneath and hooked both on the pegs by the doorway.

The men shook hands.

Jake dragged one of the two chairs toward the stove. "You look good, Woodrow."

"You look like something the dogs chewed up and spit out."

"Thanks," Jake replied, warming to the teasing. "I didn't need to come up here to be insulted. There's folks a lot closer to Rawlins that would be more than happy to do the job."

"Yeah, I'll just bet," Woodrow confirmed with a chuckle.

Jake settled his weary body into the chair, while Woodrow perched on the edge of the desk. Jake could see him out of the corner of his eye. He held his hands up to the stove, letting the heat warm his fingers and inch its way up his arms.

"I've got Ben Allshards outside."

"Yeah?" The marshal's pale blue eyes widened in his round face and he looked toward the window and the horses standing head down in the storm. When he looked back, his mouth was drawn in a thin white line, and his brow was slightly knit. "What happened?" As he spoke, he opened a desk drawer.

Jake saw Woodrow produce a bottle of whiskey and two metal cups from the drawer. "Drink?"

"Yeah." Jake joined him at the desk.

Woodrow splashed whiskey in both cups and handed one to Jake.

"So what'd he do?" Woodrow raked one hand through his thinning, graying hair.

"Him and a partner held up the bank at Broomfield." Jake took a long drink, nearly emptying the cup. The whiskey burned his tongue and the back of his throat. He needed a drink, something to ease away the cold and the regret. Killing a man wasn't easy.

He helped himself to another splash of whiskey. "Partner got away...so far."

Woodrow dropped into his chair, the metal swivel squeaking. "You going after him?" He tipped back, making his plaid shirt pull tight over his rounded stomach.

"Naw." Jake wandered over to the window to look out at the body draped over the packhorse. Water streaked down the canvas and the soles of the man's boots. "The man's in the next county by now and out of my jurisdiction. I'm gonna send Bill Hurley—"

"Sheriff in Laramie County." Woodrow filled in the information by way of understanding who Jake was talking about. "Good man."

Jake sipped his whiskey. "I'll send Hurley a wire. It's his job now." He returned to the stove and sank into the chair, his feet stretched out in front of him, the half-full cup resting on his chest, his faded blue shirt stained dark down the front from the rain. Muscles in his back and neck slowly relaxed.

Woodrow leaned forward, elbows propped on the edge of the paper-strewn desk. "You get the money?"

"I got lucky." It was a hell of a thing to call killing a man lucky. But he knew that Allshards had had a choice. He made the wrong one—he'd gone against Jake McConnell.

The two men sat in silence, the kind that comes from being longtime friends and from being lawmen. Feeling safe and relaxed for the first time in a while, Jake let his eyes drift closed. Lord, he was tired. He hadn't realized how tired until just that second.

Outside, lightning sizzled overhead like fireworks on the Fourth. Thunder rattled so close, he could feel it in his teeth. And that rain, hell, the rain pounded on the metal roof.

"Sounds like a stampede going on up there."

"Yeah."

Woodrow motioned with the whiskey bottle. "More?"

"A little."

Woodrow asked, "You know who Allshards's partner was?"

"I'm guessing it was Ingles. Those two usually ride together."

"You know—" Woodrow shuffled the mound of assorted paper on his desk "—I think I've got a poster around here on them two...."

"Woodrow—" Jake straightened "—you couldn't find your hat in a room full of elbows. One of these months I'm going to come in here and you'll be gone, buried in the paper."

Woodrow gave up on the looking. "Fast as I put this stuff away, some government weasel down in Cheyenne, with nothing better to do, sends me more. Why, in the old days when me and your pa was riding together—"

"I know. In the old days when the world was flat—"

"Never mind, you young pup!" Woodrow broke in, laughing.

And Jake laughed, too. It felt good to laugh again, better to be with a friend. "Before we get down to some serious name-calling, I think I'll call it a night." Jake let his feet slam to the floor and stood all in one motion. "I'm headed over to the telegraph office to let the Broomfield bank know I got their money." He hefted the saddlebags. "I'll stop by the local bank and get them to lock it up until we can send it out on the next stage." Jake shrugged on his slicker, still wet from the storm. "Will you rouse the undertaker out and get him to take care of the body?" He settled his hat comfortably on his head, then gathered the rest of his gear and his guns.

"Sure." Woodrow came around to Jake, giving him an affectionate pat on the shoulder. "Son, you look tired."

"I feel like I could sleep for a week." Too long on the trail mixed with whiskey on an empty stomach—he thought if he didn't get to bed soon, he'd go to sleep standing right here.

They started for the door. Woodrow grabbed his tan hat and navy blue coat, the one with the torn left pocket. He pulled them on as he spoke. "You remember about the trouble, don't you?"

"Trouble?" Jake halted, hand curled around the smooth brass of the knob, the door barely open. "What trouble?"

"You mean you didn't get my wire?" Woodrow was doing up the last of his jacket buttons.

Jake forced himself to focus. "What wire?"

"Hell, I sent it a week ago."

"You're the marshal here." Jake leaned down on the knob. "What kind of trouble needs the county sheriff?"

"It's Earl Hansen out to the Bar W and Amos Carter over to the—"

"MJ. Yeah, I know," Jake interjected. It was his business to know the ranchers in the county, and the MJ and Bar W were two of the biggest. "What about 'em?" He was feeling annoyed.

"They've been going at it over water rights."

"What do you mean, 'water rights'? They've been friends for years, as far as I knew."

Woodrow shrugged. "All I know is Hansen and Carter had a blowup and Hansen went and built a dam cutting off Carter's water."

"Did you talk to 'em?"

"Course, but they won't listen to me. I figured maybe you being the *county law*..."

"Oh, yeah, that's me, all right—big shot." He was too tired to talk and too tired to care right now. He opened the door. "Well, those boys shouldn't be having any trouble with water on a day like today."

"That's for sure." Woodrow made a derisive sound in the back of his throat.

Jake stepped out onto the sidewalk, Woodrow right behind him, both men ducking their heads and turning away from the beating rain. Jake had to hold on to his hat brim to keep it from flapping in the wind. "I'll come around tomorrow and we can talk. Okay?"

Lightning split the gloom of the gray sky like a flash of gunpowder and was followed by the explosion of thunder.

"Sounds good."

Woodrow grabbed up the packhorse's rein and reached for the lead on the gelding. Jake shot him a questioning stare.

"Let me," Woodrow said, talking loudly over the storm. "I'm headed to the livery anyway."

"A man's not much of a man if he can't put up his own horse," Jake countered, rain soaking through the wool of his trousers and icing his recently warmed skin beneath.

"A friend's not much of a friend if he can't help out once in a while."

With a smile and a pat on the shoulder, Jake said, "I owe you."

"I'll hold you to it." Woodrow left, leading the horses.

Jake trudged off to send the wire telling the folks in Broomfield their money was safe. It was the part of the job he liked. Law and order.

Clair paced back and forth, back and forth along the length of the bar, her heels drumming a steady rhythm on the uneven wood floor. Every so often she'd pause long enough to glance over at the marshal's office.

How long did it take to identify a body? How long did it take to write a voucher for the bounty hunter's money?

Just go, why don't you? she thought, as though her wishing would make it so, would make him leave.

Anxious, downright worried, she started pacing again, the hem of her skirt picking up the dust with every step. She'd about reached the far end of the bar when the front doors banged open, the wood slamming against the wall and sending her heart up into her throat. Clair whirled around faster than a carousel.

It was him.

He filled the doorway like some dark menace and sent her mind racing. Was he after her? Had he seen a Wanted poster somewhere?

Well, there was no escape now. She had to play out the hand she'd been dealt. Good sense and a little healthy caution made her move discreetly behind the bar. She needed a protection—of sorts.

"Hell of a storm out there," the man said in a voice that was deeper than a well bottom and smooth as fine whiskey. Her nerves prickled at the sound and the closeness of him.

He kicked the door closed with his booted foot and took off his slicker and hat, which he tossed on the nearest tabletop as if he hadn't seen the Closed sign displayed in the front window. She had the distinct feeling his type didn't bother with things like signs or warnings. His type did what they damn well pleased. A reckless temper flared and before she could stop herself, she said, "Can't you read? We're closed."

"Since when?" he challenged. "This isn't Sunday."

If he was angry, he didn't show it. In fact, when he turned to look at her the man was smiling. Who would have expected that? Not her. She'd had the misfortune to meet a few bounty hunters over the years and not one of them had ever smiled. Leered, frowned, snarled, even, but smiled—never.

Her pulse took on a funny little flutter, then settled. This was crazy. Maybe so, but he was looking at her all soft and easy and way too familiar. Her pulse fluttered again.

"No, it's not Sunday, but we're closed, all the same."

"How come?" he asked again.

He took a step in her direction and she was glad for the bar between them. His face was all chiseled planes and smooth curves like the wild countryside he'd come in from. Several days' growth of dark beard covered his square jaw and framed his mouth like a mustache.

His hair was black as coal and gleamed from the wet. There were deep furrows where he'd finger-combed it back from his face. The overly long ends curled around his ears and neck and skimmed the top of his collar.

But it was his eyes that held her. Even in this dim light she could see they were black as midnight and just as wild. She was transfixed, intrigued by his unrelenting gaze. A restlessness stirred in her like some long-forgotten memory—eager, exciting, promising.

Bounty hunter, remember?

Sure she remembered. She tore her gaze away, pulled herself up to her full height, all five feet eight inches, and said, with all the authority she could manage, "I don't have to explain to you. I said we're closed." She was feeling awkward and uncomfortable and it was more than just his being a bounty hunter, though Lord knew that was enough. She grabbed up a rag and absently started wiping a glass.

For a full five seconds he looked straight at her as though he was giving her declaration some thought.

She kept right on wiping that glass. She polished the darned thing as if it was Irish crystal instead of green glass.

He moved in close, his chest pressing against the edge of the bar, his fingers curving over the polished wood trim. He flexed his shoulders like a man who was tired. "Look, lady, it doesn't matter to me if you're closed or open. Where's Bill?"

"He's not here. We're closed."

His mouth, the one that had smiled so seductively, now curved down in a hard, fierce line. A muscle flexed in his cheek. "I got that, lady."

Stay calm. He doesn't know anything. He's looking for Bill, remember?

"Bill left on the stage yesterday. If you leave now, you could catch him, I'm sure."

Jake arched one brow in question. "You think I'm going back out in this to go chasing after Bill? Woman, are you crazy, or what?"

"You're the one who was asking about Bill. So go after him if you want to see him." There, she thought, feeling more churlish than cautious.

At that moment the rain turned particularly heavy. Lightning flashed close enough to illuminate the room in a bolt of white light. Thunder crashed.

Jake saw the woman jump, heard her sudden intake of breath. If he hadn't been so tired he would've jumped himself.

"You all right?" he asked, wondering if it was entirely the storm that had her on edge.

"What? Yes. Sure. I'm fine," she said with not a bit of conviction. "Now you have to leave." She put the glass down and picked up another.

For the first time he really looked at her. Up until now all he'd been thinking about was sleep. However, he began to think about just how pretty she was— blond hair, blue eyes, delicate features that hardly fit the usual saloon-girl image.

He propped one foot on the brass railing and settled in for one or two more questions. "Are you from around here?" He didn't get up this way much, but he was sure he'd have remembered her.

"No" was all the answer he got—almost all. "*We're closed,*" she repeated emphatically.

"You keep saying that. You know, I could start to take this personally."

"Good," she retorted, her tone brusque enough to make him curious. She had on a yellow blouse that had seen one too many washings. The long sleeves were rolled up and the collar was high under her chin. She had on a black skirt. He'd seen that before she'd hightailed it behind the bar. It was long and full and revealed absolutely nothing of her womanly curves.

Ah, now, why would a saloon girl want to conceal anything? Her skin was winter pale, not powdered or painted, and her hair was pinned up in a haphazard way that bespoke more practicality than come-hither.

The more he looked, the more curious he got, and since the subtle approach hadn't worked thus far he decided to go straight for the gut. "All right, woman. Who are you? Why did Bill leave?"

She blinked twice, then said, "Drink?" With a flurry of motion she retrieved a glass from the shelf behind the bar.

Jake regarded her through narrowed eyes—narrowed mostly because they hurt, like the rest of him. He needed sleep. "What? No, I don't want a drink." He ran the flat of his hand over his face, trying to wipe the exhaustion away. Maybe if he could clear his mind some of this would make sense.

When he looked again she was pouring liquor, the drink he'd just turned down. With a sigh he ignored the glass she was intently shoving at him. "I asked your name."

"Why?"

"Is it a secret?" He could be as tenacious as her.

"It's none of your business. Now, have a drink if that's what you came for, then leave. I keep telling you we're closed."

Thunder rumbled overhead and she flinched. He saw her fingers tighten on the glass, saw her gaze dart to the window.

"You're sure you're all right?" he asked one more time.

"Yes." Her tone was curt.

Okay, he'd had enough. Without another word he retrieved his hat and coat from the table where he had tossed them. He looped his slicker over his shoulder, the muddy hem banging against his pant leg, smudging the black wool with mud. "I'm going to bed."

"Goodbye," she said, her lips curving up in the closest thing to a smile he'd seen since he'd walked in. "Come in again sometime, *when we're open*."

Of course, Clair didn't mean a word of it. She was hoping he'd get on his horse and ride out of town, never to be seen again. Bounty hunters were trouble. Bounty hunters with suggestive smiles were a whole other kind of trouble. She wasn't in the market for either.

She circled around the bar intent on following him to the door and closing it firmly behind him.

She was making a beeline for the front when she realized he was headed up her stairs. "Hey, hold on there." She skidded to a halt and planted her balled fists at her waist. "Where do you think you're going, mister?"

The man never stopped, just kept plodding up the stairs, his boots making one hollow thud after another, like a man climbing to the gallows. "Like I said, I'm going to bed." Gripping the oak banister, he glanced back over his shoulder long enough to say, "Care to join me?"

It was a brazen, impudent remark and she should be offended. She *was* offended. The nerve of the man!

Never mind the wicked grin on his face, never

mind the dimples that were barely visible through the beard.

The man has dimples!

Rogues and scoundrels and charmers had dimples. Bounty hunters did not. Even so, it took two tries to get her voice to work. "I most certainly don't wish to join you! Now get off my stairs and out of my saloon!"

He turned on her, gunfighter slow, and she actually took a step back, banging into the wall by the front windows. Her eyes were riveted to his.

"What do you mean, it's *your* saloon?"

She was in it now. That temper of hers was on a rampage. "I—" she thumbed her chest near the top button of her blouse "—own the Scarlet Lady."

He came down a step, then paused again.

There was no sign of humor or kindness in his eyes or tone when he spoke, and she instinctively knew this was the darker side of the man, the side that killed people. "All right, honey, let's have it. What's going on?"

Clair's temper knew when to beat a retreat, and this was definitely time. In a voice that was mild, maybe even a little shaky, she said, "I own the Scarlet Lady."

"Since when?"

"Since yesterday."

"You buy it?"

"I won it."

"How?"

"In a card game."

He closed in on her like a predator on the hunt, standing on the bottom step so that he towered over her even more. "You're a gambler?" There was a bit of the incredulous in his voice—and disdain.

Who the hell did he think he was to judge her? "Yes," she returned, refusing to flinch. "I'm a gambler. What of it?"

"And you tricked Bill out of the place, huh?"

"No. I won the saloon fair and square, not that it's any of your business, and if anyone tries to say different I'll—"

"Hold on, honey. I believe you." He held up his hands in surrender, but since they were both holding weapons, a shotgun and a rifle to be precise, he didn't look very meek.

"Don't call me honey," she snapped back.

"Fine." He started back up the stairs again speaking as he went. "Look...whatever your name is...I have a deal with Bill. When I'm in town I sleep here...up there." He pointed to the second-floor landing and the two furnished rooms that were there.

Panic merged with that temper of hers. She'd moved in here right after Bill had left, figuring to save the rent money. "You can't sleep here."

He was still climbing the stairs. "Lady, I'm not arguing with you. I've been on the trail a week, the last three days without enough sleep to fill a shot glass. I'm *going* to bed."

"Find another place."

"No."

"I'm ordering you to leave," she said with all the authority she could muster, which was usually enough to send a bleary-eyed cowboy on his way. This man had the audacity to laugh.

"Honey, you want to stop me, then you're gonna

have to shoot me. As a matter of fact, I wish you would, just to put me out of my misery.''

Tempting as that was, she resisted. These days she had an understandable aversion to guns.''I could call the marshal and have you thrown out.''

He was nearing the top of the stairs. "Go ahead and call the marshal. It won't do you any good.''

"And just why not?'' she hollered after him. "I doubt the marshal has any sympathy for bounty hunters.''

"Bounty hunter? Is that what you think?'' He paused on the landing long enough to look down at her. "I'm no bounty hunter. I'm Jake McConnell. I'm the sheriff of Carbon County.''

Chapter Three

Morning came as cold and gray and wet as yesterday. The rain and gloom were bad enough; having a sheriff, of all things, sleeping in the next room—well, that was nothing short of a disaster waiting to happen.

With a flounce of sheet and quilt and nightgown she rolled over in the bed and was rewarded with a chill where her feet touched the sheet her body hadn't warmed yet.

"Damn man," she muttered, punching her pillow, trying to get a little fluff out of the feathers that were long since matted down to the thickness of an envelope.

Her hair fell across her face and she swiped it back. Muscles in her back hurt and her eyes felt as if there was gravel in them. That was lack of sleep, she knew. That was his fault, too.

Of all the things the man could be, he had to be a sheriff! Jake McConnell. Yeah, that was his name.

She rolled over again, trying to get comfortable. Useless. As for him, she wished now he was a bounty hunter. At least bounty hunters and gamblers were both on the fringes of the law. Gamblers and lawmen were natural enemies, like rabbits and wolves. She was feeling decidedly like the rabbit, and she didn't like the feeling, not one bit.

Out of nowhere she was assailed with images of another sheriff. Him holding her down, tearing her clothes, forcing up her skirt...

No! She refused to think about that. She refused to give in to panic or fear that washed over her faster than a flash flood.

Throwing back the covers, she scrambled to her feet, her toes flexing against the chill of the bare floor. A couple of short steps and she was at the window. The sash worked easily and she leaned down to take a deep breath of fresh, sage-scented air. The rain was finer today, the drops like tiny pellets, which stung her face and dampened the front of her nightgown, making the cotton cling to her bare flesh beneath.

She forced herself to think about the rain and the cold and the wagon that was rumbling along the street below, anything but the terrifying images that continued to haunt her when she least expected it.

Enough, she told herself. She owned a saloon now. She was making a new life. She had to let go of what she couldn't change, and move on.

No regrets. No turning back.

With a resolute determination, she shoved her sleep-tousled hair behind her shoulder. It was morning, the start of a new day, a new beginning. A day filled with possibilities and chances to be taken. What was a gambler if not a chance taker?

The creak of door hinges and boot steps on the bare wooden floor caught her attention and she turned toward the closed door to her room. She knew he was out there, on the landing, moving around. Would he knock on her door? What would she do if he did? There was a moment of uneasiness, then she remembered that he hadn't bothered her during the night.

For that matter he could have made advances in the saloon, could have done just about anything he'd wanted—they were alone, then as now. He hadn't.

So he's not a lecher. So what? Are you going to invite him to tea?

Hardly. She knew quite clearly the danger she was in. Having a sheriff under the same roof was like having an open flame in a fireworks factory. There was bound to be an explosion. The only question was when.

Well, maybe she could put that flame out.

She knew a couple of things. First, he wasn't here looking for her. Because if he was, and he'd recognized her, then he would have said or done something last night.

A smile threatened, but she knew she wasn't in the clear yet. He was not the local law. No, she'd seen the town marshal yesterday, an older man who looked as though he ought to be someone's grandfather. Local law, she'd convinced herself, was too remote to be aware of "things," of people wanted in faraway places like Texas, for instance.

But a county sheriff, well, that was different. *He* would get the posters and such, if there were any.

In the meantime, she had an immediate problem. How to stay away from him until he left town. He was probably downstairs just waiting for her so he could ask some more of those questions he'd had such a supply of last night. Lawmen.

She listened at the door, trying to hear if he was moving around. Nothing. Silence.

She went back to the window and lifted the shade with one hand. Son of a gun, there he was crossing the street. She pulled back the shade more, wanting to get a good look. No time for mistakes.

Nope, it was him, all right. He was so tall and broad shouldered, she couldn't miss him if she wanted to. And she did—want to miss him, that is.

But he was there, trudging across the street, headed straight for the marshal's office. Could it be? Her stomach clenched in anticipation. He'd left. Just like that. No words. No questions. Just gone.

Her spirits soared.

"Lord, I'm sorry I doubted you."

She saw him go into the office. Yes! This had to be it. He was leaving. He was probably going over to say goodbye. He was probably anxious to get going; there were other places he needed to see, maybe criminals he needed to take back to Rawlins.

Relief washed through her. "Yes!" she said to the empty room. All that worrying, all that losing sleep had been for nothing.

Well, this called for a celebration—coffee. She made quick work of getting dressed in a royal blue skirt and pale green shirtwaist, and ignored her corset completely. It was a celebration, after all.

She washed up in the bowl on the washstand and twisted her hair up in a serviceable knot on the top of her head. She'd change later for business, assuming the storm let up enough to have some business. In the meantime, she'd do a little of that fixing up she'd been thinking about.

Grinning like a kid with a brand-new peppermint stick, she strolled out onto the landing. The door to his room, or rather, *her* extra room, was open a foot or so. She would have to see about fixing it up. Maybe she could rent it to someone—not a sheriff or marshal or bounty hunter, but someone. A little extra money would help with expenses.

Using only the tips of her fingers, she pushed the door open as though she expected him to jump out at her, then chided herself for her foolishness. In a blink she noticed that his shirt, the blue one from last night, was draped around the curved-back chair, the hem dragging on the dust-covered floor.

What the devil? His shirt. His saddlebags.

That joy of hers dissolved faster than sugar in hot water, which was exactly what she was in. It didn't take a genius to figure that if his things were here, then he'd be back.

Her temper got the best of her. She had half a mind to pack up his things and toss them right out on the sidewalk, rain or no rain, sheriff or no sheriff.

Good move. Let's make the lawman angry. That's a sure way to keep from calling attention to yourself.

"Damn the man."

Breathing a little harder, she stood there glaring at the rumpled bed he'd slept in. That was *her* bed and *her* room and *her* saloon. The man had no right, sheriff or not.

Why, just look at the way he'd tossed that quilt off the end of the bed. It wasn't his quilt, so what did he care? Never mind that it wasn't hers, either, until yesterday.

She stormed in and picked it up, intent on putting it on the bed. Instantly she was assaulted with the feeling that she had invaded his privacy, which was ridiculous, but she felt it all the same.

Her eyes went immediately to the straw-filled mattress, to the shape of his lean body perfectly outlined there. She dropped that quilt faster than a stick of dynamite and took a half step back.

Her eyes were riveted on the bed. Heart racing, she was starkly aware that his bed was against the wall, the same wall that her bed was against, the same wall that was the only barrier that kept them from being intimately close.

She suddenly wondered what it would be like to open her eyes and see Jake McConnell there first thing in the morning. There was something about him that stirred her up just a bit, and… Tiny nerves in her skin fluttered to life, prickling as though skimmed by an electric charge.

Stop it right now!

On a sharp breath, Clair marched from the room. She was not going to think about dark-eyed men with the devil's own smile. She was not!

That familiar ache was building behind her eyes and muscles were knotting along her shoulders. Coffee, she needed some coffee. She marched down the stairs with the precision of a West Point cadet.

Fortunately, Bill had a supply of coffee and a few cans of food, but the storage closet was dark—bordering on well-bottom black—and trying to read the labels was next to impossible. She heard the wind howl outside an instant before the closet door slammed shut and cut off any and all light.

Alone in the dark, a childhood fear surfaced in a gut-wrenching instant.

She threw down the can she'd been holding and lunged for the door. "Open," she commanded, as though there was some power holding it shut. She tried the knob. It turned, but the door didn't move.

"Come on," she demanded, more loudly and urgently this time. "Open, will you?"

Panic took shape and form like a demon lurking in the darkness, waiting, watching, ready to pounce.

Heart racing, breath ragged, she jiggled the knob again, twisting hard, her skin nearly tearing on the brass knob. "Open!" she ordered once more. With all her weight she pulled on the door and this time the door obeyed.

With a creak and groan, the door flew open and she half fell, half stumbled into the empty saloon, managing to stay on her feet only by her grip on the knob and some fancy footwork.

She stood there, bent slightly at the waist, trying to regain her breath, her composure. Eyes shut, she waited for the panic to melt away.

When, finally, she felt in control again, she spared the threatening cave a look.

With a shake of her head, she forced a little laugh, mostly to dispel the last of the demons. Demons always went away when you laughed at them.

"Dumber than a prairie dog," she muttered to herself. Now, there was something she hadn't heard in a while. Sully had always said that, usually to her.

Sully. Why, she hadn't thought of him in years.

She put a chair in front of the closet door this time, took a lamp from the bar with her for light and found the coffee and the pot.

The stove, which she'd started earlier, was going nicely and she fetched water from the rain barrel out back. A couple of scoops and she set the pot to boiling.

Clair always liked her coffee strong and hot. She liked to feel the steam against her cheek and wasn't above blowing on the liquid, even if it was not ladylike.

But Sully was different.

Sully had liked coffee mild—not too mild, but mild. She never was quite sure what that meant, but she certainly knew when she got it wrong. Sully got angry if his coffee was too hot or too strong. Wouldn't want Sully to get angry. She shook her head in disgust—or wonder, she wasn't sure.

She took a seat at the table closest to the stove and let her mind wander back a few years.

She'd met Sully in New Orleans. Clair had been seventeen and green as spring grass. Sully was tall, dark and handsome and had a way of talking that could charm a preacher's daughter right out of the church. Sully always knew what to say to get his way—with her, and with about any other woman, she had come to realize too late.

She went to check on the coffee and tossed a small piece of firewood into the stove, using her skirt as hand protection when she closed the door.

She stood there warming herself, listening to the metal crack and snap as it expanded with the heat. Rain sprayed the windows, and the distant rumble of thunder echoed off the mountains.

Sully had always liked warm weather. He'd never have made it around here, not in this damp cold. Of course, there was no danger of running into Sully here or anywhere else. Poor Sully, she'd heard he was dead—shot by a jealous husband, no doubt.

She'd felt bad when she'd heard, though why, she wasn't sure. Lord knew he'd lied and cheated on her, used and abused her and always had a reason they couldn't get married.

Four years. That's how long she'd stayed. That's how long it had taken her to wise up and figure out that she could make it on her own, that she'd be better off on her own. It simply came to her one day, one morning. She woke up and knew she didn't love him anymore, that if this was what love was she wanted no part of it.

Sully hadn't taken her announced departure gracefully. It had taken a month for the bruises on her face to heal.

The coffee boiled over, brown liquid foaming and sizzling on the hot surface. Thoughtlessly, she grabbed the handle. "Ouch!"

Searing pain shot up her fingers and through her hand. Remembering to use her skirt as protection, she dragged the pot off the burner then plunged her hand into the bucket of water, gritting her teeth as the cold of the water covered the burn. Her eyes fluttered closed as she moved her fingers in the water.

Another minute and she lifted her hand out to take a look. She could see her palm was as red as flannel but not a blister in sight. Thank goodness for small blessings. The pain eased off to almost nothing.

Just thinking about men is trouble.

Well, no more. Ever since Sully, she'd sworn off. She didn't think about men, didn't want a man, didn't need a man. Instinctively, her eyes lifted to the top of the stairs.

Nope! She wasn't thinking about him anymore. He could come and go—especially go.

With that thought firmly in place, Clair went to check on the storm. The sky was still gray, but optimistically lighter, and the rain was more of a mist than anything else.

No one much was stirring and the street was more like a lake bottom. She had the distinct feeling few, if any, men would be venturing out just to have a drink or play a hand of cards.

That being the case, she might as well leave that Closed sign in the window and do some housekeeping. Nothing like hard work to keep her mind off...things.

Cleaning required soap so, after retrieving her coat and some money from upstairs, she ventured outside, made a dash along the plank sidewalk and ducked into the mercantile, which was three doors down on the same side.

Large and square, the store had wooden counters on three sides. The walls were white wood and the counters a shade of pale blue. The glass in the cases gleamed from recent cleaning, and all the wall space was lined with shelves, floor to ceiling. They were well stocked with everything imaginable, including brightly labeled canned food—mustard to canned oysters. The countertops were stacked high with rolls of calico and gingham, and near the back, barrels held an assortment of brooms and rakes and shovels like some strange bouquet.

A narrow-faced young clerk watched intently.

"Morning." She brushed the rain from her hair and smiled.

"Morning," the clerk answered, his somber expression split with a broad grin that revealed a broken bottom tooth. "Miserable weather to be out."

"Yes, it sure is." She strolled along one counter, looking at the needles and thread and carved hair combs displayed under the glass. Window-shopping was a weakness.

"Can I help you with something?" He came over to where she was standing by the calico. He was tall and gawky in the way of boys before they fill out.

"Yes. I'd like a cake of lye soap and—" she scanned the shelves "—and, now that I'm looking, a few other things."

Twenty minutes later the wooden counter was stacked with sugar, flour, salt, coffee, eggs, bacon, butter and dried apples. She added a broom to the order, another bucket and lye soap.

"Whew! I only came in for one thing." She laughed.

"Well, that's how it is sometimes, and we're glad—that is, my pa will be glad. It's his store. I'm Larry Nelson." He offered his hand.

She accepted. "Pleased to meet you. I'm Clair...ah...Smith," she added falteringly. No sense tempting fate.

Larry ran the tally on a notepad, his red brows drawn down in concentration. "Comes to $7.15." He beamed. "You passing through or settling in?"

"Settling in," she told him, liking the sound of it.

He put the pad down and reached for a ledger book. "You want me to start an account?"

"That would be nice. Thanks."

"No trouble." He flipped open the well-worn book. "Name...Clair Smith. Miss or Missus?"

"Miss."

"Where are you living?"

"The Scarlet Lady."

He stopped midmotion and looked up at her through his brows. "Really?"

"Yes." She looked him square in the face.

"Scarlet Lady it is." He marked the book again.

"Seven dollars and fifteen cents is your total. We ask for half of your first purchase now and balance on the first of the month. After that you pay at least ten percent if you don't pay it off."

"Sounds fair enough." Clair relaxed a bit and paid him four dollars.

Larry stacked her groceries in a wooden crate. "You want help?"

"If you don't mind?"

"Glad to do it." He didn't bother with a coat, and as he hefted the box, he leaned in closer. "Any excuse to get out of here." He punctuated his words with a wink. In a louder voice he called toward the back, "Ma, I'm helping a lady with her groceries. Back soon!"

"Okay," came a high-pitched female voice in reply.

Together they left. "Don't you like working in the store?" Clair asked as they hurried to her saloon. She held the door open for him.

"It's okay. I was hoping for something a little more exciting this summer, is all."

"Ah," she muttered, following him inside. "You like excitement, huh?" What young man didn't?

He put the crate on the nearest table, then scanned the room as though he'd never seen the inside of a saloon before. His gaze settled on her. "Everybody's heard Bill left. The word around town is that he was bamboozled by a woman gambler. You don't look like a woman who would cheat a man."

Coming from almost anybody else she'd have taken offense, but Larry was young and the young had a refreshing way of coming right to the point.

"Well, thanks, I guess."

"Oh, I didn't mean anything," he rushed to assure her.

She chuckled. "If you want to know, I won the saloon."

Amusement flashed in his eyes. "Really. So it's true. You are a woman gambler."

"Afraid so."

"What's it like being a gambler?" He pulled out a chair. "I mean, do you get to go to a lot of places? Must be kinda exciting, huh?"

"Sometimes." She took off her coat. "It can also be hard work and lonely."

He seemed to consider this for a moment, then said, "I can see that. I'm off to college in the fall. I can't wait to get out of here."

"Why? Is Broken Spur such a bad town?"

"It's just pretty quiet here and I'd like to see a little more of the world, so to speak."

Clair sat down next to him. "Ah, that excitement thing again."

"Yeah." He grinned.

She smiled back. "So, Larry, tell me something. Do the people in this town really think I cheated Bill out of his place?" If they did, she'd never have any business and she was done before she got started unless she could find a way around the problem.

Larry shifted uncomfortably in his chair. "Well, ma'am, you know how it is. A woman running a saloon... Folks naturally think... Well, we never had a wh—" His eyes went wide. "Oh, I'm sorry. I didn't mean—"

"It's okay, Larry." She touched his shoulder lightly, her hand feeling his bony shoulder through the thin white cotton. "I've been called worse."

"I can't imagine that, ma'am," he replied.

She could. It was part of that job of hers that Larry found so exciting. Still, Clair was enjoying talking with him, realizing that he was the first person she'd talked to all day.

"Just so you'll know, Larry, I'm a gambler. Nothing more." She picked up a sack of flour and a sack of coffee and headed for the storage closet.

Larry spoke up. "Here, let me help you put this stuff away."

Twenty minutes later they had the supplies put up in the storeroom. She was grateful.

As they walked back toward the front doors, she said, "What about you? Do you think I would cheat him out of his saloon?"

"Hey, a man makes his own decisions about things. Nobody held a gun to Bill's head and made him wager the saloon." He arched one brow, a teasing glint in his eyes. "You didn't, did you?"

Clair took his remark with good humor. "Anything but."

She pulled open the door to let him leave. "Say, Larry, you wouldn't know anyone who needs a job, would you?" An idea was formulating in her mind.

"What kind of job?"

Rain spattered on the plank sidewalk and bounced up against the partially open door.

"I need a barkeeper. Someone I can trust. Someone who can work fast, keep orders straight."

"Well," he said, moving around out of the doorway and the chilling breeze. "I'm looking for work."

Clair cocked her head to one side. "I thought you worked at the store?"

"I do, but if I could find something to do that

would generate some extra cash, it would be a help. You know, I work for free in the store, but a man needs a little spending money when he's on his own."

"What would your father say to you working in a saloon? Long hours. Late nights."

"He wouldn't like it," Larry replied with honesty. "As a matter of fact, he's not keen on me going off to school, but I talked him into it."

"How old are you?"

"Eighteen and a half," he told her, puffing his chest under his white shirt as he did.

"And a half, huh?"

"Nineteen come October."

"Well, that makes you more than a half, doesn't it?"

He beamed. "I suppose it does."

She liked him. He was warm and friendly and enthusiastic. The fact that he was local—and, she thought, probably well liked and thus able to give a certain credibility to her and the place—worked just fine. Besides, she'd like having someone to talk to.

"Would you like the job, then? I can't pay much. Eight dollars a week to start, then we'll talk again in a month or so if business is good."

Larry grinned. "When do I start?"

"Today's Saturday. How about Monday night?"

"Monday's good." His head bobbed up and down with each word. "What time?"

"This is night work. Can you stay awake?"

"Sure. I'm usually up half the night reading, anyway. Ma says I'll be blind by the time I go away if I keep this up, so she'll be glad to know I'm giving my eyes a rest."

"Larry, you're a treasure. Okay. Monday through

Thursday, six to midnight. Friday and Saturday, five to two in the morning. How's that?''

"Great!" He turned and was halfway out the door when she stopped him.

"Larry? What about your father? Do you want me to speak to him?"

"Naw. I'll tell him. In fact, I can't wait." With that he bolted out the door.

Chapter Four

The marshal's office was cold and dank from the smell of the water-soaked wood. That stove in the corner was going, but a man had to stand next to the thing to feel any heat.

Unfortunately for Jake, he and Woodrow weren't near the stove. They were over by the window, hunched over Woodrow's desk studying the county map.

Jake leaned in closer to get a better look at the creek that was the source of the water dispute. He traced it with his finger, mentally noting location and direction.

"Okay," Woodrow was saying. "So now you know all that's going on."

"The question—" Jake straightened, flexing his tired back as he did "—is what to do."

"Beats the heck outta me."

They'd been at this for hours, going over the details—territorial law, land deeds, ranch sizes, herd sizes, location in relation to the creek and its headwaters. Trouble, Woodrow had told him, had been mostly threats, some pushing and shoving by both Hansen and Carter and their ranch hands.

"As soon as this rain stops—" Jake poured himself a cup of reheated coffee "—I'll ride on out there, pay both of them a visit and see if I can't talk a little sense, or a little law, into 'em."

"I'll be ready." Woodrow told him.

Jake took a taste of coffee and wished he hadn't. It was thick as molasses and tasted like coal tar. He put the cup down. "No, you're staying."

"Says who?" the marshal demanded, looking for all the world like a kid who'd been told he couldn't eat cake for breakfast. "I'm backing you up."

"I don't need backup," Jake replied, thinking that as much as he loved Woodrow, his friend was getting on and Jake didn't want to take any chances. "It's out of your jurisdiction, remember. That's why you sent for me."

"Now, look, you. I ain't scared to go against them boys and I ain't too old, if that's what you're thinkin'." He squared his shoulders, the cotton of his plaid shirt pulling tight across his chest. "I sent for you 'cause I figured it was the only way I was gonna get to see you anytime soon, but if you think—"

"I don't think anything."

"I ain't senile, ya know. I can still put a bullet where I want it, if it comes to that, and it just might. Them two are riled."

"That's exactly what I'd like to avoid. We don't need this to blow up into another Lincoln County. What a mess that is."

"Exactly, so—"

"Look, I'm the outsider here. I don't have to face these folks every day. If they don't like me, well, so much the better—it doesn't matter. If they get too angry at you, then they'll give you trouble every chance they can, and you don't need that."

"Humph. I don't give a damn about them. I'm still able to do my job and—"

"And I wish you'd let me do mine." Jake strolled closer to his old friend. "All I'm saying is that if I get in trouble, I'd like to know that you're back here to bring the cavalry, so to speak, if I need it."

Woodrow screwed up his face in skeptical thought, but finally he relented. "Okay. But I'm doing this against my better judgment."

"Thanks," Jake interjected before Woodrow could go off down another path.

"Just remember I've been pulling your irons outta the fire ever since Chugwater."

"Yeah, I remember." In an instant the memory flashed in Jake's mind as though it was yesterday. He'd been riding with his father—who was U.S. marshal in California at the time—and Woodrow, his father's number-one deputy. Ben McConnell was a hands-on kind of lawman who'd rather be dead than stuck behind a desk.

They'd been trailing a killer. Jake was supposed to stay with the horses while they went into the saloon to ask about a certain felon they were after. But Jake, being too eager for his own good, had left the horses and snuck around the back to have a closer look. Next thing he knew he had a gun pressed up against his ribs, an arm strangle-tight around his neck, and he was being dragged toward those horses he shouldn't have left.

He was a goner—he knew it as sure as sunrise. Jake's father, Ben, came barreling out the back door and skidded to a halt, dust swirling around his ankles. Jake could still remember his father's face, totally expressionless, his blue eyes flat and hard as Jake had never seen them. He didn't look at Jake, didn't look anywhere but at the man holding a gun to Jake's head. Ben stood there, an easy target, and tried to convince the outlaw to give it up. Any second Jake knew that outlaw was going to open fire and kill them both.

Then out of nowhere, or so it seemed, Woodrow managed to outflank the man. Jake never saw him and neither did the outlaw. All Jake registered was the thump of metal hitting flesh and skull, a groan, and then the man sagged to the ground.

It had taken him a full ten seconds to understand that he was alive. He was all right. Woodrow had saved him, but his father had faced down an armed man, risked his life. Jake was gut-wrenching scared—and more than that, he was ashamed.

When it was over, his father never yelled, never criticized. "Son, if you go and get yourself killed, your ma is never gonna forgive me." Then he'd hugged Jake. Jake was seventeen years old and his father had never hugged him before, never hugged him again, but he did that day. Jake had always worshiped his father, and so the following year, Jake had become a lawman, too, and spent the rest of his life trying to live up to the no-nonsense tradition his father had demanded.

"...going to Allshards's burying?"

Jake blinked to clear away the memories. "Uh, oh, sure." He dragged over a chair and sat down, his legs crossed at the ankle. The heat from the stove warmed him through the faded denim of his trousers.

"You coming?" Jake asked.

"Thought I might, as well. A man ought to have someone there when they say words over him."

Jake agreed. It was a pitiful thing, a man dying and being buried without a soul to mourn him, without anyone to mark his passing. A man should have someone.

Oh, hell, what was he doing sitting here ruminating like some old goat? At thirty-three he ought to have a few good years left.

Unless someone somewhere puts a bullet in you.

The wind picked up outside and got itself caught in some unseen crack in the walls, making an eerie whistling sound as it moved through.

"Like a banshee's wail," Woodrow muttered, his gaze fixed on the window and the storm outside.

Jake shot his friend a look. "Since when do you know about banshees?"

"Since my Irish mother told me, that's when."

"Now, Woodrow, don't you go getting all spooky on me."

Woodrow busied himself with folding the map, the paper crinkling and snapping as he worked.

Jake was suddenly feeling a little edgy, and got up to move around. He always felt better when he was moving—maybe that's why he'd never settled down. Maybe he'd never met anyone he was interested enough in... Then again, there was a certain woman with the biggest blue eyes he'd ever seen and a voice as smooth as fine whiskey...

Whoa, there, McConnell.

It took a bit of effort to pull back those errant thoughts of his and focus on the business at hand. "So, any idea how this water trouble got started?

Hansen and Carter have been up there a while, how come all of a sudden they're at each other's throats?''

"Well," Woodrow said with a drawn-out sort of sigh, "Billy Hansen—"

"I know Billy. Nice kid."

"Well, the rumor is that Hansen wanted Billy to marry Sally Carter. You know, old families united, ranches merged, that kinda thing."

Jake shrugged his understanding. "What was the trouble? The kids weren't buying?"

"Don't know. No one seems to know. Billy called on Sally and the next thing Carter ships Sally off on the train for Chicago. Anyways, them two started in prodding each other until—"

"So this is about Sally Carter? You didn't say that before."

Woodrow's brows arched upward like a couple of birds taking flight. "Didn't I?"

Jake paused by the window. "What else didn't you think of?"

"Don't know." Woodrow made a thoughtful little noise in the back of his throat. "I was thinking that if Billy did something..." A light of sudden realization flashed in his eyes and he looked straight at Jake. "You don't think Billy got the girl—"

"Pregnant." Jake finished the sentence. Great minds thinking alike, or at least lawmen's minds thinking alike. Feuds had been started over less. "Has anyone heard from Sally? Maybe some girlfriend?"

Woodrow rubbed his chin, his blue eyes narrowing. "Until this minute I never gave the possibility a thought, what with her leaving and all." He smacked his hand hard on the desk. "I think I'll just go on over and talk to the Hocksettler girl. She and Sally were close, and if anyone would know, she would.''

''Good.''

Woodrow pulled on his coat and slapped his battered old tan hat on his head, his graying hair protruding out around the band. ''See, you can't do everything yourself. I'm good for something.'' With that he slammed out the door.

Jake watched him cross the muddy street to the hotel. All the while he was thinking. If Sally was pregnant, well, men had been killed for less in this part of the world, but... He let the thought sort of stretch out in his mind.

It didn't make sense. If Hansen wanted Billy to marry Sally and if Sally was in a family way, the logical thing would be to let 'em get married, so why...

Damn. How come nothing was simple anymore?

When it comes to women, nothing is simple. His gaze flicked to the Scarlet Lady saloon.

Talk about things not being simple. She—he realized he didn't even know her name—she wasn't simple. Frustrating and confusing, yes. Simple, absolutely not. She'd met him straight on, never backed down, never hesitated. He liked a woman with fire, even if she was a gambler. Hell, the gambler part only added to his interest and her mystery.

That must be why he'd lain awake for quite a while last night thinking about her, listening to her come up the stairs, go into her room. With every sound, he'd imagined what she was doing, undressing—what article of clothing she was removing. That was what had his fingers twitching.

McConnell you've been too long without a woman.

He chuckled. Perhaps that was true, but something deep inside him said that maybe it was something more. Jake's curiosity was piqued. He was up for the challenge. A smile curled along his lips.

Now seemed as good a time as any to get started.

Two steps outside, rain splattered him in the face and took some of that confidence right out of him. "I'll get even," he muttered to no one in particular. But swiping away the water, he realized he hadn't shaved, hadn't bathed, hadn't done much to wash away weeks on the trail. Not a good way to go...solve a mystery, he lamely told himself.

No matter what, he needed to get cleaned up, and Steinkeller's Bath Emporium was just the place. It was a fancy name for a barbershop and bathhouse but, he thought, angling across the street, he could use a little fancying up.

Clair was on her knees scrubbing the walnut paneling along the back wall when a deep male voice said, "I always did like to see a woman work."

"What the devil—" She turned so quickly she lost her balance and landed flat on her behind. Her blue skirt flounced up around her knees, giving him a clear view of her stocking-clad legs and pantalets and who knew what else. "You scared me to death," she snapped back at Jake, shoving her skirt down as she did. "What do you want?"

"I'm sorry. Here, let me help." He offered her a hand up, which pride made her refuse, and so she was left to scramble up with all the grace of a drunken chicken. Darn the man. He hadn't been here one minute and already she was angry.

"What are you doing here?" She glared at him.

"I live here," he retorted, one brow arched in surprise. Rain dripped from the brim of his black hat and splattered on the floor—her newly *washed* floor.

She shoved her hair back from her face with her forearm. Soapy water trickled down and dripped off her elbow onto her skirt and annoyed her even more. "You most certainly do *not* live here."

He tossed his hat onto the closest table and shrugged out of his slicker. "Okay, then, I'm staying here until I leave town. How's that?"

"When?"

"When what?" He was inspecting the spot on the wall she'd been washing.

"*When* are you leaving?"

His smile was immediate and soothed and inflamed her raw nerves all at once.

"Aw, honey, you hurt my feelings."

"I've told you not to call me honey. My name is Clair Smith. As for the feelings part, I didn't know you had any. If you did, then you wouldn't have ignored my order that you leave last night."

Lord, the woman was something when she was riled, which had been most of the short time he'd known her. He wondered if she was just as out of control at other times, like making love, for instance. His body stirred.

"So-o-o." He looked around with an appraising stare. "I see you've been busy."

"I have been busy." She blew a wisp of hair out of her face, but it fell right back. "Of course, when people keep tracking on the floor..."

Jake glanced at the muddy footprints he'd left, then at her, and then he laughed. "Honey—" it just slipped out "—it is a saloon, not a drawing room, you know? I mean, what would you have me do, leave my boots outside?''

Damn straight, she thought to say, but almost at the same instant she realized he was right. She looked around as though seeing the room for the first time. It was a saloon, and if anybody else had walked in here she knew she wouldn't be ranting about boots and muddy floors.

Still, she wouldn't let him get the best of her. "I have an idea." She inched up closer, getting almost in his face. "Why don't you take your belongings and your muddy boots and stay outside?" She made an imperial gesture, pointing with one slender, wet finger toward the closed double doors.

He never budged, never even acted as though he'd heard a word she'd said. Trouble was, she was too close to him and he was looking straight at her; his eyes were soft as velvet and just as compelling, and before she knew it she was frozen in place. Delicious shivers skimmed the back of her neck. Her arm fell lightly to her side.

His mouth quirked up on one side in a lazy, confident smile that was one hundred percent male. Something warm and tight stirred deep inside her. Her breathing went all ragged and shallow. Blessedly, he spoke and broke the spell.

"Now, honey—" His smile moved up a notch and there was a definite knowing gleam in his eyes. "Does this mean you aren't glad to see me?"

"Glad to see you!" The man was too arrogant for words, but a few choice ones were right on the tip of her tongue when she realized there was something different about him.

"Good Lord, you shaved," she blurted out before she could think to stop herself.

That smile of his turned into an all-out grin that was full of boyish charm and dimples and made little lines appear around his eyes. "Why, yes—" his brow pulled down in a mock frown "—I believe I did." He rubbed his chin as though checking the truthfulness of his words. "Do you like it?"

Like? What wasn't to like, the woman in her answered. His face was all smooth curves and deep ravines and totally rugged—like the man himself.

Her gaze flicked down long enough to see that he'd changed clothes, too. Pine green shirt tucked into denim trousers that were faded from too many washings and hugged his lean legs as though he'd put them on wet and they'd shrunk to fit.

When she looked back there was the devil's own glint in those eyes of his. A sensual warmth traveled out along her suddenly trembling nerves.

He shifted, resting one shoulder against the wall. "So how about some help?"

It took her a couple of seconds to get her brain to register his words. "What?" She blinked and made herself step back.

His smile remained firmly in place, and she couldn't help thinking it ought to be illegal for a man to be this handsome or this confident.

She was staring like a schoolgirl, she knew, but couldn't seem to stop. He, on the other hand, was rolling up his sleeves. "Help? You want help?"

"Help?" she stammered. She couldn't possibly have heard him correctly.

Apparently she had, because next thing she knew he was busy unbuckling his spurs from his scarred black boots. He glanced up. "Honey, are you all right?"

"I'm fine," she muttered, giving up on her demand that he stop calling her honey. "What are you talking about?"

Casually he strolled over to the bar, deposited his spurs with a thud and then unstrapped his gun belt and put it there, also.

"You want help cleaning?" he said again in the patient tone parents use with a little child.

His offer and his actions all sank in at once. "You're kidding?"

"Nope." He gave her a wide-eyed look of hurt. "I never joke about work. I can see you're intent on cleaning, and though for the life of me I can't understand why, I figure giving you a hand is the least I can do to sort of pay my way."

Not waiting for her answer, he moved around her, grabbed up the bucket she'd been using, and strode for the back door.

"Where do you think you're going with that?"

"To get fresh water. Don't worry. I'll be back."

Was the man serious? Was he going to get down and wash walls?

A few minutes later he loped back in, bucket in hand. Water glistened in his hair and darkened the tops of his shoulders. He grinned at her, that slow, easy smile that sent goose bumps racing up her legs.

"Okay. Where do you want me to start?"

He didn't really wait for an answer, just picked up where she'd clearly stopped.

"Since when do sheriffs wash walls, or clean at all, for that matter?" She couldn't keep the suspicion out of her voice.

He was up to his elbows in dirty water, and as he squeezed out the cloth, he said, "My mother cleaned our house from top to bottom twice a year, spring and fall." He went back to scrubbing, making big curving swaths on the walnut. "No one escaped. Everyone worked—Mother, Father, me and my sisters." He shoved the bucket along and followed, bracing on one knee.

Clair was standing there like a foreman at a factory. "You have a family?"

He laughed, but kept on working. "Well, yes, it's the usual way for us humans. Of course, having older sisters, I sometimes wondered about that. When I was really little they used to try to dress me up—" he glanced over at her, his face all screwed up in disgust "—in girls' clothes. Can you believe it?"

Actually, she couldn't. Looking at this man, dark and powerful, it was nearly impossible to think of him being overwhelmed by anyone, especially sisters. The man had sisters! Suddenly he seemed much less imposing, less threatening. She relaxed a bit.

"I am having a hard time imagining you in girls' clothes."

"Well, don't think on it too long." He chuckled. "It wasn't a pretty sight, I can tell you." He rinsed the rag again, the water splashing as it ran back into the bucket. "But I got even."

"What did you do?" She was drawn into the story and the man telling it.

"Ah," he responded brightly, "I outgrew them. Yup, I'm six-three and they're...oh, Katie is here—" he motioned midchest "—and Mary Alice is here." He motioned a fraction lower. "So now they're my *little* sisters, even if they are older, which, by the way, they don't like me to mention.''

Before she knew it she was involved in the conversation. She totally forgot who he was, what he was. "Where are they now?"

"Katie's married and lives in Colorado. Mary Alice is in California with my aunt Gladys, but she's looking for a husband and I pity the man who gets corralled by her.''

"Why?" she asked, genuinely curious.

"Why?" he repeated with feigned shock. "Well, the woman is bossier than a schoolteacher and stubborn..." He shook his head woefully. "Of course, they say the stubborn streak runs in the family." He angled his head around for a quick glance at her, amusement dancing in his eyes. "Personally I don't see it, but, well..."

"All things considered, I think 'they' may be right," Clair replied, laughing. The darned man had outmaneuvered her and now here she was laughing with him.

How could she be angry or even afraid when he was down on his knees scrubbing her walls, talking about his family as though the two of them were old friends, as though they'd known each other for years?

She gave up and went to help him. Those were her walls he was so diligently washing, after all, and no one ever said Clair Travers didn't do her share.

"You don't have to do this, you know," she finally said, pushing the bucket along, the wood scraping on the floor.

"I know."

"Why, then?"

"Because you need help.''

Instinctively she knew he meant it, and it occurred to her then that no one had ever helped her just because she needed help. No one except him.

"Thanks," she said sincerely, and felt the first crack in her defenses.

"You're most welcome, ma'am," he returned in a teasing tone that made those darned goose bumps scamper over her legs again.

Another thirty minutes or so and they'd finished. He insisted she rest while he emptied the bucket and put the cleaning supplies away in the storage closet. She sank into the nearest chair. Muscles she hadn't used in years were making themselves heard, mostly along her shoulders and down her back. She rolled her neck, rubbing knotted tendons as she did.

The back door slammed and he strode back in. Her gaze went to him immediately. He went straight to the walls and strolled along inspecting the newly washed wood with all the intensity of a general inspecting the troops. Eyes narrowed, occasionally he'd lean and touch some spot, then make a show of checking his fingertip to see if there was dirt present.

"Hmm," he muttered gravely. "Hmm."

Clair felt the laugh start down in her chest. The more she watched him, the sillier he looked and the sillier she felt. Without hesitation, she laughed, really laughed for the first time since she couldn't remember when.

"I was wondering what it would take to get you to laugh."

When she opened her eyes he was there, right beside her, down on one knee, looking up into her face. As he had one hand on the table and the other on the back of her chair, it was as though she were locked in his embrace. She went very still.

"Anyone ever tell you that you have a laugh that makes a man think about...things he shouldn't think about?"

Chapter Five

Clair felt the heat rise in her cheeks and she didn't need a mirror to know she was blushing. Lord, it had been a long time since anyone had made her blush. While she was trying to recover, he stood and came around behind her.

His large hands curved over the tops of her shoulders.

Clair flinched and with a start tried to twist away, but he held her gently in place.

"Just relax. I won't hurt you." He started to massage her shoulders, lightly at first. His fingers flexed on her aching muscles, pulling at the cotton of her shirtwaist, making her collar tug at her neck until she undid the top two buttons. He rubbed the tendons at the base of her neck.

"Feel good?" His voice was soothing, tantalizing.

"Yes." She gave in to his sweet touch, rolling her shoulders under his hands as though to help, to make sure that he touched her everywhere. Heaven.

Her eyes drifted closed. She relaxed back in the chair. "Nice."

"I'm glad," he murmured.

The steady patter of the rain drowned out all sound but his voice and the slow, steady beating of her heart.

His thumbs glided up the back of her neck, and she rolled her head forward to give him better access. His fingers slipped into her hair. Pins fell unnoticed to the floor. Clair surrendered to the sensual world of his touch.

"Your hair is soft as silk."

His voice was dreamy and seemed far away. His hands drifted down to her shoulders again, then down her spine, his thumbs working magic on the stiffness between her shoulder blades.

More relaxed than she'd been in months, she let her head loll back against him. The edge of his belt buckle pressed against the back of her head and she was aware of his breathing.

"Sleepy?" he asked so softly she almost thought she'd imagined it.

"Hmm."

Dimly she wondered what it would be like if he rubbed lower, if his hands massaged the small of her back where it throbbed from too much bending. His hands would be gentle, she knew, and—

Instantly her eyes snapped opened and she bolted out of the chair. Breathing hard, she whirled around to face him.

"What's wrong?" he asked, his hands gripping the back of the chair she'd just vacated.

"Nothing." She strode for the bar. "Would you like a drink?" She snatched up a bottle and two glasses. "I think I'd like one."

He stared after her for a moment then said, "Sure. What's my choice?"

"There's, ah, whiskey…beer…I think I saw a bot-

tle of wine around here somewhere...." She rummaged around as though she had thousands of choices
to look through back there. She needed a chance to
catch her breath and still the frantic beating of her
heart. "The whiskey is—" she took a sniff of one
bottle and crinkled her nose "—not very good."

When she straightened he was leaning over the bar.
There was a sort of half smile on his lips. She had
the uneasy feeling he knew exactly what she'd been
thinking.

Her pulse took on a funny rhythm and she wasn't
all that surprised to notice that her fingers trembled
when she reached for a glass.

Casual as you please, he lifted the bottle from her
less-than-steady hand and sniffed the contents as she
had done. "This is fine. Better than most I've had."

He poured. She watched, suddenly fascinated by
his hands, remembering the way they had felt on her.

Snatching up her glass, she spilled a little liquid,
ignored it and walked to the window, taking a sip as
she did. Her brain was working overtime. Change the
subject. What subject? Never mind, just change it.
She was acutely aware that they were alone together
and that the Closed sign was still parked in the window. She wished now she'd opened for business.

"I think the rain is letting up," she said, pleased
her voice sounded calmer than she felt.

"Really?"

Out of the corner of her eye she noticed he wasn't
drinking, just watching her. "Yes."

"Too bad." He toyed with the glass.

"Why?"

"I like stormy...weather."

She made the mistake of looking at him more fully. The glint in his devil-black eyes was unmistakable.

"Sheriff McConnell, are you trying to…charm me?" *Seduce* was the word she carefully avoided, though it was the one she thought most fit.

"Would you mind if I was?" he replied in a soft tone that sent those damnable goose bumps skipping up her legs again.

"I give you credit. I don't think anyone ever washed walls for me before. Is this an approach that you've used with ladies before?"

"Actually, I confess, I've never washed walls for a woman before." He chuckled. "Is it working?"

"No," she lied, hoping he didn't hear the catch in her voice.

He made a show of sighing. "Too bad. I guess I'll have to try something else to win you over. I thought we were making real progress there." He motioned toward the chair she had been seated in minutes ago.

"Oh, the neck rub was nice, but you're wasting your time if—"

"I have the time."

"Then you might consider spending it somewhere else, with someone else." She hadn't forgotten, not for long, anyway, that being with him was dangerous—in more ways than one.

He tossed back his drink in one long swallow, making a small grimace as the whiskey hit the back of his throat. "You know, you keep talking about me moving on. I just got here."

"Well, I assume you have duties…other places— a home, perhaps, a wife, children who miss you."

"If you want to know if I'm married—"

"I don't."

"Well, in case you change your mind, I usually live in Rawlins, and I live alone. No wife. No children."

Secretly, she was glad. She shouldn't have been, but she was. She strolled over to the end of the bar and he closed in to meet her.

Clair put her glass down, though she clung to it as if it offered some kind of defense against him. "You mean you aren't there in Rawlins very often?"

"I'm not anywhere very often. I'm the sheriff of this county. That's about, oh, fifteen thousand square miles of Wyoming."

"That's a lot of area to cover." She took another sip of whiskey. He still hadn't made any overt gestures and, feeling braver, she decided to ask the burning question once and for all. "So then, you aren't here...in Broken Spur, I mean...looking for someone?"

"Like who?"

"Oh, anyone." Her tightening grip on the glass was her only outward show of nerves.

After what seemed an endlessly long time he said, "Water rights. I'm staying here because of a dispute over water rights."

That was it? Water rights? She wanted to cheer.

He wasn't looking for her!

She was grinning like a kid on the last day of school and she had half a notion to haul off and kiss the man. She didn't. Instead she walked over to a table and sank onto one of the chairs.

But she kept on grinning, and if he noticed he didn't ask why. Somehow, she managed to make conversation. "Water rights, huh? Someone's complaining they've got too much water, is that it?"

"You'd think so, wouldn't you, but no. Actually a couple of the locals have decided one has too much and isn't willing to share with the other."

"Ah." She was only half listening, groping to keep up her end of the conversation. Her mind was still reeling with the welcome news that he wasn't looking for her.

Jake followed her to the table, bringing the bottle and his glass with him. Taking a seat, he said, "Since we're asking questions, how about telling me what brings you to Broken Spur?"

"Oh, nothing in particular. I was just passing through." He might not be looking for her, but she wasn't going to give him any reason to change that.

"And you won the saloon?" He shifted, his boots making a scuffing sound on the bare floor.

Clair toyed with her drink, revolving the green glass around in her fingers, the whiskey occasionally sloshing and making rings on the scarred tabletop. "True."

"Was it poker, faro...?"

"Poker," she confirmed. "Aces over a jack high straight."

"What made Bill put up the place?"

"Beats me. The man was intent on besting me at poker, and I guess his male pride overcame good sense, what with several men watching and all. He kept upping the ante. I tried to talk him out of it, but he wasn't having it, so-o-o..."

"You're a good poker player, then, I take it."

"It's how I earn a living, so, yes, I'm a good poker player." She was proud of what she did and how well she did it.

He helped himself to a half glass more. "So what happened after that?"

"Next morning Bill signed the deed and left. He said he'd been wanting to go to California and that he hadn't wanted to sell out to Slocum."

"Yeah, I know Slocum. He's your competition and he'll play rough if he thinks he can get away with it. If you have any trouble let me know—or Woodrow, Marshal Murphy."

"Thanks. I appreciate the warning, but us ladies—" she gestured to the open room "—will do just fine."

"Ladies, huh?" He chuckled.

"Of course. We Scarlet Ladies have to stick together."

Jake leaned back in his chair, perusing the room and her in one quick motion. He liked her, liked her a lot.

"Just so you know, Miss Smith," he said, "I have a real fondness for things scarlet."

She shoved back her chair. He stopped her with a touch.

"So you own the saloon and..."

She slipped her hand free of his, but remained seated. "I thought I'd fix it up, do some cleaning—"

"I got that part."

"Pull down that awful wallpaper—"

"Take down some of the pictures and put up lace curtains..."

He was teasing her again, all soft and friendly, and it would be so easy to slide right into his game, but she couldn't. "I'm not foolish, Sheriff. I know what a man likes."

"Do you really, Miss Smith?"

It was a provocative question if she ever heard one, and she'd heard plenty in her life. If she was such an old hand at this, how come her nerves went all tingly and thready?

One minute they were talking about the saloon, the next...

She ignored the question and wished she could ignore the man as easily. "So, as I was saying..." She plunged ahead. "I think the place can be made presentable and I can make a living here."

He raked her with an appraising stare. "You know, Miss Smith, I think you could do anything you set your mind to doing."

"Thanks." She was trying hard not to like him, but failing miserably at every turn.

"No thanks necessary. Would you do me a favor?"

"Depends."

"Would you call me Jake?"

"All right. Jake." The sound of rain was a distant second to the sound of defenses crumbling.

He shifted, crossing his legs to rest one booted foot on the opposite knee. "How'd you come to be a gambler, anyway? Not a usual occupation for most women."

"I'm not most women," she replied.

"I can see that. What I meant was that most women—" he chuckled at his repeated use of the words "—choose marriage."

"How do you know I'm not married?"

He hesitated for the barest second and she gave him high marks for his quick recovery. "Are you?"

"No."

"I'm glad." His voice had a husky tone.

When she didn't answer, he continued. "Then why not—"

"Because, like I said, I have to earn a living. I have to eat and sleep somewhere, and that takes money. Doing what I do, where I work, the men I meet aren't usually looking for permanence, if you know what I mean."

Jake did and nodded in reply. "But still, women are in short supply out here and ranchers or farmers—"

"Are looking for someone to cook and clean and pull the plow when the mule dies."

He laughed. "That bad, huh?"

She chuckled. "No, not really, but there is one truth to it. I mean, it's the nature of life on a ranch or farm. It's not for me."

"Gambling's easier, huh?"

"Not hardly. You try sitting in a saloon night after night, tobacco smoke so thick your eyes water until you can barely make out the cards. Every couple of weeks, moving on, a new game, a new town, never having a home or anyone—" She broke off, realizing she was revealing too much about herself. He had a way of making her feel at ease. Dangerous.

"Or what?" he prompted.

Warning bells were sounding in her head.

"Why all the questions, Sheriff?"

"Occupational habit, I guess, and I'm genuinely interested."

Those warning bells were loud enough to start an avalanche. "Why?"

"Why not?"

There was a challenge in his tone that made her temper flare. "Okay, Sheriff. Fine. You want details.

Here's details. I was on my own at fourteen. I learned to gamble on the docks of New Orleans.'' Her tone and demeanor were defiant, challenging. ''By the time I was seventeen I was earning my living working in saloons and gambling halls from New Orleans to San Francisco. I've worked mining camps and cow towns and places most men won't go alone. I've been pawed and prodded and generally manhandled. I've played faro and monte and just about any game where I can win a dollar. Have I had sex before?'' She gave a harsh laugh, thinking of Sully. ''Yes, Sheriff, I'm no saint, don't pretend to be. But am I a whore? No! Now, does that answer all your questions?''

Without warning he reached out and took her hand, his expression serious.

''I'm sorry if my questions offended you. My mother raised me better,'' he said sincerely.

''But listening to you,'' he continued, his grip tightening on her hand, ''it seems that you and I have some things in common.''

''I doubt that,'' she said, liking the warmth of his touch.

''Well, like you, I'm on the move most of the time and I don't own a thing, except for a few acres of land west of here that I bought one of those times I was feeling like I needed someplace to call home.'' He wrinkled his brow and chuckled. ''Crazy, huh?''

''No,'' Clair said quietly, startled by his honest revelation. She knew exactly what it meant to have a home, or not to. That's why the Scarlet Lady meant so much to her.

Pulling free of his grasp, this time she did stand and walk over to inspect that newly washed wood paneling, to inspect the peeling wallpaper, to do anything except sit there and be drawn into a web he wove much too easily around her.

Looking thoughtful, Jake swiveled in his chair, one arm hooked casually over the curved back, his chin resting on the back of his hand. "It seems, scarlet lady, that these days we are both pretty much alone in the world."

There was a moment of uneasy silence, then abruptly he stood. In four long strides he was there beside her. "How long will it take you to get ready?"

She shook her head at the sudden change in him and in the conversation. "Ready? Ready for what?" she cranked her neck to look up into his downturned face. He was too close—way too close for comfort.

"Why, dinner, of course. It's Saturday, and Nellie Wills always makes pie on Saturday. I assume that with the rain and the state of your cleaning you aren't planning to open tonight."

"Actually, I was."

"Naw. It won't be worth it for a couple of locals. Besides, you don't want to miss Nellie." He produced a silver pocket watch, clicked open the cover and checked the time. "It's five o'clock. Can you be ready in twenty minutes?"

Without waiting for her answer, he had her by the arm and was propelling her toward the stairs.

"Whoa." She dug in her heels. "What's this about dinner and pie and who's Nellie Sills?"

"Wills. Nellie Wills. She owns the restaurant, and today is Saturday and—"

"I got that part."

He grinned. "Okay, then, get going. I'm hungry enough to eat a horse."

"What on earth makes you think I'm going to dinner with you?"

He was instantly contrite, about as contrite as a kid with his hand in the candy jar. "You are hungry, aren't you?"

"Well, yes, but—"

"Me, too. Working makes me hungry. Hurry up. I'll wash up out back and we'll be on our way."

Thirty minutes later Clair had changed and, against all rational wisdom, decided to keep the saloon closed and go to dinner with Jake. He was right—the dinner, the pie and Nellie Wills were all wonderful.

Jake, she discovered, might not live here but he knew almost everyone in town or they knew him. The restaurant was a quarter full—couples mostly, town folks and their wives, most likely. If people stopped to greet him, he always introduced her, said she was the new owner of the Scarlet Lady. It didn't take her long to realize what he was doing. He was helping her, giving her his official stamp of approval, so to speak.

It was an incredibly generous thing for him to do, especially after the way she'd snapped at him, and the man had still washed her walls. He confused and astounded her.

They lingered over coffee until three hours had passed. The rain had stopped by the time they strolled back to the saloon. The sidewalk was a grayish black from the water, the planks curled at the edges, so that she had to watch her step. Jake took her arm and she felt for all the world like a couple, like those she'd seen in the restaurant—a couple out for an evening then going home together. It was a nice feeling.

"Looks like it'll be clear by tomorrow," he said, sparing the sky a glance before he pushed open the door for her. He stepped back and she preceded him inside.

Wordlessly he walked her to the bottom of the stairs, like a gentleman caller returning his charge safely home for the night. She stood one step above him.

"Jake..."

"Yes?"

"Thanks."

He took off his hat. "For dinner? Sure. Anytime."

"No, for what you did there. For introducing me, for helping me."

"My pleasure."

For a long moment she looked down into his up-turned face and then... It seemed so natural, so easy. She kissed him. Just a gentle brush of her lips on his. But his lips were warm against hers. She felt more than saw him toss his hat aside before his hands drifted to her waist then slid around, pulling her against him. He lifted her from the stairs, her body pressed length-to-length against his, her feet suspended inches from the floor.

She clung to him, her fingers curled into the muscles at the tops of his shoulders. The world, like the floor, dropped away. The silence of the room wrapped around them like a cloak, shutting out all thought, all fear.

The kiss turned more urgent, more demanding, setting off a lightning storm in her like nothing she'd known before. Jake's fingers dug into her ribs as he held her. When his tongue laved at her lips, demanding entrance, she instinctively welcomed him. The jolt of desire that flashed through her was hotter than summer in the desert.

Never fully releasing her, he let her slide down the front of him, her skirt catching on the buckle of his gun belt, his hands gliding up under her arms while his thumbs brushed the sides of her breasts, setting off a heart-pounding rush of desire she was totally unprepared for.

As her feet settled on the floor, she made a small moan of protest, not wanting this moment to end, not wanting to let him go.

Jake heard the little sound, felt her arch into him. Knew she felt what he was feeling and knew that she didn't have to worry—no way was he letting her go. Muscles tensed with sudden urgency.

His grip tightened fractionally before he let his hands play across her slender shoulders, down to the curve of her narrow waist and back again. Somewhere in the recesses of his mind, he realized she wasn't wearing a corset.

He moved against her. Her breasts were firm and enticing, pressed as they were against his chest. The woman was heating his blood faster than fire. She felt good, really good. Lord, how he wanted her. Lust surged in his body and his brain. All he could think of was being naked against her naked body and...

Greedy, hungry, he ate at her mouth, laved at the tender inside. She tasted like coffee and sweet apples. She felt like heaven.

Lifting his mouth from hers just enough to speak, he said, "Let's go upstairs, honey, where we'll be more comfortable." With that, he started to turn her toward the beckoning stairs and the rooms beyond.

The reality of his words hit her like a splash of

cold water. Clair blinked, then blinked again. The faint voice of warning echoed in her brain. Fear overwhelmed desire. Her world filled in around her—the saloon, the rain, the lawman who was holding her.

What the devil are you doing, Clair?

"No," she said, as much for herself as him. She pushed him hard. "Who do you think you are?" she raged at him, clinging to the rage like a lifeline. "Let go of me! Who do you think *I* am!"

With passion clouding his brain, Jake felt his temper flare. "I thought you were a woman who wants to get naked as much as I do."

Desire disappeared faster than gold in a mining camp. "Why, you arrogant bastard! I do not want you." She pulled free of him.

He looked momentarily taken aback, his eyes wide with suppressed passion. Then he seemed to recover. "Woman, you can curse me all you want, but I know what was happening here. You want me as much as I want you."

Without thinking, Clair reached back and swung on him, but he caught her hand, trapping it in his larger one. Black eyes locked with blue, and then he released her.

"Stay away from me!" she flung at him, and with a flounce of black cotton she spun on her heel and stormed up the stairs. Breathing ragged, Jake watched her go. He heard her door slam, hard enough to break the damned hinges. He had half a mind to go after her, to tell her…

"Damn!" He snatched up his hat from the floor and slammed out the front doors.

Chapter Six

It was early morning and Jake was on his way out to the Bar W, slogging his way through the mud soup of a road and spending an hour on a twenty-minute trip.

A bobwhite warbled out his song and sprang up from a sage bush in a flutter of feathers and squawked protest. The gelding shied and Jake, being in a dark-tempered mood that lingered from yesterday, jerked hard on the reins. The horse balked and tossed his head in righteous complaint.

"Sorry, boy, I didn't mean to take it out on you."

Sun glinted on the water that pooled along the roadside. Jake squinted and adjusted his hat lower in a futile effort to shield his eyes. He was riding straight into the sun. The weather had changed overnight and was bright and cheerful. Jake wasn't.

Of course, he knew his mood had nothing to do with the weather or horse or birds. His mood had everything to do with the woman—Clair.

Jake twisted in the saddle, the leather creaking as he did. Hand braced on the horse's sun-warmed back, he looked in the direction of town—not that he could see it or her, but she was back there, all right.

He knew exactly where she was. Right this minute she was in the Scarlet Lady, probably cursing him six ways from Sunday—and, you know what, she was right. He'd been way out of line yesterday.

Facing forward again, he casually adjusted the leather reins through his fingers and settled comfortably in the saddle.

He'd spent the night in his room, although he'd been sorely tempted to knock on her door. Clair had been up long before him this morning, though. She'd looked tired.

He'd tried to ignore their trouble of the night before—no sense bringing up bad feelings and all. So he'd spoken to her. She'd turned her back. He'd done everything he could think of to coax and cajole her. Nothing. Not a sound, not a smile, not even a frown. She had walked around him as though he were invisible and, to tell the truth, he wished he had been.

There she'd been, sleeves rolled up, skirt tucked around her legs, scrubbing tables and humming some unrecognizable tune that seemed to get louder with every word he spoke.

Finally his temper had got the best of him and he'd stormed out. He had work to do.

So why are you thinking about her now?

Damned if he knew. Maybe because she got him so riled. Maybe because she was the damnedest woman he'd ever met.

There was something about her, something elusive, something exciting, something that kept his thoughts going back to her and that kiss.

It was a hell of a kiss. His body tensed slightly at

the rich memory. No matter what she said, what he'd done, the lady had liked that kiss. What's more, she'd kissed him back, and that was more than male pride talking. She'd kissed him the way a man wants to be kissed, as though she'd been waiting for him all her life.

Oh, she'd gotten her message across to him earlier. She was no nun, but then Jake McConnell was definitely no monk, either—sinners both, he supposed. That, too, was another bond, of sorts. It seemed they had a great many things in common. Who'd have thought? Sure as hell not him.

He shifted in the saddle, easing his spine, his hand resting lightly on the horn. A slow smile pulled up the corners of his mouth.

Lady, this isn't over. Not by a long shot.

He spotted the gate to the Bar W and turned in. The house was visible at the end of the quarter-mile roadway. He circled around the barn and corral where a couple of cowboys were busy breaking what looked to be a particularly ornery bronc.

The breeze fluttered the blue-speckled bandanna at his neck and he pushed it down into the open neck of his green shirt. The sun warmed the leather of his shotgun chaps and his denim-clad legs beneath. Looked like it might be a hot one today.

Two men, perched like a pair of blackbirds on the top log of the fence, turned and stared.

"Jerry. Nat," Jake said by way of hello. He reined up at the hitching post in front of the house, a one-story fading white clapboard. The roof was wood shingles and looked to need repair after the bad winter they'd had.

Earl Hansen came out on the porch. He was a tall

man, well over six feet, barrel-chested, with shoulders like a bear. Jake had known Earl off and on for about four years and, on the whole, liked him well enough.

"Sheriff," Earl said, sunlight highlighting his thinning brown hair.

Jake swung down, saddle leather flexing and groaning with the change in weight. "Morning, Earl." He started up the path, spurs jingling, pebbles crunching under his boots as he walked. "Turned out to be a nice day, don't you think?"

"Depends."

"On what?" Jake asked, stepping up on the porch.

"On whether you've come to tell me that Amos Carter is six feet under."

It was Sunday and, though there was no church in town, out of respect Clair kept the saloon closed until two in the afternoon. The storm was gone outside and the sky she could see through the dirt-smudged window was pale blue with puffy white clouds drifting across the sun.

As was her habit on Sunday, Clair had gotten up early. She hadn't read the Bible because she didn't have one, but she'd said a prayer of thanks for all her good fortune and then gone downstairs to finish washing the tables and chairs and the bar.

He'd come down shortly after her. She'd ignored him. He'd finally given up and left. Good. She'd let her guard down last night, but this morning was a different story and he might as well get that idea straight right now.

Once he was gone, she had set to work with a vengeance—idle minds could get a person in a lot of trouble.

She had taken down what she considered the more provocative paintings of women in various stages of undress. She'd decided to leave a stuffed elk head on the back wall. Jake's remark about lace curtains flitted annoyingly through her mind and she was tempted to put up a pair or two just to spite him.

She quickly snatched back that idea. He was not to be considered or thought about or in any way allowed to get too close to her again. Instantly she thought about their kiss, and her hand fluttered to her lips with the heated memory.

She straightened, chided herself for her foolishness and went back to work. She refilled all the bottles behind the bar with the limited assortment of rye, whiskey, bourbon and rum. She washed the bar towels by hand and draped them over a chair in her room to dry in the sunlight.

By four, she was tired and dirty and, except for one man, there hadn't been any customers. As much as she was grateful for the time to do some work, she wasn't foolish enough to think that she didn't need customers to keep this place going. All her work wouldn't be worth beans if she didn't get some business in here, Sunday or no Sunday.

Her hair came loose from the pins and she put it up again. She wandered to the front doors that were propped open as a way of letting people know she was ready for business.

Outside, a few people were stirring. Across the street a woman was looking intently at a yellow gingham dress displayed in the window of Ruth's Dress Shop. An energetic little boy was tugging on her hand, evidently anxious to move on—dresses not being of any interest at all—but his mother seemed to admonish him and a moment later they went inside.

It was a perfectly ordinary scene, nothing unusual at all, and yet for reasons she didn't understand she was suddenly assailed with feelings of sadness and loss, feelings so intense she actually had to take in a steadying breath. Such a scene would never be Clair's. No, Clair was destined to be alone because she wasn't willing to settle for less than love and she knew she'd never find it—not a woman like her.

Into her mind flashed visions of a certain broad-shouldered cowboy of a lawman with eyes a woman could easily drown in and—

Stop it!

Her chin came up in a defiant gesture and, stepping back, she closed the door on the thought, on the man and on any regrets. She was who she was, and there was no sense wishing otherwise.

But try as she might, she couldn't quite dispel the image of the man, easy and laughing, his hands working magic on her shoulders, his mouth working magic on her nerves.

Kissing Jake was insane. The kiss had been a momentary lapse in judgment, a weakness brought on by exhaustion. Yes, that was it. Anyway, Clair wasn't a fool. Jake was dangerous, about the most dangerous person within a hundred miles. The odds were a million to one against her, and even she knew when to back away from the game.

Okay, so he'd be around for a few more days. She'd be busy working. She would hardly have time to do more than say hello.

The rumble of a wagon in the street and the sound of voices passing by roused her from her musings.

She jolted as though being suddenly awakened. Hey, lollygagging around here wasn't going to get it done.

"So," she said out loud, looking around, "what are we going to do to get some customers in here?"

Something different was called for, something to set her saloon apart from the other. Liquor was important and Clair knew that what she had wasn't the best, but then again, the best was probably out of the financial reach of most of the men around here, so why bother, at least for now.

Men came into a saloon for a place to talk, catch up on news and gossip, to relax away from work and sometimes family. They liked to talk politics and the price of cattle. They wanted to play pool and eat and drink. They liked music with their food and entertainment.

There was no way to get a pool table in here even if she had the money, which she didn't. Hiring musicians was doubtful and took time she didn't have. Her money wouldn't last forever and she needed some income.

"But..." she said out loud, her eyes lighting up with an idea. "I could..." The more she thought about it, the better it sounded.

"Scarlet Lady, I think we're in business."

First things first, and that meant a bath. After she got some water heating, she went to Nelson's, explained her plan to Larry and charged enough salted ham, cheddar cheese, crackers and pickled eggs to feed fifty men.

She displayed the items carefully on the end of the bar, the one in plain view from the open doors. Using the back of the Closed sign, she printed the words Free Lunch.

* * *

After her bath, Clair made a quick check in the mirror, gave herself a couple of firm pinches on each cheek and headed downstairs. She put the sign in the window. It was nearly five o'clock and, stepping out on the sidewalk, she could see men going into the Lazy Dog, her competition.

The breeze fluttered her hem and cooled her bare shoulders above the black-lace-trimmed neckline of her dress.

A woman strolled past, gave her a hostile glare and pronounced, "Harmph."

Clair barely noticed. She was focused on her destination. Her nerve faltered. This plan of hers had seemed a lot better when she was inside the Scarlet Lady; as it was, well, it was brazen as hell.

Maybe, but she had to do something to let customers know she was ready to do business. Fists clenched, jaw fixed, she strode down the sidewalk. When she got closer she heard men's voices carrying out through the open doors. This was it. Now or never.

The customers you want are in there, and they think you are a conniving cheat who robbed good ole Bill of his saloon. You've got to show them they're wrong.

She took a deep, steadying breath and walked inside.

All talking ceased. At least she had their attention. She turned her most radiant smile in the direction of the man behind the bar. "Good evening," she said as though she came here every night. She strolled around the room. The men watched with undisguised interest. It was exactly what she wanted. Once they got a good look, they'd see she was perfectly ordinary, not too ordinary, but not someone to be shunned—she hoped.

The man behind the bar, the notorious Slocum, said, "What the hell are you doing in here, woman?"

So much for friendly competition—and she remembered Jake's warning about Slocum playing dirty. Clair could take care of herself.

She feigned a look of wide-eyed shock at his bluntness. "Why, Mr. Slocum, I'm just visiting, is all. This is a public establishment, isn't it?"

"Visiting, is it?" He came around the bar as though he was being chased by fire and skidded to a halt inches from her face. "Get outta my place. I know what you're up to, and it won't work!"

She pretended hurt. She had the attention of every man in the room.

"But, Mr. Slocum—"

"I'm telling you to get moving or else," Slocum snarled.

Clair was tempted to put a knee right where it would do the most good, but she restrained herself. Instead she made her chin quiver and blinked and gulped and generally looked for all the world as though she were devastated. "You mean I can't even come in here?" she asked in a helpless little voice that would have made a New York actress proud.

"You heard me!" His eyes bulged and his face was mottled red.

"But why?" she simpered, making her voice crack.

"Yeah, why?" One of the customers, a man in a brown suit whom she'd met briefly at dinner the other night, spoke up. "Why, Slocum?"

"You ain't got no call to yell at her." Another

man, one she'd never met, spoke up in her defense. This was going better than she'd hoped.

Clair made a show of pulling a handkerchief from her bodice and dabbed appropriately at her eyes. "It's all right, gentlemen," she said demurely. "I'll go back over to the Scarlet Lady." She said the name quite loudly. "I only came over here because, well, a lady gets lonely all by herself with no one to talk to. It's just me and the Scarlet Lady. I guess I'll have to eat all that *free food* by myself...all alone." Another look of rejection and she left.

Bold and saucy, she sauntered back to the Scarlet Lady and waited. She didn't have to wait long.

Two of the men drifted in shortly after she'd returned. They stood two steps inside the doorway.

"Come in, gentlemen," she encouraged brightly. "Make yourselves at home. Have a bit to eat if you like." She gestured toward the banquet she'd put out. It was around dinnertime, after all.

"Free food?" one asked.

"Absolutely," Clair replied, and the men honed in as if they hadn't eaten in a week. "What will you have to drink?"

"Beer," they said practically in unison. Clair served. Larry had volunteered to come in later as a way of escaping his mother's piano recital.

Three more men ambled in. "Help yourselves to the food, gentlemen," she repeated, and took their drink orders.

But even with the food and drink, the men were whispering as though they were in church—no way to run a saloon. Men needed to feel comfortable.

"So what do you boys think about the price of cattle this year?" she asked.

That was enough. The men started talking and complaining and she relaxed.

Larry came to work right on time and by nine the place was two-thirds full. She didn't offer to play cards, thinking she wanted them to get used to her and the saloon. Customers first, then cards.

It was about ten-thirty when the barman from the Lazy Dog came in. He surveyed the room with a proprietary interest then headed right for her. Clair stiffened, but she didn't back down. He was on her territory now.

He was wearing a stained white shirt and black trousers that were two inches too short. "Woman, you want trouble, I'm just the man to give it to you."

"I'm running a business here, Slocum. Either buy a drink or leave." She met his angry, beady-eyed glare head-on.

"You stay out of my place and stop stealing my customers." He slammed his fist on the bar and got a lot of unwanted attention for his trouble. He plastered a ferret-faced smile on his face as though to assure those closest that all was well.

Clair didn't feel like smiling. "I didn't steal your customers. They can go wherever they like. It is a free country."

"Look, lady, maybe you don't understand." He leaned in and the scent of bay rum wasn't enough to overcome his lack of personal hygiene.

Larry sidestepped over. "Everything all right? Because I could—"

"Fine, Larry," she told him, appreciating his willingness to help, but she didn't want a fight in here. "Everything's fine. Thanks."

His brows pulled down and he hesitated before he went to serve a customer.

Slocum growled, "Let me set you straight. I—" he thumbed his chest "—will put you outta business, one way or another."

"Go ahead and try, Slocum," she retorted. "You don't scare me. Besides, it looks like you're the one who's worried."

His brown eyes got all small.

"Me? I'm not worried." He angled around and spoke loudly, so loudly that everyone in the room could hear. "Word's out on you, sweetheart. How you cheated poor old Bill outta all his money and then when he didn't have any more, you got him to bet the saloon and—"

"You're a liar, Slocum."

"What?"

"You heard me. I said you're a liar. I didn't cheat Bill and I have witnesses that would say it's true." She might as well tell it all, get it straight. "It was his idea to play poker, his idea to wager his saloon."

"Sure, sweetheart," he said in a smug tone that dripped with sarcasm. "If you say so. After all, we all know what women who work in saloons are. They're just whores who get a man's money one way or another."

He raked her with an insolent stare. "I'd ask how much to get to know you, but I don't fancy wagering my saloon and—"

"Get out, Slocum!" she cried. "Do it now or I'll—"

"You'll what?"

"What's going on here?" Woodrow's sharp voice cut through the scene like a sword. He strode into the room and headed straight for Clair and Slocum, lamp-light catching on the badge pinned to his brown wool vest.

Woodrow had been making the rounds when he'd seen Slocum headed this way, and he could tell by the way the man was walking that he had a head of steam up.

"Slocum? You're in the wrong place, aren't you?"

Clair was seeing red. She was seeing this bastard Slocum drawn and quartered—slowly. It took a second for her to realize that the tall, gray-haired man striding toward them was the town marshal. Great. Trouble with the law. *Here it comes.*

"Look, Marshal," she began, and was surprised when he didn't accuse her of doing wrong. Instead, the man got right in Slocum's face. When he spoke again he addressed Clair. "You having trouble, ma'am?"

Ma'am? Did he say ma'am? No lawman had ever given her the benefit of the doubt before. "Ah, no, not really." She didn't want any more trouble. She sure didn't want anyone arrested, which might mean she'd have to go to court. As much as the thought of Slocum behind bars appealed to her, she said, "No trouble. Mr. Slocum was *just leaving.*"

The marshal wedged himself between Slocum and the bar, a sort of show of strength, a sort of daring the man to do something—take a swing, perhaps. Slocum edged away. "You sure, ma'am?"

"I'm sure."

"Hey!" Slocum piped up. "What are you getting on me for? She's the one." He pointed a thick finger in her direction. "Why don't you arrest her? She's the cheat and the whore, everyone knows—"

"I ain't seen her cheat." Woodrow cast about the room. "Anyone here got any complaints about cheating...or anything else?"

A cowboy she'd met the first night spoke up. "She don't cheat. I was here when Bill bet the place, and she tried to talk him out of doing it, and that's a fact."

"There ya go, Slocum. The woman don't cheat."

"Are you gonna believe some drunken cowboy over me?" Slocum bellowed. "If I go to the town council and tell 'em—"

"They'll laugh in your face," Woodrow retorted. "Now get the hell outta here."

Slocum straightened his shirtfront and spared those present an icy glare before he stormed out of the place.

The saloon was as quiet as a tomb. All eyes focused on Clair and the marshal.

Woodrow spoke up. "All right, boys, show's over. Better get back to them beers before the foam's gone."

Those present immediately did as they were told.

Clair waited as the marshal turned back to her.

"Miss?" Woodrow said politely. "Don't pay Slocum too much attention. He's more talk than action."

Clair's gaze was boring a hole in the doors where the blasted man had stormed out. Who did he think he was, coming in here, calling her a whore? Why, if she'd had a gun...

Memories of a gun in her hand, her finger on the trigger, the deafening explosion, the scream as the bullet penetrated flesh...

She gulped in a lungful of air and willed the memories away. Fingers trembling, she grabbed the bar for support.

"What were you saying?"

Larry came up beside her. "You okay?"

"Yes. Thanks." She gave him an affectionate pat on the shoulder and he went back to work.

"Marshal, can I buy you a beer?" she said when she finally got her temper under control.

"No, ma'am, I never take something I can pay for myself, so I'll buy my own if you'll join me?"

"Excuse me?" A local sheriff who was not only fair but honest—didn't even want a free beer. What kind of town was this? "Beer's free, Marshal, if you—"

"No, ma'am." He tossed two bits on the counter. "Join me?"

"Marshal, it would be my pleasure."

Chapter Seven

Jake and Earl had been talking quietly for a while—a little too quietly for Jake's comfort. Other than that comment when he'd arrived, Earl hadn't said another thing about Amos Carter.

Jake had decided to ignore the remark and take it slowly. He was seated on the settee and Earl was in the chair opposite.

They made some small talk about horses and cattle and the latest news from Cheyenne. They talked about statehood and the governor and even those rascals in Washington. They talked about everything except what was on both their minds.

They shared a couple of glasses of very fine Irish whiskey. Earl always did have good taste in whiskey, Jake thought.

His near-empty glass in his hand, Jake said as matter-of-factly as he could, "How's chances of us working out a compromise on this water issue?"

Earl looked at Jake so long he was about to repeat the question when the man said, "There's nothing to work out."

Jake tossed back the last of the whiskey and refused another, putting the crystal glass on the low walnut table in front of the settee. "Well, seems like there is."

"That's your opinion."

Jake took a few seconds to collect his thoughts. This wasn't going to be easy—he could see that now. Elbows on knees, he studied the faded blue and red flowers in the well-worn carpet. "Billy around?"

Earl's expression turned dark at the mention of his son. "Why?"

"I wanted to ask him a couple of questions." Jake looked up. He fingered the brim of his hat, which was lying on the settee beside him.

"Cut to the chase." Earl's thick brows converged into almost a single line with his frown. "What have you been hearing, McConnell?"

"I heard there was some trouble between him and Sally Carter." Woodrow hadn't found out a thing by talking to the Hocksettler girl. She claimed all she knew was that Sally was with her aunt in Chicago, going to some girl's school and being homesick. She'd even showed Woodrow Sally's last letter.

Earl finished off his whiskey. "You could say that there was some trouble."

"What would you say? I'd like to hear your side of this dispute."

"Hell, Jake, don't be pussyfooting around here. You know as well as I do that it's all over this county that Carter up and sent his girl back east when he found out her and Billy had been courting."

"You mean he was going over without her father's consent?" This might be 1879, but young ladies— good girls—still needed their father's permission to be courted.

"How the hell would I know?" Earl answered.

"Come on, Earl, if this is about pride and hurt feelings, then we can work it out. All we have to do is sit down and talk."

"I've talked to him and I'm not doing it again. Bastard ordered me off his place, ordered Billy to stay off, too."

"But you and Amos Carter have been friends for years."

"That's right, and now Carter goes and gets on his high horse—with me!" Earl glared at Jake. "I'm not taking that kind of affront, especially not from him!"

"That's all well and good, but courting or not has nothing to do with water rights. When you cut off a man's access to water, you're breaking the law, and that means you and I are gonna go head-to-head." He didn't try to keep the hard edge out of his voice. He wanted Earl to know he meant business. "If I can get Carter to come in and talk, would—"

"I told you, McConnell, I'm done talking." Earl surged to his feet. "In the meantime, let the bastard sue me if he wants."

Jake's temper was on the rise. "It'll take till fall to get on the court docket, maybe longer." He knew from the last territorial bulletin that there was a shortage of judges and an abundance of civil suits. "Come on, Earl, you can't mean to stand by and watch four thousand head die of thirst."

"Like I said, if he don't like it, then he can sue me. If I'm wrong, well, then..." He shrugged.

The front door opened and Billy, the object of their discussion, strode in. At twenty, he was a nice-looking young man. Shorter than Jake and thinner, his dark auburn hair curled out around the edges of his sweat-stained brown hat. His clothes, blue plaid shirt and denim trousers, were dirty, like the clothes of a man who worked for a living. "Jake." He tossed his hat down on the leather-covered chair by the door. "I just rode in and heard you were here. Everything all right?"

"No." Jake stood and offered Billy his hand. He'd always liked Billy. The kid, who wasn't a kid anymore, was the call-'em-like-you-see-'em kind of person that Jake felt comfortable with. Probably because he was that way himself.

"What's going on?" Billy's blue-eyed gaze flitted from Jake to his father and back again.

Jake spoke up first. "I'm telling—" he emphasized the last word "—your father to take down the dam he built. If he doesn't... Well, you talk to him."

Billy visibly sighed and grimaced. "Pa, I told you not to—"

"Never mind what you told me." His father cut across his words, waving a dismissive hand. "*I'm* still running this ranch."

"It's not right, Pa."

Earl made a grumbling sound in his throat, then paced over to the fireplace, empty and cold now, ashes from an earlier fire thick on the stone bottom.

Jake picked up his hat and held it loosely in his left hand. "You know, Earl, I could arrest you and take the dam down myself." The problem there was that the dam was on private property, and until there was a court order his hands were tied.

"Go ahead, McConnell," Earl said, his expression smug. "There's laws about trespassing, destruction of property."

"Earl, you're playing fast and loose with the law and I don't like it."

"Maybe so, but there's not a thing you can do about it and we both know it."

Billy took up the cause. "Dammit, Pa, Mr. Carter is threatening a range war—you know what he said."

"I ain't afraid of him. Let him come for me if he's got the nerve."

Billy continued, "Well, looks like you're gonna get your wish, 'cause there's already been trouble on the north range. That's what I come to tell you."

"What kind of trouble?" Jake demanded.

"Nothing much," Billy assured him. "Some name-calling between a couple of our men and a couple of his, is all, some threats, a challenge...you know."

"Yeah, I know." Jake knew only too well. "This is it. That rain will hold things off for a while, but another month and there's gonna be real trouble if you don't tear down that dam and let the water go."

Earl faced Jake, feet braced, his jaw set. "That man insulted me and mine and I ain't takin' it. You understand me, McConnell? As far as I'm concerned, you can tell Amos Carter to go straight to hell."

With that, Earl stormed from the room. Jake and Billy looked at each other.

"Jake, me and Sally never meant for this to happen."

Jake slapped his hat on his head. "I know, Billy."

"He's my father and I love the ornery old coot, but he's wrong in this. I've told him so, but he won't listen. I've thought about going out there and tearing the dam down, but I know as soon as he found out he'd only have the thing put back again."

Jake had a bad feeling about this.

* * *

Jake stopped by the MJ on his way back to town. Carter wasn't in a very charitable mood, and was less so after Jake told him he hadn't made any progress.

Short and stocky, Amos Carter craned his neck up at the late afternoon sun then looked hard at Jake. "The way this weather's warming it won't be long before them water tanks are empty. When that happens, I'm not going to let this ranch go for lack of water—water I'm *legally* entitled to."

Jake leaned forward in the saddle, looking down more fully at Carter's weathered face. "Move the cattle south. Squirrel Creek is there and—"

"And won't keep my cattle in water for more than a week. You know that creek is dry by July."

"It's better than nothing."

"So this is it, McConnell? You caving in to Hansen? What'd he do, buy you off?"

"Watch it, Amos," Jake said. It was enough.

Amos shaded his eyes with his hand at the edge of his hat brim. "If it comes to him or me, well, I can put twenty men in the saddle and I can bring in more."

Jake's horse shifted, pawing at the muddy ground. Jake soothed him with a pat. "You talking hired guns, Amos? I wouldn't like to hear you're bringing in hired guns." This was going from bad to worse in a hurry.

"Like it or not, if I don't get water by the end of this month..." Carter turned and walked toward his house. "You're warned," he called over his shoulder. "And so is Hansen. Tell him I'll be coming!"

"Let the law handle it, Amos," he shouted.

"What law?" Amos flung back, then disappeared into the house.

It was well past nine when Jake led his horse into town. The animal had thrown a shoe and Jake had been forced to walk the last eight miles in ankle-deep mud. He was tired and he was mean.

He stopped by the livery stable and put his horse up, telling Sam to have the gelding's shoe replaced in the morning when the blacksmith came in, then he forked over two dollars and left.

He went first to Woodrow's office, but he wasn't there. Probably gone home, Jake thought. He needed a drink. He needed...a friendly face.

The Scarlet Lady was busy when he walked in. Larry, the kid from the mercantile, was decked out in a spotless white apron and was serving drinks as though he'd been doing it all his life.

Several cowboys from the Bar W stood at the bar. That, Jake figured a touch churlishly, was because *she* was at the bar, and men being men...

She was wearing satin tonight, burgundy satin with black lace trim, and her hair was pinned up, soft wisps falling around her neck and ears. He thought she looked beautiful. He'd thought she looked just as beautiful when she was scrubbing walls.

McConnell, you've got it bad.

If she noticed him she didn't show it—no smile, no nod. Great. He was still on the black list. What the hell would he have to do to bring her around? He was thinking about just heading up to bed when he spotted Woodrow.

"Jake. Over here."

Jake went to join his friend.

Woodrow raked him with a look and said, "What the hell happened to you?"

"Horse threw a shoe. Had to walk into town." Jake dropped into a chair and thumbed his hat back off his forehead.

"How'd things go out at the MJ?"

"Don't ask."

"That bad, huh?"

"Yeah."

"Well, I'm buying. What'll it be?"

"Anything." Jake wasn't really interested in drinking, and until two minutes ago he hadn't been interested in socializing—but that was before he'd seen her.

Woodrow returned with two mugs of beer clutched in one hand. He plunked them down with a thud, foam sloshing over the rim and pooling on the tabletop, the one she'd been so intent on cleaning this morning, he thought with a little surliness.

Jake took a long drink. "Looks like business is good."

Light flickered from the overhead lanterns. A misty gray cloud of cigarette smoke hung in the air along with the unmistakable scent of men who didn't appreciate the need for an occasional walk through a creek with a bar of soap.

Three cowhands—Charlie, Ed and Ralph—from the MJ wandered in.

"Marshal. McConnell," they said as they passed by and set up at a table near the back.

Jake watched Charlie fetch a bottle and glasses from the bar for himself and his friends. He saw the sharp looks they exchanged with the boys from Hansen's Bar W.

Bar W at the bar. MJ at the back. An uneasy prickling teased the hair at the back of his neck.

"Does look busy, don't it?" Woodrow interrupted his thoughts and Jake focused his attention on his friend. "Did I tell you Slocum was in here?"

"What did he want?" Jake looked over the rim of his glass.

Forearms on the edge of the table, Woodrow leaned in closer, talking under the general din. "He was giving her a bad time." He motioned with his head as if Jake wouldn't know who he was talking about. Fat chance of that. Jake was very aware of "her."

"What do you mean, 'a bad time'?"

"Hold your temper." The marshal held up a placating hand. "She handled him fine. Told him to get out." Woodrow fell back against the curved chair and grinned.

"Well, I'll be damned," Jake muttered.

"If you say so," a soft female voice said, and they both looked up to see her standing there.

A gentleman stood for a lady, his mother had taught him, so Jake did just that because she was a lady and he wanted her to understand that he felt that way—an apology of sorts. Woodrow, mouth open in shock, fumbled around a minute before he managed to shove back his chair and mirror Jake's stance.

"Evenin'," Woodrow said with an easy smile that warmed his eyes.

"Good evening," she replied.

Jake's gaze found hers and held for a breathless heartbeat, then she tore her eyes away. "Marshal, I wanted to thank you again."

"Anytime. Just give a holler."

A raucous round of laughter erupted from the table

in the back. There was an awkward moment of total silence between them. "Well, enjoy your evening."

She'd begun to turn away when Jake said, "Clair? Can you stay for a—"

"Ah, no, I don't think so."

Jake was already dragging back a chair. "Please stay."

It was amazing how that one word, how the huskiness of his voice, merged together and started a sudden coiling warmth deep inside her.

"Jake," she began wearily, "if this is about—"

"It's about whatever you want it to be about. Nothing more." His expression was thoughtful, gentle. "I'm sorry, Clair."

The air between them went suddenly still. He'd said it so unexpectedly, she was taken off guard. If she'd had to bet money, she would have given a hundred to one against him ever admitting he'd been wrong. But there he'd gone and surprised her—again.

He was still standing, hand on the chair he held out for her. He looked dark and powerful, and yet there was a tiredness around his eyes, weariness in his tone that tugged at her. Oh, it was pure folly, she knew. Staying here with him was more dangerous than walking on ice. But all the same, she said, "All right, Jake, I'll stay."

Right on cue he produced that familiar grin of his, the one that was all temptation and knowing promise, and he helped her with her chair.

Jake put his hat on the extra chair and settled in on her right. He didn't say a word; no mention of last night or this morning. Even with Woodrow there, she'd thought he'd make some mention, try to explain, justify perhaps. He didn't.

The flickering yellow-orange lamplight highlighted his face, a day's growth of beard shadowing his jaw, his hair matted from his hat. His shirt was green, pine needle green, and hugged his shoulders perfectly. Instantly she remembered clinging to those same broad shoulders while he'd lifted her from the stairs as he'd kissed her.

Her gaze flicked to his mouth and quickly to his eyes and there was a glint there, as though he knew what she was thinking. Electricity shot out through sensitive nerves and she felt a knot of anticipation form in her stomach.

She was lost in thought and feeling.

Woodrow cleared his throat loudly. His gaze flicked from Clair to Jake and back again. "You two okay?"

"Sure."

"Fine."

They both spoke at once, like children caught out behind the barn, and—both evidently having the same thought—they chuckled at their foolishness.

It wasn't entirely foolish to Jake. He'd been thinking about Clair, and being somewhere alone with her was certainly a very urgent thought.

"Would you like something to drink?" he asked politely.

"No. Thank you, though, for asking."

The noise of the saloon seemed a distant hum, nothing more. Clair let her fingers trace a gouge in the surface of the table while she tried to think of something to say, something more than...I missed you.

It was then that the shouts reached her ears. Men's

voices raised above the others, curses, threats made and challenged.

Before she could react, a gunshot slammed home in the wall above the painting behind the bar. The sound was nearly deafening in the enclosed space. What the hell was happening? She saw Larry dive for cover behind the bar.

Clair was on her feet. "What are you doing?" she yelled. "Stop it. Stop it!" They weren't going to break up her place—not tonight, not when things were just going right.

All around her customers were ducking behind an overturned table or running for the door. No!

"Wait," she entreated, grabbing at their sleeves. They rushed past intent on saving their hides.

Fury overwhelmed good sense and she whirled around to face the troublemakers, who were squaring off in the back of the room. "Now, look, you men, you—"

A hand grabbed her wrist and yanked hard, pulling her off her feet. "Get down, woman!" Her knees hit the floor. Pain ricocheted up her thighs. "Hey," she complained, her skirt puffing out around her. Jake was holding her wrist. "Let go of me."

About that time another shot cut off all talk, and there were more loud voices.

"...son of a bitch..."

"...can't say that and..."

She tried to get up, but Jake had her pulled hard up against his chest, both of them cowering behind a table. Woodrow was taking cover behind another table a couple of feet away.

Clair squirmed. Jake held tight. "Woman, are you

deliberately trying to get yourself killed, because if you are..."

She managed to twist around. "This is my place, and I'm not letting them break it up." She pushed at his hand gripping her around the waist like a vise. "Now, let me go so I can—"

Another shot, this one slicing into the floor inches from them. The scent of gunpowder was strong enough to burn her nostrils.

Suddenly Jake said, "Don't move. Do you hear me? Don't move."

Reluctantly she nodded her agreement.

Jake released her and edged up to peer over the table. "All right, you men, this is Sheriff McConnell. Put your guns down now and no one gets hurt."

Squirming around, his boots crunching on the broken glass, he spared Woodrow a quick glance. "You ready?"

Woodrow leveled his gun on the edge of the table, pointing straight in the direction of those gun-happy cowboys. "Ready."

On a deep breath, Jake surged to his feet and strode to the back as if he had the entire cavalry backing him up instead of one marshal. Heart racing, he kept his gaze focused and his hand close to his gun. Right now he was playing the odds, figuring that they were more interested in blasting away at each other than at him.

He angled around an overturned table and spared only a quick appraising glance for the men sprawled on the floor, hands over their heads. Sure, as if that would protect them. Jake closed in on the trouble in three long strides and sized up the situation.

The Bar W boys, Nat and Jerry, were fortified behind the bar, and the MJ hands were lurking in the corner using a table and a couple of chairs for a shield.

"Cattle killer!" Charlie, the MJ hand, hollered, and popped up long enough to fire off another shot. Jake dived for the floor, his hands skidding on the rough floor, his cheek hitting a chair leg. Damn. Teeth clenched, he rolled over and came to his feet in one furious motion, his anger high.

"Drop the guns," Jake growled, pulling out his Smith & Wesson. He came up behind the MJ cowboys so fast they didn't have time to react. "Do it or I swear I'll shoot you where you stand!" At the moment, he thought he might.

Out of the corner of his eye he saw Woodrow hurry Clair behind the bar, then discreetly signal that he was moving on the Bar W ranch hands. Good that Clair was safe—sort of. Walnut never stopped a .44.

Fortunately, the cowhands were so distracted by Jake, they didn't notice Woodrow outflanking them.

Breathing hard, Jake kept his back to the wall and his eyes on the trouble. "Okay, this is the last time I'm telling you boys to put down those guns."

"I ain't doin' it, Sheriff," Jerry countered, his .44 wavering dangerously in his unsteady hand. "Them coyotes called me and the boys here cattle killers." His thin, weathered face turned fierce and there was an intense look in his eyes that made Jake nervous.

"Yeah," Nat chimed in, still concealed behind the bar.

"Well, you are cattle killers!" Charlie retaliated, and Ed and Ralph moved in, guns drawn, to back up their friend.

This was about to get really ugly, and in one blurring motion Jake came down hard with his gun barrel on Charlie's hand. The sharp sound of bone crunching echoed in the quiet room.

"Damn, McConnell," he moaned as the gun sailed four feet through the air and slammed to the floor with a thud.

"I told you boys to put those guns down! What, do you think I'm joking here?"

Charlie started backing away, shaking his head adamantly as he moved. "Not me, Sheriff. I ain't going to jail, not while them sons of bitches are loose."

Suddenly Charlie made a lunge for Jerry. Jake stopped him with an elbow in the gut and Charlie dropped to his knees clutching his stomach and cursing. "Son of a bitch." Ralph and Ed moved in to help their pal, their feud momentarily forgotten.

"Are you gonna drop those guns or not? It doesn't matter to me."

It wasn't a question, and they all knew it. Guns hit the floor like hailstones.

Jake kicked them away with the toe of his boot, the guns sliding over by the wall. "All right, Woodrow, let's get these boys to jail for the night."

"My pleasure," Woodrow said, and they jumped, clearly surprised at how close he was behind them.

Seeing that everyone was accounted for, Jake relaxed. No one dead or dying. He slipped his gun back into the well-worn holster.

Behind him, Jake heard the men helping Charlie to his feet, heard the scraping of boots, the muttering of curses. He was keeping his eyes on the Bar W boys when—

"Jake, look out!"

He heard her warning too late to avoid the punch

that blindsided him. Pain shot through his eyes and cheek, and the acrid taste of blood pooled in his mouth.

In one motion he turned, hauled back and slammed his fist into Charlie's face with a jaw-breaking force. The man careened into the wall. Dazed, he slid downward toward the floor. Jake dragged Charlie to his feet. The sound of tearing cotton punctuated the move.

Charlie's blue eyes snapped open in surprise. He grabbed Jake's wrists, trying to break his hold. "It ain't me, Sheriff, it's them. They the ones what oughta be—"

The other two made to move. Jake saw it coming. He pulled his gun, shoved it hard under Charlie's chin and spun around.

Back to the wall and holding Charlie like a shield, Jake faced them. "Now, you boys back off. There's a law in this town about gunplay and I'm gonna enforce it." When they hesitated, he shoved the barrel of his gun a little harder under Charlie's chin, making him crane his neck high.

"Do what I'm telling you," Jake growled.

"Do it," Charlie pleaded. "He'll kill me sure if you don't."

They did as they were told.

Jake flung Charlie away from him, and he half stumbled into the Bar W boys, who were staring openmouthed at the scene.

"Hey, watch it!"

"Get off me!"

Disgusted, Jake said, "Woodrow, get these fools outta here, will ya?"

Turning to the men, he ordered, "All right, let's go. Come on, get a move on."

Sheepishly, still grumbling, they started for the door.

Customers appeared from their hiding places like prairie dogs coming out of their holes. Men looked surprised, confused, frightened. The unmistakable burnt scent of gunpowder hung like a cloud in the air.

Breathing hard, Jake raked a hand through his hair and got a sharp pain for his effort. "Damn," he muttered, examining his knuckles that he just now realized were cut and bleeding pretty badly. He sucked on the blood and spit it on the floor.

He felt a hand on his shoulder and turned, fist drawn. It was Clair.

She looked all worried and pale and she threw herself into his arms. He hadn't seen that coming, but he was nothing if not a man who reacted fast. He grabbed her and held on. "What's this about?"

The satin of her dress bloused around his legs as she clung to him, her face buried in the side of his neck. Her breath was warm on his skin above his collar. His anger was disappearing fast, replaced by something just as dangerous.

"You could've been killed," she was chiding him. "Are you crazy, walking up to those men like that?"

"Me?" Jake felt her tremble, felt her hands clutching at his shirt and his skin beneath. He tightened his grip. "You should talk."

Over the top of her head, he gave all the men a smug little wink. His smile got him a pinch of pain from that bruise on his cheek. "Ouch."

At the sound of the complaint, Clair looked up, into his face. Wait. What was she doing? *Oh, no!* She pushed free of him, but it was too late. Every man in the place was staring, and Jake was grinning.

She was embarrassed and angry—at him, at herself. "Look what you've done to my place," she ranted to the crowd in general. "Just look!"

Men who weren't even involved looked sheepish. Woodrow chuckled and took to prodding the prisoners. "Come on, you galoots, let's go."

"It ain't my fault," Charlie grumbled. His pals were giving him a little help walking. "I didn't start it, lady, and—"

"Who's going to pay for this?" Clair demanded. "Someone has to pay!"

"It ain't *my* fault," Jerry declared as he and the rest of the troublemakers were herded out by Woodrow.

"Let's go," the marshal said. "You can cool your heels in a nice drafty jail."

Clair was busy righting tables. "I'm telling you, someone is going to pay for every bit of damage," she grumbled as she worked. Some of the customers helped her right the chairs and tables.

Jake picked up a chair or two himself before he said, "All right, folks, that's it. No harm done."

"No harm!" She turned on him, her eyes wide, her breathing ragged. "Just look at this broken chair and—"

"Go home," Jake told them, ignoring her tirade. "It's late. Everyone go home. The place is closed for the rest of the night."

The men obliged.

Clair straightened with the speed of lightning. "Closed? Closed! You can't close me down!"

"I just did, honey," Jake said calmly.

She advanced on him with fire in her eyes. He always did like a fiery woman.

"You can't. You hear me, you can't do this!" She poked him in the chest with the tips of two fingers. Jake grabbed those two fingers and held on, held on to her.

The last of the men exited and Larry, the bartender, gave Jake a parting wave before shutting the door.

They were alone.

Jake reached out one hand and fiercely pulled her to him. She slammed into his chest with a suddenly expelled breath, her lips parting with surprise.

"What the devil do you think you're doing?" she demanded, her face inches from his as he held her arms lightly behind her waist.

"I'm doing what I've been wanting to do all night." Then he kissed her—and not a soft, coaxing kiss, either. No, this was long and slow and deep. This was giving no quarter. When, delicious minutes later, he raised his head, his lips only a breath from hers, he looked into her wondrous blue eyes, felt her trembling in his hands and he knew.

He knew that his world would never be the same again.

Chapter Eight

"Ah, come on, Sheriff, dammit, let me go! I'm gonna lose my job!"

"Shut up, Jerry," Woodrow hollered. "I'm not gonna tell you again." Morning sunlight filled the office and took the chill off the air.

Jake was helping Woodrow. Not that he really needed any help; the marshal had the situation completely under control. It was Jake who needed the help.

Yeah, after that kiss, he needed a lot of help.

Self-preservation had made him spend the night at the jail. He'd told Woodrow he wasn't tired and would keep an eye on the prisoners while Woodrow went home. It sounded reasonable. It was a lie.

The truth was he'd left her there and beaten a hasty retreat. After kissing her, he hadn't waited around to discuss her reaction. He didn't want to know.

It was pathetic. Here he'd faced down a bunch of gun-toting, drunken cowboys and he was afraid of one woman. Why?

Damned if he knew. All he could say for sure was that it had taken more strength than he'd thought he

or any man possessed to walk away from her. Even
now, thinking about her, about the feel of her in his
arms, the taste of her, the silk of her hair gliding sen-
suously through his fingers, his body stirred to life,
and he shifted to quell the feeling.

How he'd wanted her. Had any man ever wanted
a woman as much as he wanted Clair Smith? Couldn't
be.

"The boys got a little outta hand last night."
Woodrow's voice cut into Jake's thoughts and, almost
glad for the distraction, Jake said, "A bit of an understatement, don't you think? Those idiots coulda
killed somebody."

"Somebody, or a particular somebody?" Woodrow
had seen the way the woman had thrown herself into
Jake's arms, and Jake hadn't seemed all that surprised—more like pleased.

"Never mind being so nosy." Still, he glanced
across the street once more, anyway.

The front door creaked as Billy Hansen walked into
the office, his boot heels making a scuffing noise as
he did. Thumbing his brown hat back, he looked disgusted as he said, "Jake, I hear some of our hands
caused some trouble last night."

Jake faced Billy. "Nearly killed each other."

"They shot up the Scarlet Lady," Woodrow added,
also coming to his feet. "Lucky no one got hurt—
well, almost no one." He nodded toward Jake and the
deep cut and purple bruise that decorated his right
cheek.

Billy grimaced. "My God, Jake, one of our boys
do that?"

"No. Charlie Martin."

"You need stitches?" He sat on the corner of the

desk, one foot braced on the floor and the other suspended a few inches above the pine planks.

"No." Jake would rather bleed to death than have some dolt sewing him up like an old sock.

Woodrow said, "I told him I would—"

"What is this, a mother hen convention?" Jake shot an angry gaze from Billy to Woodrow and back again. "How'd you hear about this anyway?"

Woodrow answered. "I sent Tommy Beal out to both ranches before I came in this morning. No sense hanging on to them boys forever."

"I'd like to keep them forever," Jake told them both, loud enough for the men in the back to hear.

"Ah, come on, Sheriff," Jerry's plaintive wail came from the cell. "I didn't mean no harm. I jest got this bad temper, ya know, and these fellas pissed me off and—"

"Shut up, Jerry," Jake and Woodrow hollered at the same time, then shared a smile.

Billy wasn't smiling. "I'll pay the fines." His gaze flicked to Woodrow. "How much?"

"Five dollars each, so that's ten total. Plus damages. That's another ten."

Billy counted out the money in silver. "If there's any more trouble, they're fired." This time it was Billy who spoke loud enough for his Bar W men to hear. There was no sound from the men in the cell.

"I wish to hell your pa would tear down that dam," Jake muttered. "This isn't going to be the last, threats or no threats, as long as that dam is in place."

"I know. I'll talk to Pa again, but..." Billy shrugged, then stood. Woodrow grabbed the keys off the peg behind the desk and was just starting for the cell when the door banged open again.

"All right, Sheriff, where's my men?" Amos Carter stood, feet braced, in the doorway for two seconds, then marched into the room as if he was leading a cavalry charge. When he spotted Billy, he stopped dead still.

Jake's hand instinctively drifted to rest on the worn handle of his gun. If there was trouble he was prepared.

Amos took one look at Billy and the bluster went out of him like a kite losing the breeze. Quickly he schooled his expression and in a voice that was flat, he said, "Hello, Billy."

"Mr. Carter," Billy replied, his tone equally guarded.

"Look, Billy," Carter continued, "whatever happens, I want you to know I have nothing against you, but if your arrogant jackass of a father doesn't back off—"

"I'll thank you not to talk about my father, Mr. Carter. Anything you do to him, you can bet I'll take real personal."

Carter seemed to hesitate. Abruptly, he turned on Jake. "All right, McConnell, where's my men?" His mouth was drawn down, his jaw was set. "Come on. Come on. Get 'em out here. Let's go!"

"Now look, Amos—"

"Boss, is that you?" Charlie Martin called from the back.

"Yeah, Charlie," Amos called back. "You boys okay?"

Jake moved between Amos and his men. "Maybe you ought to be asking if the lady who owns the Scarlet Lady is all right? Maybe you ought to be asking if there were any damages? *Maybe* you ought to be asking if the next time there's trouble someone's gonna get killed?''

Jake gave both Amos and Billy a hard look to drive home the point.

"Never mind the list, McConnell," Amos snapped, already reaching into his trouser pocket. "What's the damages?''

"Fine's five each plus breakage over at the saloon.''

"There's the fifteen for the boys and another fifty for the damages." He tossed money on the desk. "There wouldn't be any damages, though, if Earl wasn't such a goddamned—''

"Watch it," Billy warned.

Carter's expression got serious. "All right, Marshal, let 'em out.''

Woodrow picked up the money, stuffed it into a desk drawer and went to release the men. Carter was already opening the office door.

Jake saw Carter's gaze settle on Billy for a brief moment more. "Billy, I..." He pulled his hat down low and left. Through the open door Jake could see Amos mount his horse and wait for his men.

A grumbling Woodrow let the Bar W men out first. There were some sheepish looks as they collected their guns and gear. "This fine is comin' out of your pay," Billy told them as they filed stoically outside.

"See, I told you." Nat elbowed Jerry.

"Aw, hell," Jerry grumbled.

"There won't be any more trouble" was Billy's parting remark to Jake and Woodrow.

Woodrow let the MJ boys out next. Jake returned their guns and belongings. "If I see you in town, if I hear of *any* trouble with one of those Bar W boys, you'll be seeing me."

"Okay, Sheriff."

"We understand."

They filed outside and Jake stood on the sidewalk making certain that they left, all of them.

When they'd gone he turned to Woodrow. "Did you see the way Amos looked at Billy? What the hell was that?"

Woodrow rubbed his chin. "Damnedest thing I ever saw. I thought when those two showed up at the same time there'd be fireworks."

The sunlight glinted on a small puddle of water in the street. Jake settled his hat more comfortably on his head and squinted. A man rode past and waved his hello. Jake waved back, but his attention was focused on his friend. "Something's crazy about this and I wish to hell I could figure it out."

Chapter Nine

Jake spent the rest of the day with Woodrow. They made the rounds of several other ranches, asking questions, trying to see if anyone knew anything about exactly why two former friends would suddenly become enemies.

No one did.

It was just after dark when they got back into town. They stopped by the restaurant and, though Nellie was closing, Jake talked her into taking pity on a couple of hungry men. She did, cooking up a steak and some potatoes for them both.

Teddy Hocksettler spotted Jake through the window and stepped in to chat. "Heard there was trouble in the Scarlet Lady last night."

"Some. Woodrow and I handled it." Jake polished off the last of his steak. Woodrow was busy chewing.

"You think having a woman…you know, that kind of woman—"

"That fight had nothing to do with her. It was a couple of cowboys arguing over cattle, is all. She didn't do anything wrong." He was feeling possessive, protective.

"Okay, Sheriff. Okay." Teddy held up both hands in surrender. "Don't get excited. I was just asking."

"I'm not excited and I'm just answering." He tossed fifty cents onto the table and he and Woodrow left. Jake figured to head on over to the saloon—to get to bed. He was tired. At least, that was what he was telling himself.

Deep down, he thought maybe he'd been avoiding her, just a bit. He had the very distinct feeling he was in for another chilly reception, which wouldn't be so bad, he supposed, if he hadn't been thinking about her most of the day and most of last night.

He and the marshal shook hands and agreed to meet tomorrow. The rain had bought them some time, but not much. "There has to be a way to get them to talk to each other again," Woodrow said, rubbing his chin.

"Short of locking them in the same jail cell, I don't know how."

"Well…" Woodrow chuckled. "We could try it."

Jake made a derisive sound in his throat. "Trouble is, I don't have any legal grounds."

"You know, seems to me that sometimes there's law and then there's what's right, and they ain't always in the same place at the same time."

"I won't break the law and—"

Woodrow stopped him with an upheld hand. "I know."

They shook hands again and Jake headed for the Scarlet Lady and bed—alone, he added, feeling a bit sullen.

The street was dry tonight, so crossing was easier. The town was quiet; all the stores were closed. The lights were already out in Nellie's Restaurant. So it didn't register at first that the saloon was closed.

What the hell? This was Monday and the place should be open. Cupping his hand, he peered through the window. Nothing. Only the dim flicker of a lamp on the far end of the bar showed that anyone even lived there.

He knew from firsthand experience there was no lock, so he let himself inside.

"Clair?" he said, speaking softly to the gray shadows that made seeing next to impossible.

Things looked pretty normal. All the furniture seemed to be back in order, chairs and tables and such.

He turned up the lamp, putting a little more light on the subject. He never liked the idea of things, people lurking in the shadows.

He took another step, the jingle of his spurs and the thud of his boot heels the only sounds. Where was she? Maybe she was afraid to open. Naw, not her. The woman hadn't been afraid last night, she'd been riled. And a sight to see, too—all flushed cheeks and tousled hair.

A provocative image flashed hot and bright in his mind, not the first he'd had about her. The woman had had a way of stirring him up, of getting him thinking about her and him and things he shouldn't be thinking about.

"Clair?" he called again. "You here?"

No answer. He cast around the room again. No sign of trouble. He checked the back door. Closed and locked.

Returning to the center of the room, he stopped.

Had she gone out? Where? Why would she? Maybe she'd gone to bed? Maybe she was sick.

He practically ran to the stairs. "Clair, honey? You up there?" he shouted. As he stood with his hand on the rail, a sound caught his attention. He halted, listening. There it was again, a small, pitiful sound, like the whimpering of an injured animal.

"Clair?" he called out, louder this time, not sure it was her.

"Yes," came the muffled response.

It sounded like her. It sounded as if it came from the back of the saloon, and he closed in on her voice. "Clair, where are you?"

"Jake? Jake!" Her voice was stronger and more urgent, punctuated by a banging on the door of the storage closet. "Jake, please! Get me out! I'm trapped. I've been here for hours!"

"Oh, is that all?" Jake practically laughed, he was so relieved. She wasn't hurt, only trapped in the closet. He worked the knob. "Is it locked?"

"It's stuck. Please, Jake, get me out of here!"

Jake heard the demand in her voice, knew she was upset. "Okay, honey. Give me a minute to work on this thing. Try the knob on your side."

She did. He could hear the metal rattling and then, "Oh, no!"

"What?"

"The knob came off."

Using his shoulder, he bumped against the door, thinking he could nudge it loose. Nothing. "Is something wedged against the door on your side?"

"No. I don't know. Maybe."

"Okay. I'm thinking." He carried the lamp closer so that he could inspect the door better, check the framing, the hinges for something bent or warped. "How did this happen? Why isn't the saloon open?"

"I had a terrible headache all day, so I was going to open late. I came in here to get something for dinner. The wind must have blown the door shut. Jake?" Her voice was small and quiet like a terrified child. "Are you there?"

"I'm here."

"Don't leave me."

"I'm not leaving," he promised, thinking for an instant that he meant more than just tonight.

"Jake?"

"I'm here." He banged around the edge with his fist, trying to find where it was caught.

"It's dark in here."

"I know." The brass was bent. "Just another few minutes."

"No, Jake, please."

He heard the catch in her throat, heard the muffled sob. He tried to soothe her. "Honey, it's all right, I'll just—"

"I'm afraid of the dark, Jake. Please."

Her voice tore at him. "Okay, stand back as much as you can."

On a quickly expelled breath, he threw his full weight against the door; his shoulder slammed hard against the solid pine. Pain ricocheted down his arm and along his ribs. The wood creaked but the door didn't give. Gritting his teeth, he threw his whole body into it again. This time wood snapped like a gunshot and gave way. Jake half stumbled, half fell into the closet and sprawled on her.

In a tangle of brooms and buckets and empty bottles, he righted himself, his hands immediately grop-

ing for her. "Clair, are you hurt?" His eyes strained
to see her, but it was dark, too dark.

"No."

He couldn't see more than a silhouette, but she was
moving, crawling over him like some crazed spider
racing for the door.

"I have to get out of here."

Her knee pressed on his ribs and her hand dug into
his hip in her frantic struggle to get out of the closet.
A broom handle banged him in the head and a mop
clattered to the floor beside him.

With an awkward effort, Jake managed to get to
his feet and reach for her. Looping his arm around
her waist, he turned and lifted her all in one motion
until he had her cradled safely in his arms. "You're
safe now," he told her, and was surprised by the sudden jump in his heart rate.

She curled kitten-soft against him, her arms looped
around his shoulders in a way that was all too intimate
and tempting. Her face was pressed hard against the
side of his neck. He felt her unsteady breath on his
skin just above his collar, felt her shudder and cling
tighter to him while the satin of her dress spilled over
his arm. "Oh, Jake..."

"It's okay. You're all right now. I've got you."

He held her against him, feeling the shape of her
slender body molding to his. Desire stirred again and
he stopped there in the middle of the saloon. The
world around them was silent except for the hard
beating of his heart.

She lifted her head away from him and looked up.
"Clair, I think this isn't a good idea." Oh, Lord, she
was so beautiful and she was here in his arms and he
wanted her. It was that simple and that complicated.

His grip tightened fractionally on her as though his body's need was overwhelming his mind.

"Clair" was all he managed before he dipped his head and kissed her—a small kiss, a skimming of lips, because she was so close and so beautiful and he couldn't help himself.

She made a startled sound that merely parted her lips in invitation, and his tongue slipped inside to lave at her mouth and tease her tongue.

He'd expected her to pull away. He'd expected her to push him or threaten him and haul off and hit him. He hadn't expected her to kiss him back, and he sure as hell hadn't expected the little purring sound that came from deep inside her throat.

He deepened the kiss, slanting his mouth this way then that, all the while holding her cradled in his arms. This wasn't supposed to happen, but heat shot through him at the speed of a lightning bolt, searing, scorching his mind and turning all that rational thought into smoldering ashes.

She was kissing him as if she'd missed him, as if she was welcoming him home. Her body tensed and twisted in his arms, and her hand threaded into his hair at the back of his head, holding him to her.

God help him, he'd never forced a woman in his life, but he was damned close, and those little sounds she kept making weren't helping.

His kiss was hot and hard and insistent, stealing the breath right out of Clair's lungs and sending her pulse rate flying. She hadn't expected to kiss him, and she sure hadn't expected to want him more than she wanted air or water. As soon as he'd touched her, every nerve in her body had flared to life. Days of denying her attraction, nights of sensual dreams all merged in one soul-rocking kiss. Blood heated, muscles threatened to liquefy and a warmth coiled tight and urgent between her legs.

Danger and fear were too well ingrained to be completely denied. She tore her mouth from him. Still locked in his grip, she somehow managed to say, "Put me down."

Jake stopped. "Damn," he muttered on a harsh breath and instantly released her. "Aw, hell."

He snatched off his hat and raked one hand back through his hair, leaving deep furrows in the inky blackness. "I didn't mean to—" Why did she keep standing so close—didn't she know what she was doing to him? Or was this some kind of punishment for kissing her, some perverse sort of revenge?

He had to move, to get out of here, if he had any hope at all of saving himself, of saving her. Because if he touched her again—and he would if he stood here much longer—well, he couldn't be responsible.

"Look, I gotta...go...somewhere...and I'll be back later. Okay? After you've gone to bed. I mean..." He slapped his hat back on his head. "I gotta go."

He started for the door. She caught up with him as he reached for the knob. Her hand on his sleeve stopped him cold. He glanced around and thought again how beautiful she was. Her hair was down around her shoulders, spilling like gold over one breast. Her cheeks, pale moments ago, were flushed and her chest was heaving above the neckline of her dress. "Look," he said, slipping free of her grasp, praying for divine intervention to keep from dragging her back into his arms. "I'm telling you straight out.

I shouldn't have kissed you. I know. You've made that clear before. I'm sorry. Okay?''

There was no warmth in that apology.

''It's not okay.''

''What?'' He straightened away from her grasp. ''I don't want to fight. I want to do a lot of things right now, most of which have to do with both of us being naked, but believe me when I tell you that fighting has absolutely nothing to do with any of it.''

Her chin came up defiantly and she looked him straight in the eyes, hers like luminous blue pools that this man would willingly drown in.

''Who said anything about fighting?''

He reached for the door again, and this time she stepped into his path. Without a word she pulled his mouth to hers and kissed him, and kissed him some more. When he finally tore his mouth away he said, ''Woman, are you crazy?''

''I guess I am.'' Her voice went all soft. ''All I know is that I don't want you to leave.''

''What?''

''I'm asking you to stay.''

''I said I'd be back later after—''

''Not after.''

''If this is some kind of game... The last time I kissed you you refused to speak to me and the time before that I nearly got my face slapped and now...''

''Now I want you to—'' she stepped up close and stroked his face with her hand ''—stay.''

Her words were right, the invitation clear, but still he hesitated.

His mouth turned down and he frowned.

Clair traced his frown with the pad of her thumb while she looked at him, her gaze open.

"Clair," he said against her hand. "If I stay I'm going to make love to you, make no mistake about it. I want you. I'm trying to do the right thing here, but—"

Her smile was inviting. "Stay."

For the span of one heartbeat he stared into her breathtakingly huge eyes while the words, the invitation penetrated his desire-clouded brain.

She wants you, McConnell. What are you waiting for?

Damned if he knew. On a sudden intake of breath, he pulled her to him. His arms went around her slender shoulders and he took her mouth in a hungry kiss that left no doubt of what was to come.

Clair understood. She wanted this. She wanted him. Fear and danger dissolved in the fire that heated her blood. She was only human, she told herself, but she knew it was more than that. It was Jake McConnell. With word and touch he'd shattered her well-made defenses until she could no longer deny her heart.

The bedroom was upstairs. In one motion Jake scooped her up and, taking the steps two at a time, he carried her there.

Inside the small room there was only a bed and a bureau; a shade was partially drawn on the front window. This time when he released her she slid down the front of him like silk over polished steel. His hardened arousal strained at the denim of his trousers while desire thrummed and pulsed through him like a living force, threatening to consume him.

For Jake there was no thought other than the simple fact that she was here with him, wanting him. How this miracle had happened he didn't know, didn't care, merely accepted, like an answered prayer.

Feverishly his mouth ate at hers. Desire, long denied, pulsed raw and restless through him, muscles tensed and flexed and ached with desperate need. He moved, side to side, never leaving her yet unable to keep quite still. His hands cupped her face, his fingers threaded into the fine silk of her hair. "I want you so much. I never knew a man could want a woman as much as I want you."

She covered his hands with hers. "Yes, Jake. Oh, yes."

He kissed her brow and chin and the tip of her nose. Desperate as he was to get them naked, he couldn't bring himself to stop touching her completely, so he tore at his shirt one-handed, dragging the cotton free of his waistband, working the buttons until, frustrated, he merely ripped the last two off.

Clair struggled with the tie on her dress, but the darned thing was knotted and she couldn't get it free. "Jake, can you?"

Jake wasn't bothering with things like undoing knots. He produced a small knife from his front pocket, tugged on the cord and slit it all in one motion. The burgundy satin pooled around her ankles. Her petticoat quickly followed.

Illuminated by moonlight that came through the front window, Jake could see Clair in her remaining undergarments. The thin white cotton camisole clung provocatively to her breasts and the pantalets outlined her long, slender legs, legs that he wanted desperately to feel wrapped around his waist.

"You're beautiful," he told her. She was beautiful and strong and smart and all the things he admired in a woman—all the things he admired in her.

Her hair cascaded down her back and he couldn't

resist lifting a handful to drape it across the front of her shoulder and down, the ends curling just below her nipple. His fingers brushed the sensitive peak through the cotton fabric and she responded with a sudden intake of breath and a seductive shiver.

He rubbed both of her breasts, his hands curving around each firm mound then sliding to the straining nub barely visible through the cloth. She moaned her delight.

He was surprised to see his hands shake as he reached for the first of the four blue satin ties that held her camisole in place. One by one, slowly, reverently, he pulled the ties free, watching as the garment opened to him like a flower.

Clair watched the movement of his long fingers with breathless anticipation as he slipped the garment free to fall to the floor, leaving her breasts bare. The night air prickled goose bumps over her flesh but did nothing to cool the heat that she felt from his undisguised stare. Nerves close to the surface tingled and ached, longing for his touch.

Jake drew in a lungful of air, trying to steady himself against the raging lust that thundered in his brain. Taking her hands, he pulled her to him, looping her arms around his waist, reveling in the feel of her breasts against the bare flesh of his chest.

She felt so good, so damned good. He cupped her buttocks and leaned into her, wanting her to feel his hardness against her cotton-clad belly, wanting her to know what she did to him, for him. He kissed the side of her neck and the top of her shoulder. He rubbed her back, his fingers playing along her spine and gliding over the deliciously smooth skin there.

Then he leaned back and cupped her breast in the palm of his hand, rubbing, twisting, before he took the rosy nubbin between his thumb and forefinger, gently squeezing, watching her face, looking for the sudden flash of delight.

Clair moaned with the delicious pleasure that surged in her. Her fingers dug into the tops of his arms. Her eyes drifted closed as she savored the sweet rapture of his touch. "Yes," she breathed. "Yes." She moved, pressing against his hand, wanting more. After another moment her eyes opened to him again.

Jake looked into her half-open eyes glazed with passion. "I've wanted to do this for so long." He squeezed the nipple again and was rewarded with a pleasure-driven moan. "I want to touch you... everywhere."

Lowering his head, he took one puckered nipple in his mouth, teasing and sucking, licking, letting his teeth tease the flesh.

Enchantment, more intense than anything Clair had ever known, streaked through her. Her desire doubled again as he moved to the other breast. Muscles clenched and flexed, while Jake never relented in his sensual assault.

"More," she ordered or pleaded, she wasn't sure. All she knew was that she wanted this, wanted him. Every touch was luscious, every feeling more exquisite than the last. She wanted it all. She wanted him to never stop. All her barriers, all her defenses had long ago crumbled. Jake. She wanted Jake.

He ran his tongue lightly along her jaw then traced the outline of her ear, sending shivers of delight over her heated body. "Do that again," she demanded, and he willingly obliged. "It's wonderful."

Breathing hard, he looked at her. "I want you to feel wonderful." His voice was deep and rich as fine velvet. "I want to spend my life pleasuring you, sweet Clair." He kissed her lightly, and then in one breath-taking motion he released the tie on her pantalets and they drifted down her legs to the floor.

Clair stood before him proudly, unashamed of her nakedness or her drumming need to have him, to make love with this man who so enticed and mes-merized her that almost from the first she'd thought only of him.

Clad in nothing but black silk stockings, she stepped toward him, and Jake held his breath. Surely this was a fantasy, a dream he was in. But she rose on her toes and kissed him and he knew then that his dream was tantalizingly real. "Let me love you, Clair."

"Love me," Clair returned in a fierce whisper.

In one motion he scooped her up in his arms. She was heaven. She was bliss and she was his. His whole body seemed electric, wilder than any storm.

Dropping to one knee, he lowered her onto the patchwork quilt that covered the small bed. She lounged there seductively, one knee drawn up, her hair splayed out around her head. With a wanton's smile, she reached for him and, hesitating only long enough to shed his boots and trousers, he went to her gladly, eagerly. He covered her with his own body, nerves alive with wanting, his skin on fire, while every fiber of his body screamed with the frantic need for release.

He kissed and touched and caressed and hoped like hell she was ready because he knew, with the small part of his brain that was still working, that he couldn't wait any longer.

Heart pounding in his chest, he sought the entrance to her core, and without hesitation he slid into her easily. She was wet and hot and wonderful. She soothed and inflamed him all at once and in that second before he started to move, he knew she owned him, body and soul.

Clair arched up in welcome. She welcomed every powerful thrust of his body, every flex of muscle. Her body hummed with the power of him as he glided in and out of her. He created a storm of fire that she could no more stop than she could stop the earth from turning. She wanted this. She wanted to make love to Jake McConnell.

Jake struggled to maintain control, but passion clouded his brain and was driving his body to move. Faster. Harder. Again and again, unable to control the need. His mouth tore at hers. His hands frantically stroked her body.

With each stroke, Clair felt him excite the hard, aching spot between her legs. Desire burned white-hot in her, and she met him stroke for stroke, clawing at his back and shoulders, her legs lifting to encircle his hips. "More," she cried out. "More!"

He obeyed, and then he felt her first tiny tremor.

He changed the rhythm—slower, deeper—and each time she felt the tremors increase, felt herself convulse around him.

"There," she moaned. "Yes, there." Suddenly it was as if all the nerves in her body were centered between her legs. She felt the glorious rush, like soaring off a high cliff.

A moment later Jake tensed and shuddered as he gave in to his own release. The world around him converged into one thought, one word.

Clair.

Chapter Ten

The morning came bright and crystal clear through the front window of the saloon. If anyone had asked Jake, he would have been happy to tell them that there had never been a more glorious day.

Jake was at the stove downstairs, trying to brew up a pot of coffee—that is, if the darned thing would ever consent to boil.

Glaring at the gray metal, he had to content himself with bracing one shoulder against the wall, his bare feet crossed at the ankles. The morning air chilled his chest where his shirt hung open; his denim trousers protected his legs.

Arms draped casually over his chest, he waited, but not patiently. His gaze drifted upward to the second floor and a certain bedroom he was extremely anxious to get back to. She was there, curled languidly on her side, sleeping, when he'd slipped quietly out.

He turned a hard scowl on the pot of coffee. "Boil, dammit."

Sunlight landed like a perfect yellow-white square on the nearly black pine planks of the floor, highlighting years of scrapes and gouges. The chill of the June breeze slipped under the double front doors where the Closed sign was still firmly in place.

Thank goodness for Closed signs.

What had happened between Clair and him last night was very good. Perfect, in fact.

The first thready puffs of steam drifted up from the spout of the coffeepot.

"Thank heavens," he said to the empty room. He was going to take her coffee in bed. He'd thought about making breakfast, then decided against it. Not that he wasn't hungry. He was, but what would satisfy his hunger a man couldn't cook in a skillet.

Sure, he knew it was pretty usual to feel a certain sense of euphoria, a calmness after making love. It was also reasonable, he knew, to feel warmth, tenderness—even gratitude—toward one's partner. Grinning like a schoolboy, he raked his hair back with one hand.

It had been a hell of a night. They'd hardly slept at all. He didn't care if he ever slept again, not if every night could be like last night—and he didn't see any reason why it couldn't. He was willing.

He rubbed his face and stretched, arms up, back arched. "Ouch. What the—" Oh, yeah, he thought with a smug satisfaction, the lady had claws. He grinned again remembering what he'd been doing when he got those claw marks.

The woman had been wild—wild and exciting and provocative and demanding and... Ah, hell, the woman was incredible.

He'd never ever felt so good in all his life, but it was more than physical. There was a feeling...something that circled in his mind just out of reach, like a long-forgotten memory. He shook his head, trying to grasp the thought, to pull it into the light, but every time he tried...

Shaking his head in frustration, he poured the coffee and headed for the stairs.

Clair snuggled in the bed, the covers softly pooled over her naked body. The sun glared bright through the windowpane and landed smack-dab on her bed. She held her hand up to block the light, then rolled over and shoved her face into the pillow.

She felt warm and sleepy and deliciously wicked. A gentleness moved through her, lush and tempting, and she stretched and flexed like a lazy cat. A smile of sensual delight curved up her lips, lips tender from kissing Jake.

Ah, yes, kissing Jake. She'd been kissed before, of course, but never the way Jake McConnell kissed a woman. Lord, the man sent her senses reeling.

Ah, Jake, what have you done to me?

She chuckled on that one. The answer was blatantly obvious and carnal and absolutely wonderful. What surprised her was just how it had happened. One minute it seemed she had been trapped in the closet, the next, Jake was there, scooping her up in his powerful arms and carrying her up here to the bedroom. Then she was kissing him or he was kissing her and then...

"Nice," she said out loud, and let her leg slide over toward his side of the bed. It was then she realized he was gone.

A momentary flash of fear was drowned out by the wood-creaking sound of someone coming up the stairs. She knew it was Jake. So she relaxed and shifted, reveling in the smoothness of the sheet against her body, the feel of the cotton on her sore muscles. Not that she was complaining.

Jake had been incredible last night...several times last night, she corrected with a wanton's smile, and that fast desire flamed in her, making her draw her knees up against the sudden warmth.

"Good morning," a deep male voice said, and she craned her neck to see him standing there. He was tall and dark and handsome as the devil himself. Her gaze skimmed over his bare chest as she remembered being sprawled on top of him, her breasts pressed against the hard plane of his chest while he...

"Good morning," she managed to say, shoving her hair back. She sat up. "I was wondering where you were."

"Coffee," he said, coming into the room.

"For me?" she purred. She adjusted the sheet over one shoulder in a bit of shyness.

"I hope you like it strong."

She looked up through her lashes. "Oh, I like some things strong," she said in a throaty voice as she accepted the offered mug. "Hmm." She sniffed the contents. "Thanks." She took a sip. "It's good."

"Of course the coffee's good." Lightly, like the brush of a butterfly's wings, he caressed the length of her exposed arm with the backs of his knuckles. "*Everything* I do is good." His voice was deep with an unmistakable seductive tone that sent shivers scampering up her arms and over her shoulders.

"No modesty here, I see," she teased, her heart taking on the shudder that was stimulating all the nerves in her body at once.

"Too *much* modesty here," he countered. Lifting the covering sheet between thumb and forefinger, he let it slide to her lap, exposing her bare breasts to him.

Still he towered over her. But his gaze was hot and unmistakable and traced her exposed breasts with a lover's appreciation. Her nipples hardened in response. Desire heated her blood and her traitorous body. She wanted him.

She held her breath and craned her neck to look more fully into his downturned face. She wanted to touch him. Her fingers actually shook with wanting to touch him. But she didn't. It was almost as if the not touching was more…exciting. The coffee rippled dangerously in her unsteady hand and she had to steady it beside her on the mattress.

"Are you hungry?" he asked, so casually anyone might have thought they were sitting in church instead of being here half-naked.

He sat down beside her, his hip pushing against hers so that she had to inch over, careful to hold her coffee cup out of the way. His back propped against the white wall, he stretched out his long, denim-clad legs, crossing them at the ankle.

Easy as you please, as though he didn't know she was fast becoming aroused, he sipped his coffee. "So, are you hungry? You didn't say."

Heart beating laboriously in her chest, Clair twisted around to face him, her toes tucked under the edge of his thigh, the denim warmed by his body heat. The sheet that had been covering her slid away, pooling like a discarded cloak around her on the bed.

"Oh, I don't know." She feigned a thoughtful expression. What she was thinking about had nothing to do with food. "Are *you* hungry?"

"Depends." He put his coffee down on the floor

beside the bed, then took hers lightly from her hand and put it down also. "What did you have in mind?"

Wordlessly, she gave in to her thrumming desire and reached out with her left hand, touching his chest just over his heart. Anticipation sizzled in the air and through her body like summer lightning.

He felt it, too, she knew, could tell by his sudden intake of breath, by the way his eyes slammed shut against the tantalizing tremor.

"I was thinking..." She traced the line of his collarbone. "That we could go over to the restaurant, get some steak—" her hand slid down his arm "—and eggs." She let her fingers slip between his in a suggestive gesture.

His grip tightened on her hand, his fingers squeezing hard. She kissed the center of his chest then blazed a path downward with her tongue. His grip on her hand was almost painful but otherwise he made no movement at all.

With her chin nearly touching his waistband, she looked up and blue eyes locked with black. "So," she breathed, kissing her way back to her starting place, "what do you think?"

Jake was having trouble thinking of anything but the woman who was driving him slowly insane. At her first touch, his heart had taken on a hard, steady rhythm. At the touch of her tongue on him, his blood had simply turned to liquid fire, heating every muscle, every fiber of his being.

He needed Clair the way he needed oxygen to stay alive. Because when he was with her he was alive, fully alive, as he'd never been before.

She was promise and light, temptation and fulfillment; that ghost of a feeling moved in closer.

She rubbed her cheek against his chest while her hands played up and down his bare arms. Every so often her fingers would curl tightly into the muscle and she'd arch into him, letting him feel the weight of her glorious breasts against him.

It was a lover's game they were playing, he knew, a game of excitement, of anticipation that was working very well on his body. His breathing was uneven and shallow, and the evidence of his arousal pulsed painfully hard against his trousers.

He had to try twice to make his voice work. "Do you really think we should go out? I mean..." She slid her leg between his and he forgot what he was trying to say. "I, ah, I... Don't you think you might cause a scandal...dressed as you are?"

"Do you think so?" she said with all innocence. "I suppose I could put clothes on, but, well—" she made a show of stretching "—it's so much more...comfortable like this, don't you think?"

"Oh, honey," he growled, grabbing her hands and pulling her hard toward him. Grinning, she sprawled on him while he looped her arms around his neck. "I'm long past the point of thinking, except about what I'm going to do to you, you hussy."

He kissed her hard and long, ravishing her mouth, letting her know what he was going to do to her tempting little body.

In one motion he put her beside him, stood and shed his shirt and trousers. She reclined on the bed, her smile seductive. The bedsprings creaked as he knelt and she grinned at him. "Sounds like we've worn something out," she teased, her gaze drifting lower, to his thrusting arousal.

"Not even close. A couple more decades, maybe."

He came to her then, his powerful body pinning her beneath him, his legs slipping easily between hers. They were not strangers now; they knew each other's bodies intimately.

So when his mouth covered hers, hurried, greedy, she welcomed him. When she felt his manhood press against her aching core, she lifted to him.

He filled her perfectly, moving expertly over her sensitized nub, making her groan with the need that doubled with every powerful thrust.

With practiced hands they stroked and fondled, each knowing the other's pleasure points. There was no sound, no sight, only the sense of touch that made them so aware it was almost painful.

Jake's fingers dug hard into her shoulders, and his chest ground into her breasts. She hugged his back, feeling the straining muscles as he pumped in and out of her while her nails dug half-moons in his flesh.

"Clair" was all he managed as he gave in to his own need and poured himself into her while she arched and cried out in her climax.

Seconds later, breathing hard, he levered up on his elbows, braced on either side of her beautiful face. Tenderly he brushed the hair back from her damp skin and looked into her eyes, still glazed with passion. Her cheeks were reddened from his whiskers, her luscious lips were swollen. He traced the outline with his thumb as though in apology. But none was needed, he knew. She had given him all that she was, had given him her most precious gift, herself.

"Beautiful Clair. My beautiful Clair," he whispered so softly, kissing her brows and the tip of her nose. He felt her constrict around him, felt her shift slightly under him in a playful invitation.

He smiled. "Woman, are you trying to kill me?" he teased, surprised to feel his manhood stir.

"An interesting question," she replied with a languid smile, her hands skimming along his ribs. Keeping her eyes open, she lifted just her head, enough to barely touch her lips to his, then settled against the pillow again.

Over the next hour they tested their desire. Playing, teasing, discovering pleasures that could be given. Clair crested each time until, at last, she was content.

Jake lay on the bed holding her close, his hand caressing her arm from shoulder to wrist and back again.

"Honey?"

"Hmm?" She was draped down the side of him.

"Are you asleep?" He caught the corner of the sheet with the tips of two fingers and pulled it up to cover both of them.

"No" came her dreamy reply. "Why?"

He kissed the top of her head, his lips lingering there as he spoke. "You are all right, aren't you?"

"You have to ask?" She drew circles on his chest, making his sensitized flesh tingle.

"It has been quite a night."

"And morning," she amended, rising on one elbow to look into his face. "I wouldn't want to forget the morning."

"No chance of that."

He kissed her lightly, quickly, and she smiled and nestled down in the curve of his shoulder again, pleased to be here with Jake.

Jake had never been so content, so calm in his life. Being here with her, holding her in his arms, making love to her was like nothing he'd ever experienced, and while he knew he should be getting up, perhaps taking care of some of the business he was paid to do, well, he flat out didn't want to. So he ignored the way the sunlight moved across the room as the hours drifted past.

She slept in his arms, but he figured it was close to noon when she woke and stretched and said, "I've got to get up." She gave him a quick peck on the cheek. "It's late." She tried to climb over him. "I've got a business to run."

Jake didn't want her to go. Sitting up, he blocked her escape long enough to catch her by the shoulders and pin her beneath him on the bed again. For a long moment he looked into her eyes, bright from their lovemaking. In that instant he knew, recognized that feeling that had haunted him this morning and perhaps since the first time he'd seen her.

He didn't have to analyze it, or think it over. He knew; unquestionably, he knew.

"Clair." He brushed the hair back from her face, already thinking of all the mornings he would do that simple act. "I've never felt like this before and I think...I know..."

This was a first for him and, while the words were sincere enough, he was having trouble finding just the right ones to tell her.

"Clair," he began again, his face a scant few inches from hers, his body pulsing with the feel of her molded length against him. "I'm falling in love with you." There, he'd said it and it felt good.

For Clair the world seemed to come to a thundering halt. Her hand stilled, resting at the top of his hip. "What? You what?"

Jake's brows drew down. There was no smile. "I said I love you."

"You love me?" she repeated, for an instant caught up in the incredible happiness of having this very special man say he loved her. "You love me?" She beamed, repeating the words not as a question but as an answer.

He grinned, that heart-melting grin of his. "Yes," he confirmed with another quick kiss on her lips. "I love you." He was suddenly more sure than of anything else in his life. "I love you very much."

Looking into his handsome face, Clair was filled with more happiness than she'd ever known, ever expected to know. Tears glistened in her eyes and she thought her heart wouldn't hold all the joy that filled her right that second.

"Now, tell me that you love me," he coaxed, his devil-black eyes dancing with excitement.

"I love you," she told him, while she tried desperately to ignore the warning voice in her head that was getting louder with every beat of her heart.

Chapter Eleven

It was midday when Jake got dressed and left. He said he had some business to take care of and, well, he'd give her some privacy to wash and dress. She had promised they would have dinner, late and alone in her room.

He'd been gone about half an hour when the voice of reality finally drowned out all the fantasy. She sank onto the bed as though she'd been hit, and wave after wave of explicit visions washed over her, each threatening to drown in the icy-cold light of day.

What the devil have you done?

One look at the rumpled sheets and she didn't have to ask. What *hadn't* she done was more like it. Fear and regret coiled and twined together, making a knot in her stomach.

"No," she breathed to the empty room. Her hand, which had been caressing the sheet, slowly curled into a tight fist. "No." She shook her head in denial. But it was too late for denials. It was too late for her.

Clair had so succumbed to the man that she'd chosen to ignore the stark danger she was in. Being with

Jake was like taking a step out of time. Together they were a world unto themselves—no past, no future.

Dammit, it wasn't fair.

He loved her.

She couldn't love him back. She couldn't!

But she did.

The man had slipped right past all those well-built defenses of hers as though they didn't even exist. She'd tried to send him away. She'd tried to put him off.

He'd ignored all her demands. Instead he'd been kind and thoughtful and generous. He'd treated her with the respect that she got from no one, certainly no man that she could remember.

With words and a look and a touch, he'd enticed her.

She stood and went over to the window, careful to stay out of view from those on the street below, and viewed the world—her world and his. Amazing how in the stark light of day worlds could seem so different. His was here, while hers...

The morning stage rumbled down the street, stopping by the restaurant to off-load passengers.

It all seemed so normal, so routine. Didn't they know that nothing was normal and her life would never be routine again?

She shook her head. Jake McConnell. Who would have guessed that when she fell in love, really in love, it would be with a lawman? Who would have guessed she would spend a night locked in his arms. A shudder moved through her.

It had been wrong.

It had been a mistake.

It had been paradise.

She spun around and paced back toward the closed door.

You can't have him, she told herself firmly.

She was Clair Travers, a wanted woman. He was Jake McConnell, sheriff.

Blindly she stared at herself in the small mirror on her bureau. Her hair was down, a wild tumbling mass of curls. Her cheeks were red from shame and her lips were bruised and swollen from their greedy love-making.

Panic threatened. She dragged in a calming breath, then another and still one more.

She forced herself to become still.

She could not change the past, but she could change the future or, at least, this part of it. He did not know anything more than he had last night. She was going to keep it that way.

Jake had left Clair getting dressed. Not that he wanted to, mind you. No, given the choice, he would gladly have stayed and watched her get dressed—better yet, kept her undressed. Ah, yes, now, there was a thought.

"Hey, McConnell! Move, will ya?" a man's voice shouted. He looked around in time to see Ed Foster reining up his team.

"Sorry, Ed," Jake called, and hurried on across the street to Woodrow's office. He'd see Clair later. He couldn't wait for this day to end.

Light struggled to brighten the office through dirty windowpanes, and it looked to Jake as though there was even more dust on the clutter Woodrow referred to as his desk.

Good old Woodrow was standing by the cells. Jake

spotted him right away. Woodrow was sucking on a peppermint stick.

"Candy for breakfast?" Jake asked.

"Sure," Woodrow retorted. "It's one of the advantages of being alone. No one to tell you what to do or when, so don't you start." He came to meet Jake, who was standing by the desk. "Besides, it ain't morning, in case you ain't noticed. It's near on to noon. Where you been?"

"I...slept in." He straightened and adjusted his hat. "Come on, you ready?" They were going out to Hansen's to try to talk some sense into him, see if they couldn't work a compromise of some sort until Carter could get his case heard in court.

"Yeah, I'm ready." He went to fetch his coat and hat.

"Well, let's go, then."

"What's got you in such an all-fired hurry?" Woodrow tossed down the candy. "You weren't in much of a hurry this morning evidently." He shrugged into his coat.

Jake was already going out the door. "Well, I am now." He was headed for the livery stable. He wanted to get this over with and get back to town, back to her.

Jake had just stepped off the sidewalk when he heard the shouting.

"Sheriff! Marshal!"

Billy Hansen reined up hard, sending dirt clods flying. His face was red and his breathing labored.

"Whoa, Billy, what the—"

"You'd better come quick."

"What's going on?" Jake grabbed hold of the horse's reins to quiet the animal.

Billy gulped in a couple of breaths. "Amos Carter was by...the house this morning. He and Pa...went at it. Carter demanded Pa pull down the dam or else."

"And?" Jake prompted, his gut already knotting.

Billy leaned down, his forearm resting on the saddle horn. "Pa said no. So Carter said he'd be back with his men and he'd blow the thing to kingdom come. Pa's in a rage, so he's rounding up our hands and—"

"How long ago?" Jake demanded.

"About forty-five minutes."

Jake turned sharply to speak to Woodrow. "You stay here. I'll try to defuse this. If I can't, if I'm not back in—" he glanced at the sun "—four hours, then round up as many men as you can and come ready for battle."

"Don't you want 'em now?"

"No. I don't wanna wait the time it'll take to get them. Besides, with a bunch of nervous men out there, if someone pulls a trigger then it's war and no stopping it."

Woodrow was nodding as Jake spoke. "Yeah. I see."

Jake was already off the sidewalk and running for the livery stable and his horse. "Four hours," Jake called over his shoulder, and prayed he was making the right decision.

"Will do."

Jake retrieved his horse from the livery stable and, together with Billy, the two rode fast out of town. At the crossroads Jake reined up so hard his horse nearly sat down in the road. Dust swirled like a fine brown cloud around men and horses.

"Where to?" Billy gulped, his horse shying and sidestepping from the sudden stop. "Our place or Carter's?"

It took Jake a full five seconds to decide. "The dam." Jake spurred Tramp and took off at a run, Billy close behind.

They got there just as the boys from Carter's place were taking a pickax to the stone-and-wood barricade, the iron ringing against the granite.

Jake was off his horse almost before the gelding came to a complete stop. "Stay here," he ordered Billy with no time for arguments.

"Hold it, Amos," he demanded, storming through the nearly dry side of the streambed, his boots slipping on the rounded rocks. He understood Amos's frustration, but no way was Jake letting the man take the law into his own hands.

Carter didn't answer Jake's order and, except for the fact that he turned around, Jake might have thought the man didn't hear him. Trouble was when Amos turned around, Jake saw that he had a double-barreled shotgun slung in his crossed arms.

Carter focused on Jake but spoke to his men. "Keep working." A box of dynamite was on the ground beside his foot, fuses already hanging limply from three of the red sticks.

Great, Jake thought. Just great. This was going from bad to worse. Billy had said Earl knew about this little party and Jake didn't know how much time he had, but he figured it wasn't much—minutes at best.

He scrambled up the stream bank, his boots sinking into the soft earth. A rabbit shot through the sagebrush and disappeared into a hole. Jake was giving serious thought to doing the same thing.

Figuring that if Amos intended to shoot he would have done so by now, Jake closed in. "You can't do this." To the four men working, he said, "Stop what you're doing right now. That's an order."

The men hesitated long enough to look to their boss for directions.

"Keep going" was all Amos said, and the men went back to work, tearing at the rock-and-wood dam. Water was already trickling around the edges and pooling in the dry streambed.

"Give me the gun, Amos," Jake demanded, his temper moving up a notch. "You're not taking the law into your own hands here. No one is."

"Go to hell, McConnell. I'm staying. This dam is coming down right now." His hand slid conspicuously toward the trigger guard.

"You gonna shoot me, Carter? You gonna kill me, is that it?" When Carter hesitated, Jake wrapped his left hand around the barrel of the shotgun, which was pointed right at his gut. "Put the gun away, Carter. There isn't going to be any shooting here today."

"You think so, huh?" Carter motioned with his head in the direction where Billy held the horses. Beyond him in the distance Jake could make out a dust swirl, then a large group of men coming fast.

Damn. There were at least a dozen, and he didn't have to think twice to know who it was. Hansen. They were riding hell-bent for leather.

Suddenly a rifle bullet slammed into the dirt at Jake's feet and brown earth sprayed his denim trouser leg.

Jake's hand went instantly to the gun tied at his

side as he dismissed Carter as an immediate threat. "Hansen, you son of a bitch, hold your fire!"

The men reined up in a billow of flying dirt that made everyone look away to keep the stuff out of their eyes.

Jake blinked and swiped at his face with his bandanna. When his vision cleared, he spotted Carter's men diving for cover behind the dam, grabbing up their weapons as they did. The unmistakable *click-click* of rifles being cocked sliced through the air.

Hansen's men yelled at their horses, swatting them out of the way. The men hit the ground on the far side of the stream, rifles cocked and aimed straight at Carter and Jake. Carter's men, behind the dam, aimed their guns at Hansen. All that was needed was one word, one nervous trigger finger and Jake knew this would all go up in a hail of gunfire that would leave a lot of men dead, including him. Well, Jake wasn't prepared to die today, not here, not for these hard-headed bastards.

Hansen was advancing on them like a general. "Carter," he snarled. "You're trespassing. You've got ten seconds to clear off my land or I'm gonna kill you where you stand." He kept coming, his hand curled conspicuously around the handle of his Navy Colt.

"Go ahead and try," Carter retaliated, shouldering past Jake to meet the challenge head-on.

Jake reacted quickly. He grabbed Carter and spun him around, giving him a hard shove that sent him sprawling on his back in the dirt.

"What the—"

Carter rolled over fast, but Jake was faster. In one

motion, he shoved his knee in Carter's chest and wrenched the shotgun free. He surged to his feet.

"McConnell, I'll get you for this," Carter threatened, bracing up on one elbow in the dirt.

"Yeah, sure," Jake snarled back. "Any time."

Breathing hard, he sighted down on Hansen. "Get the hell over here. We're gonna settle this once and for all."

Hansen looked momentarily surprised. "Stay out of this, McConnell."

One of Carter's men hollered, "Boss, just give the word and—"

"I'm the law here," Jake retorted. "Everybody stay put."

"Boss?"

Hansen stopped. Carter didn't respond.

Jake backed up a couple of steps until he could sight down on both of them with the shotgun. "Tell your men to stay put."

"Like hell I will," Hansen blustered.

"The hell you *will*," Jake flung back. "Unless you wanna die out here. You wanna die, Hansen? I don't, and I don't think Carter does, do you, Amos?"

No answer was answer enough.

Jake gestured with the shotgun.

Hansen spoke first. "Jerry, you boys wait for my signal."

"Carter?" Jake prompted.

Carter huffed and puffed and pawed the ground but he finally said, "Charlie, don't do anything unless I tell you."

Hansen's men rose slightly as though to watch what was about to unfold. Carter's men cautiously peered out from their hiding places behind the rocky barricade.

"Fine," Hansen blustered to Jake. "Now what?"

Jake backed up slowly. He was feeling decidedly outnumbered, but as long as he had Hansen and Carter at gunpoint, he was gambling that their men would not do anything stupid.

"All right," Jake told them, "both of you over here. Move it!" He wanted to get them away from the men—none of this showing off or afraid to back down in front of their cowboys. These two were going to listen to reason, dammit, or he was in just the mood to pound it into their thick skulls.

"I'll come over there, Sheriff," Hansen announced, standing by the side of the stream. "It'll be easier to put a bullet in that bastard's head."

Jake watched intently while Hansen stomped through the ankle-deep stream, water splashing and whooshing around his brown wool trousers and staining the front of his faded tan shirt. Unsteadily, he managed to climb up the embankment.

Out of the corner of his eye Jake watched Carter inching his way in Jake's direction.

"Put your gun away, Earl," Jake ordered. Hatred was like a flame in Hansen's eyes, and the gun in his hand seemed almost forgotten, he was so intent on closing in on Carter. The two men glared at each other with a fierceness that fighters in the ring rarely displayed.

One took a threatening step forward. The other matched it. Within seconds Jake had to move in between them, a hand pressed flat on Carter's chest to keep them apart.

"Stop it, both of you!" He shoved them away from

each other. "I'll arrest you both, goddammit!" The two postured and flexed, but they obeyed.

"All right, you two," he said through clenched teeth. "I know exactly what started this and what the problem is." He glanced from one to the other in a way he hoped would make each think Jake was talking to him. "Either you tell him or I will."

Confusion flashed in Hansen's eyes. But not in Carter's. There was something else there, something in the way he suddenly refused to meet Jake's eyes.

Jake pressed his bluff. "Amos, do you want to tell him, or do you want me to do it?"

The silence stretched between them tighter than any barbed wire fence.

Finally Carter said, "You don't know anything, McConnell."

"Wanna bet?" Jake replied.

Carter shook his head adamantly while Hansen looked more confused than angry. "Will somebody tell me what the hell's going on?"

Carter turned and walked a couple of steps away.

Jake's frustration merged with his anger and he rounded on Hansen. He was pushing his bluff and hoping he didn't get called. "There's a reason why Billy and Sally can't be together." He shot Carter a telling look and said a silent prayer. "You sure you want me to do this instead of you? I mean, it's your family and I think—"

"Shut up, McConnell! I won't have you or nobody talking about Sally or my wife." Carter closed in fast on Hansen. "Millie was *my* wife," he growled, his face just inches from Hansen's. "Just remember that, you son of a bitch, and Sally's *my* daughter, you understand me? No matter what you did."

"Me? What the hell are you talking about?" Hansen's face turned dark with rage. "What's Millie got to do with this?" His beefy hands closed into fists and he continued to glare at Carter while he spoke to Jake. "Is that little runt saying that Millie and me was doing something behind his back? Because if he is, then—"

"Then what?" Carter flung back.

Hansen straightened, taking a menacing step in Carter's direction. Carter rushed to meet him. "My God. The woman's gone, dead and buried a year now, and you're saying that she and I was fooling around behind the woodshed. Is that what this is about? Because it's a goddamned lie! There was no finer woman than Millie and I won't have you talking bad about her."

"You're twenty years too late to be worrying about Millie, you selfish bastard." Carter lunged at the man, grabbing his shirtfront. Buttons ripped and the fabric tore as Hansen pushed back.

Jake moved fast, managing to get between them. Carter's hat went flying, carried twenty feet away on the breeze. No one cared.

"Pa!" Billy came splashing through the stream. "What's going on?"

Jake was a little busy dragging Carter off Hansen to answer the kid. Braced between the men as though they were bookends, he held them apart.

Breathing hard, Hansen said, "I don't know what this has got to do with Billy courting Sally, but I'm not going to stand here and let you disparage Millie. If you won't look out for her memory, then I sure as hell will!"

"I *am* looking out for her memory. I'm doing what

she asked me to do. I'm keeping you from trying to marry off your son to a daughter that's half yours.''

Everyone went very still. Jake had imagined a lot of things, but this hadn't crossed his mind.

Hansen froze in place. ''What are you talking about?''

Billy stood beside his father, his thin face drawn and grim.

Carter was in a rage, and got right up close to Hansen.

''All right, Amos,'' Jake warned, making a move to separate them again. Carter stopped him with a look.

''Don't worry, Sheriff,'' Carter growled, his body practically shaking with fury, ''I ain't gonna hurt him, though I should've. I would've twenty years ago when he come back, but Millie wouldn't let me, didn't want no trouble. Millie was like that, which is why this bastard could use her then go off to the gold fields leaving her pregnant.''

Hansen took the news like a blow to the chest. He stumbled and half stepped back, shaking his head in disbelief or denial, probably both.

''What?'' Billy mumbled, his own shock apparent.

Hansen regained his composure and in a softer voice said to Carter, ''She never told me. If she had I would've—''

''What?'' Carter challenged, years of anger and hurt no longer to be denied. ''What was she going to do? You were gone, she was alone, no way to get in touch with you. She came to me. She always came to me when you let her down.''

Hansen removed his hat, wiping his brow with his

forearm. The breeze did little to cool the men or the fury.

Jake took it all in. So that was it. Carter had sent Sally, his daughter, away because she was Billy's half sister. No wonder Carter was on the rampage. What a secret to have kept for all these years.

"Why didn't she tell me?" Hansen asked—almost pleaded.

"It was too late, and when you came back married…"

"But Millie and me never talked about us getting hitched. We were just, well, you know, friends."

"Yeah," Carter answered, venom dripping from his voice, "I know about being friends." He glanced over at the dam. "Real good friends."

Jake moved up closer and said, "But all these years you've been friends."

Carter spared him a look. "Millie wanted it that way."

Hansen was clearly lost in thought. "I'm sorry," he told Carter, his gaze flicking to Jake then back again. "I never meant to hurt Millie…or Sally. With my last breath, I'd never hurt either of them." He snatched off his hat in an agitated gesture, thrusting his hand through his hair as he did. "I'm sorry for my part in causing her and you any hurt." He extended his hand in apology. "Can you forgive me?"

The moment stretched taut between them. "I promised Millie no one would ever know, and now…" There was a catch in his voice.

Hansen's head came up with a start. "No one will ever hear of this from me, I guarantee it." He shot a warning glance at Jake and Billy.

"Absolutely," Jake acknowledged.

"Of course," Billy assured them. "Mr. Carter, does this mean Sally can come home?"

Earl arched one brow in question.

Amos looked back, his emotions obviously more under control. "I guess it does."

"Good," Earl said, then abruptly turned to his men. Raising his voice to a shout, he yelled, "You men get over here and tear this dam down!" To Amos he said, "This battle is done."

The men shook hands in earnest.

Chapter Twelve

Clair had waited until she saw Jake ride out of town. Having him gone made her leaving simple. After she'd dressed and packed her few belongings, she'd swallowed her pride and gone to Slocum at the Lazy Dog. She sold him the Scarlet Lady at the ridiculously low price of three hundred dollars and tried not to hate him for winning.

The morning stage waited like a personal carriage that would carry her away from Broken Spur and away from Jake. The sun was bright, obscured only by a few large puffy white clouds that occasionally drifted through the intense light. The air was fresh and clean, and for all the world it was a gorgeous day—but not for Clair.

She used eight dollars to buy her ticket, handed her carpetbag to the stage driver and climbed inside the coach, already occupied by a feed and grain drummer and another woman who offered that she was on her way to meet her husband in Cheyenne.

Clair merely nodded. She wasn't in the mood for conversation, polite or otherwise. How could she be expected to talk when there was a pain slicing through her chest as real as any knife?

"Hang on, folks." With a shout and a snap of the whip from the driver, the stage pulled out, lurching up and down until a rhythm of constant rocking settled in. Dust swirled past, as did the treeless countryside. The baritone voice of the stage driver shouting obscenities at the team carried back to her.

Clair braced her feet and hung on to the open window for support, though the actions were more from instinct than conscious effort. Everything seemed only dimly real. She wasn't thinking or hearing or feeling. No, she was feeling. She was feeling a great deal.

Tears welled up behind her eyes and she blinked hard. She would not cry. She wouldn't. She dabbed at her eyes with a pale blue handkerchief she had tucked into her sleeve.

She'd head south first, she thought, trying to distract herself, to think of something else, someone else. Rawlins would be her first stop, then...then she wasn't sure. East maybe, Cheyenne City, or maybe north to Fort Laramie or even Deadwood. She wasn't sure. She didn't care. All she knew was that she was moving, going. Leaving him.

Oh, Lord, she'd never known leaving someone could hurt so much. She tried hard not to think about him, but with every rumbling, crunching turn of the wooden wheel, thoughts of him stole back into her mind. Rich, enticing thoughts of Jake and the love they'd shared. Those darned tears threatened again.

She tried to stop the memories, tried to think about something else, anything else, tried not to long for him with every breath. She failed miserably, the same way she'd failed in her attempt to send him away that first day.

But she'd been helpless from the first, she knew that now. Seemingly against her will her eyes fluttered closed and she was rocked with explicit sensations that had nothing to do with the movement of the coach: his jet black eyes all soft and deep when he looked at her, the warmth of his lips when they covered hers, the way his touch inflamed her body.

She swallowed hard against the traitorous memories. She was in love, helplessly in love with the worst possible man in the world, or so it seemed.

But no matter how much she loved him or he loved her, sooner or later he'd discover the truth about her, about her being wanted, and then what? His was a life of law and order, of right and wrong. Hers was a life of survival at any cost.

Suppose she had stayed, would she have told him the truth? Would she have kept it from him and hoped he never found out? Would she have asked him to live a lie, run away with her, give up his life for her? If she asked, would he say yes? Perhaps more to the point, would he say no?

This—running away—was all the choice she had. She'd play out the cards life had dealt her, but she knew she'd never be the same now that she'd been loved by Jake McConnell.

Jake was feeling pretty good about life when he got back to town. He'd never been in love and he was warming to the idea. All the way back into town he'd been having thoughts about things he'd never taken seriously before, things like marriage and family. Clair's children.

He noticed the Scarlet Lady wasn't open when he rode past. She'd said she was going to open, but then, he thought with a pleasant stirring of his blood, maybe she couldn't get herself out of bed after all.

Maybe she was waiting for him. Ah, now that was a nice thought—Clair all warm and rosy and naked in that bed. A smile tugged at his lips and he figured he would stop, give Woodrow a report, the fastest report in history, and then...

Dismounting in front of the marshal's office, he went inside. "This day just keeps getting better and better." He was grinning.

"You think so?" Woodrow said, solemn faced, from his spot behind his walnut desk.

Jake wondered what that was about, but didn't want to take the time to ask. He didn't bother to take his hat or coat off. He wasn't staying. "I just wanted to let you know that Hansen and Carter have worked out their dispute. The dam is coming down and there will be no more trouble."

"Okay." Woodrow didn't move or smile.

Jake's brow drew down. "What's the matter with you? I said there wasn't going to be a range war and all you can say is 'okay'?" It was then he noticed that Woodrow had cleaned his desk. Papers were stacked in neat piles and he could actually see the desk top. "What's the matter? All that cleaning wear you out?"

"Something like that."

Jake was in no mood to play guessing games. "Well, I'm headed over to the Scarlet Lady and—"

"She's gone."

Hand on the doorknob, Jake stopped. He looked at his friend over his shoulder. "Who's gone?"

"The woman. Clair. She's gone. Left on the early stage."

"What are you talking about?"

"She's gone."

A feeling of dread coiled in Jake's gut. "You're crazy. Is this some kind of joke? Because I don't think..." He turned the knob and opened the door enough so that sunlight sliced across the office floor and landed like an arrow in the far corner.

"She came in here and gave me this note for you. Said she had to leave. Said she was going to miss me." Woodrow's fixed gaze never wavered, and Jake could see his friend wasn't lying.

Yet there had to be a mistake, a misunderstanding. She wouldn't leave—not after this morning, not after he'd told her how he felt, not after she'd said she loved him, too.

He stared at the note in Woodrow's hand, avoiding it as though it were a death sentence. That dread in his gut pulled in tight and hard. He didn't want notes. He wanted her. She wouldn't do this. She wouldn't. He knew her and—

He bolted out of the office and practically ran across the street. He slammed open the front doors of the Scarlet Lady.

"Clair!" he shouted, standing four feet inside the empty room.

No answer.

He took the steps two at a time and stormed the bedroom where only a few short hours ago they'd made love, where they'd pledged love.

Empty. Evidently as empty as the words she'd spoken, the promise she'd made. Dammit to hell, she wasn't gone. She wasn't.

He tore down the stairs and raced back across the street, throwing open the door to Woodrow's office so hard it banged against the wall and sprang back at him, hitting him in the shoulder as he strode inside.

Woodrow didn't say a word, just handed him the note. Jake's hands shook as he slid the pale yellow paper free of the envelope.

> Jake—
> I'm leaving. I can't explain. Please understand and forgive me.
>
> Clair

That was it? No explanation, no excuse, no promise to return? Just a few meaningless words scribbled on a piece of paper as though he were some ranch hand she was dismissing or, worse yet, had grown tired of.

He read the note again and again, trying to find something more, some tone, some hint of regret or apology or...love. Yes, dammit, love. They had said they were in love, hadn't they?

Forgive, the note said. *Understand.* He didn't understand.

He crumpled the note and tossed it on the floor, not bothering with the wire wastepaper basket.

Woodrow's voice was quiet. "Jake, let her go. Whatever happened between you two—"

"What time did the stage pull out?"

"Shortly after noon."

Jake checked his pocket watch. "Three hours head start." He looked at his friend. "She isn't going to get away with this. If she has something to say, let her say it to my face."

"Jake." Woodrow's quiet tone stopped him. "There's one more thing."

Jake cocked his head to the side. He didn't like the sound of this. "What?"

"I found this when I cleaned up my desk."

Woodrow handed him a thick piece of paper that Jake recognized as a Wanted poster. "What do I care about some Wanted poster now?"

"You'll care about this one."

Jake snatched the paper and read out loud. "Wanted, Clair Travers, lady gambler, for —" Jake looked up, then said the word out loud. "Murder." He read the description. It fit Clair. His mind rebelled. "This could be a hundred people."

Woodrow gave a little shrug. "Maybe."

Jake knew it all fit. A woman gambler, the description, that name...Smith, her vagueness about her past. He'd chalked it up to privacy—maybe she'd been running from some boyfriend or something. Aw, hell, he hadn't given it much thought at all.

He kept staring at the crumpled note lying like a rattler on the floor, and at the poster he held in his hand.

Anger overcame all other emotions he didn't want to think about or feel, especially feel.

Nobody played him for a fool. Nobody.

Thirty minutes later he had filled his saddlebags with enough supplies for a week and had his rifle in the scabbard of his saddle. The woman, Clair, had several hours' head start on him, but he knew the stage route, knew where it was headed.

Woodrow offered to come along. Jake refused. He didn't want company. He wanted to be alone when he caught her—and he *would* catch her if he had to track her to hell and back. Rage burned in his brain, blocking out any hope of reason.

All he knew, all he wanted to know was that she'd lied to him. About who she was. About loving him. He snapped down hard on the horse's cinch, making the animal shy and sidestep.

Clair wasn't getting away from him, not like this, not this easily. Somewhere in the distant recesses of his mind he knew this mission didn't have a goddamned thing to do with Wanted posters. Dammit, a man doesn't say he loves a woman every day—not this man, anyway.

He swung up into the saddle and rode south.

Clair got off the stage in Rawlins, and forty minutes later was headed east on the Union Pacific. This was what she should have done in the first place, head east, get lost in some city like Omaha or Chicago, maybe even all the way to New York.

Of course, none of that held much of an attraction now—nothing did. It was as if all the life had gone out of her, as if she was going through the motions and yet was numb deep inside, where it mattered.

She tried to shake off the feeling. After all, she'd spent most of her life alone, taking care of herself, and usually she'd done all right. This time she'd wagered her heart and won, only to lose everything she'd ever dreamed of having—home and family.

If only she'd never gone into that Texas saloon three months ago.

No regrets. No turning back.

Yes. That was her motto, her litany, as sure and certain as any church chant.

No regrets. No turning back.

She settled more comfortably in the velvet seat, the train rumbling as it moved along, soot and gray streaking past the closed window. Clair leaned her head against the glass and watched the wide open prairie turn to grassland, watched the train carrying her farther and farther from him.

Jake.

Thank you for loving me.

No one ever had before.

Only Jake.

"Cheyenne City next stop," the conductor called loudly as he moved down the aisle.

Arriving in Rawlins, Jake was grim faced and feeling deadly calm as he hunted up the stage driver, finding the man enjoying a beer in the local saloon. As Jake stormed into the place, Ned Patterson was laughing over a story one of his companions had told.

He asked the driver about Clair, about the woman with the golden hair, and Ned made the mistake of not responding quickly enough.

In one lightning-fast motion, Jake grabbed two fistfuls of Ned's shirtfront and hauled the startled man to his feet. All sound stopped as those present turned to see what had their sheriff in such a black mood.

Jake didn't care what people thought and wisely no one asked—other than Ned, who said he was eager to tell Jake anything he wanted to know.

It took Jake only a couple of very specific questions this time to get the answers he wanted. Well, not the ones he wanted, exactly. He wanted the driver to say Clair was here, in town, somewhere close, so Jake could get his hands on her lovely little body.

Unfortunately, Ned had to tell Jake that he'd seen the woman and had directed her toward the train depot. No, he confirmed, he hadn't actually seen her buy a ticket or board a train, so, yes, he supposed she might be in town.

Jake made the rounds of the four boardinghouses, the one and only hotel and several more saloons. No one had seen her.

When there was nowhere else to go, he went to the train station. He knew the answer even before he asked the question, but he asked it anyway.

As he'd figured, the clerk said she'd been there. He wouldn't forget a looker like her. She'd bought a ticket, taken the 5:40 train east.

"Thanks," Jake muttered, not feeling the least bit grateful.

Behind him the sun turned to an orange ball and started its descent in the west. The breeze had a slight chill as it swirled around the side of the wood frame building and fluttered Jake's hat so that he had to grab the brim to steady it. There'd be no train again until tomorrow morning, and he was of half a mind to ride to Cheyenne. Trouble with that was that Cheyenne was a two-day journey on horseback, while it was overnight on the train. With the head start she had, she'd be there and probably gone long before he arrived.

Sullen, he made the decision to wait for tomorrow's train. Standing on the edge of the platform, he stared at the tracks stretching out in front of him.

Abruptly, he started away, turning the corner of the depot. More alone than he'd ever been in his life, he gave in to the sadness that haunted him. Head down, he leaned into the building, the clapboard siding rough against his hands that slowly curled into tight fists.

His muscles tensed and suddenly, in a fit of rage, he slammed his fist into the wooden wall, the wood creaking. Pain exploded in his hand and shot up his arm. He didn't flinch.

"Damn you, Clair Travers. Damn you for what you've done to me."

At the last minute Clair decided not to take the train to Omaha. Maybe she was simply tired. More likely, she couldn't bring herself to go farther east and farther away from him.

So instead she bought a ticket on the stage and after waiting most of the afternoon she left for Deadwood, one of those wild towns, home to the likes of Bill Hickcock and Calamity Jane and a host of others whose names and pasts were never questioned. Maybe she'd never be questioned there, either.

The ride on the stagecoach, which she shared with a young couple, was a rocking, jostling, teeth-gnashing affair. Dirt swirled into the open windows and down her throat and she wished for a little of that rain she'd been bemoaning only a week ago in Broken Spur.

If she was making wishes, and apparently she was, then she'd wish for a couple of other things. She'd wish she'd never won that saloon and never met Jake McConnell.

But Jake was the best thing, the only good thing that had ever happened to her. Wishing she'd never met him would be like wishing she'd never learned to breathe, to feel her heart beat, to feel alive.

But—she snatched back her thought—it was not to

be. No. She and Jake McConnell were about as wrong for each other as two people could be.

Oh, she'd thought about her decision since the moment she'd left. It was all she'd thought about, it seemed. The more she thought the more confused she got. No matter how she twisted and turned the thing, it always ended up the same. He was the law and she...wasn't.

She stared listlessly out of the window of the moving coach, only half seeing the open prairie and the pine-forested mountains looming ahead.

It had galled her to sell the saloon to Slocum, feeling somehow she'd betrayed the Lady. But what had to be, had to be. Looking back, she thought it was amazing how fast she'd accomplished it all. No goodbyes, except to Woodrow and Larry. No explanations. Just gone the way she'd arrived—alone. Tears threatened again.

She snapped herself back into awareness. She had made a mistake and now she'd done what she had to to set it right. It was that simple.

"Whoa! Hold up there!" she heard the driver holler above the jangle of harness and the creak and groan of the wooden coach. "Whoa, damn you!"

The door to the coach flew open and a man stood there.

Sunlight glinted off his badge. His eyes were hard as obsidian and filled with raw anger. "Hello, Miss Travers," Jake said, his tone flat and unemotional. "Get out of the coach. You're under arrest."

Chapter Thirteen

He's here! was her first thought, and joy flashed
bright and sure in her mind at the sight of him.

Guilt and remorse merged inside her with an overwhelming speed and intensity. She wanted to reach
out to touch his stern face, to coax that devastating
smile that she'd thought of so often since she'd last
seen him.

That he'd found her somehow didn't surprise her
all that much. She hadn't tried to cover her trail, and
all it would have taken was him asking a few questions—something a lawman would be good at, the
voice of warning prompted. Someone had most likely
seen her getting on the train or the stage and after
that…

In that instant his words, his command, registered
in her brain and she whispered, "So you know the
truth."

"Yes, Miss Travers, I know the truth."

Black eyes locked with blue and the moment
seemed suspended in time until a man's voice called
out to him.

"Hey, Sheriff, what's going on?" The stage driver

leaned over the side of the coach, the springs creaking and flexing with the shift in weight. "This gonna take all day? I got a schedule to keep, ya know."

Clair watched as Jake straightened, hands gripping each side of the narrow doorway as though to block any escape. Not that she was thinking of escape. Even with him knowing the truth, all she wanted was to throw herself into his arms. She was so tired—of running, of being alone.

"Get out of the coach. You're coming with me." He settled his hat lower on his forehead, casting his face in shadow. A thin film of dust coated his green shirt and his denim trousers where they were revealed behind his sweat-stained leather chaps. He stepped back, one hand resting lightly on his gun where it hung at his side, while the other hand held the door open.

The coach horses danced and pawed the ground. The harness jingled and clanged as they moved, and the coach rocked back and forth awkwardly, making her footing unsteady.

"Oh, Jake, I—"

"Get out of the coach," he told her curtly, and held out his hand to help her down.

The others in the coach stared.

"What's wrong?" the young woman passenger asked. She was a frail little wisp of a thing, her eyes wide with fright, as though Jake had just announced that Clair was carrying cholera.

"Nothing for you to be concerned about," Jake assured her brusquely.

Clair took his offered hand, hitched up her blue linen skirt and stepped from the coach.

"But..." the woman started again, clinging to her husband.

Jake slammed the door, cutting off any further discussion.

Standing on the road, he continued to hold Clair's small hand in his. It was reflex that made his fingers curl over hers, his thumb brushing once over her knuckles. Her hand felt good, soft and...

He released her suddenly. "Let's go," he commanded, clinging to anger and his duty.

The breeze lifted the hem of her skirt, revealing white petticoats. She struggled to push the fabric back into place and when she looked up again, he thought, in that fleeting instant, that she'd never looked more beautiful.

Jake didn't know what he'd expected when he saw her again, but whatever it was, this wasn't it. No way was he prepared for the sudden lightness that made his breathing unsteady or for the muscle-tensing need to touch her.

It was all he could do not to pull her into his arms and shake her, to demand to know whether she had lied about loving him.

Abruptly, Jake skirted around her and strode for the front of the coach, where the driver was watching the scene unfold with openmouthed interest.

Jake shielded his eyes and called up, "Where's her luggage?"

"In the boot." The driver started to tie off the reins and get down. "One carpetbag—blue."

Jake stopped him with a wave. "I'll get it."

He recognized the bag he'd seen in her room, and a couple of minutes later had the boot secured and the bag in hand. He strode for the two horses he had waiting nearby. "Thanks," he called over his shoulder.

"That's it?" the driver asked evidently curious. "What's she done?"

"I thought you had a schedule to keep," Jake countered, not willing to discuss Clair or what she'd done...to him.

With a shrug, the man slapped the reins hard on the horses' rumps and they lurched in the harness. "Git up!" The stage lumbered away, the driver glancing back every so often until they were out of sight. Clair stood straight and tall, refusing to back away from him or the truth about herself. He knew and, strangely, she was glad.

They were alone.

Only the sound of wind skimming along the sage-dotted landscape and the distant call of a meadowlark broke the strained silence. Clair fixed her gaze on Jake. He wasn't looking at her. No, he was busy checking cinches and saddlebags. He seemed to be busy doing everything *except* looking at her.

So she swallowed her pride. "I wanted to tell you." It was the only thing she could think to say.

"I'll bet." His tone was sarcastic. He brought a chestnut mare up alongside, tied the carpetbag on the back and said, "This one's yours." He held the reins lightly in his hand as he stood beside the horse.

The wind picked up, tugging one side of Clair's hair free of her pins to whip around her face and across her eyes. Annoyed, she shoved it aside and made no attempt to put it up again. She wasn't interested in how she looked; she was interested in him, this man she'd thought about endlessly for the past week.

Her body hummed with the longing that seeing him set off. It was absurd, of course—a woman on the run from the law actually glad to see a sheriff. But she was glad to see *him*.

"If you let me tell you what happened—"

"No need." His tone was clipped and held no warmth. He flipped up the stirrup and went about checking the horse's cinch, which he'd already checked, but he kept his back to her.

He was so closed, so cold that genuine fear coiled in her stomach. "But I..." She reached out and touched his sleeve, the green cotton sun-warmed beneath her hand. He jerked free as though he'd been burned.

"But what, Miss Travers?" He said her name like a curse. "You'd like to make a fool of me again? I *never* make the same mistake twice, although in your case—" his gaze raked over her body like an insult "—I believe, unfortunately, I already did."

If he'd struck her, she couldn't have been any more stunned. Was he really saying he didn't care what they had shared? Her temper rose in response. "So you aren't even going to listen, is that it? No 'benefit of the doubt.'"

"No." He hurled the word back at her. He pulled a folded piece of paper from his shirt pocket and handed it to her over his shoulder. He kept fussing with that damned cinch. "Everything has already been explained so that even I can understand."

It was reflex more than anything else that made her unfold the paper. She knew what it said, yet seeing the words printed in bold type sent an unexpected shiver down her spine.

Clair Travers wanted for murder.

In the recesses of her mind she'd never thought of that desperate act as murder. Self-defense, yes. Survival, absolutely. But murder, cold and calculating? Never.

Her gaze rose to him. "It's not what it looks like."

"Nothing ever is what it looks like with you." He made a derisive sound in the back of his throat. "Why, there was a morning when I thought... Never mind what I thought. Did I give you a good laugh, Miss Travers?" He snapped the stirrup back in place and rounded on her. "Let's just string the stupid lawman along—" his tone was mocking and so bitter "— and see how long it takes him to figure out he's being played for a fool."

Clair was stunned by his accusation. "Oh, Jake, no—" Wind swirled around her legs and tugged at the hem of her skirt. Clair turned her back on the wind and on him.

"You're wrong, Jake." She spoke over her shoulder, holding the hair out of her face. "It wasn't like that. I never lied to you."

He arched one brow in skeptic response.

"Not about that. Not about loving you."

"If you say so, sweetheart." Right. She'd lied to him about who she was. She'd pledged love, and then the instant his back was turned she'd left, run off without a word, without even trying to talk to him, to tell him. She'd used him once, but not again, he silently pledged, too hurt and angry to think otherwise.

"Jake, please. You have to listen. I do—"

"Forget it, Clair," he snapped, his hand slicing through the air as though to cut some invisible rope between them. "You don't have to pretend anymore." If he was so sure, then how come it was killing him to stand here looking at her? How come he wanted her as much as he had that night? "It's done. We're done," he said, as much for himself as for her. He clung to his anger and his cold determination, familiar feelings that he understood, feelings that blocked out other more painful ones. He would do his job. Yes, that was it—his job. He would not think, would not feel.

"Oh, Jake..." she breathed, the words nearly lost on the gentle afternoon breeze.

"Don't bother." He shook his head adamantly. "You're wasting your time and mine."

Clair had never seen Jake like this. The gentle lover she remembered was gone, and in his place was this stranger. She felt more alone than before he'd come.

Tears threatened and her stubborn pride made her walk away. She'd be damned if she'd let him see her cry. She'd be damned if she'd let him know how his words had hurt.

Jake let her go. He knew she was crying, just as he'd been aware of her every move, every gesture since he'd first opened that stagecoach door. But he was determined to resist. "All right, Miss Travers," he called. "Get on the horse. We're leaving."

"Where to?" she asked, walking slowly toward the waiting mare.

"Does it matter?" He gave her a leg up and she sat astride, her skirt pouched out around her legs as he adjusted the stirrup length. Instinctively she collected the reins, threading the thick leather through her fingers.

Memories of another time, of straddling another horse, flashed vividly in her mind. Men pulling at her as she struggled to escape, and briefly she thought about doing that again. But she knew this time there would be no escape, not from Jake. He'd already proven that fact.

So she stoically repeated, "Where to? Broken Spur is quite a way and—"

"We aren't going to Broken Spur," he said, swinging up into the saddle, the hard leather creaking under his shifting weight. He settled in comfortably, his hands holding the reins resting lightly on the horn.

"Where, then?" She looked at him cautiously, fear circling in her mind like a predator.

He tugged down hard on the brim of his black hat. "I'm taking you to Texas."

Clair sat stiffly in the saddle as they rode side by side. The horses' hooves made a steady clip-clop on the hard earth. The afternoon sun was warm on her face; perspiration beaded on her forehead and the back of her neck. White clouds skimmed the tops of the mountains to her left. Any other time this would have been one of those perfect spring days that people waited all year for.

But for Clair there was nothing perfect about today.

"I'm taking you to Texas," he'd said, so matter-of-factly she'd almost thought she'd misunderstood him. She knew she hadn't. With his statement, her fear had turned to heart-pounding terror.

Her mind raced helplessly as she tried to think of something to say, to do, to change his mind, to convince him. But what? She was trapped as surely as if she were already locked in a cell.

She was scared, but fear soon turned to anger. She didn't deserve to be treated this way by him. She had been as honest as she could have been without hurting him, she reasoned. Hadn't she even left to protect him? It was the hardest thing she'd ever done, leaving him, and now here he was acting as if she'd skipped off without a backward glance.

Her temper was on the rise.

Of course, if he'd bother to listen, then this could all be resolved—sort of. But no, he'd made it clear he didn't *want* to listen.

He felt betrayed. *He* thought he'd been lied to. None of which was true. She loved the man. Angry as she was, scared as she was, she loved the man. Good Lord, she'd cried her eyes out, lost sleep, worried and fretted until she had thought she'd go crazy, and did he care what she'd been through? No!

She stiffened in the saddle, turning on him an icy glare that he seemed completely oblivious to. That made her angrier. She wasn't going to beg him to talk to her.

So they rode in silence all the rest of the day. Occasionally Jake would stop, rest the horses, let her take care of necessary matters, but then he'd continue on. There was no long discussion.

By sunset she didn't know how far they'd come, but her shoulders ached and she rolled them back and forth in an effort to ease the stiffness. Didn't help.

An ache pounded behind her eyes and in her temples. Her legs hurt where they rubbed against the unbending leather. Still they rode on and she, her temper long past boiling, refused to tell him, to ask him to stop.

About the time the sun was below the horizon, she spotted a stand of cottonwood trees off to the south, a bright green ribbon against the brownish landscape. The trees meant shade and, she knew, water—cool water to soothe the dry burning on her face and hands from the hours in the sun. The horses must have smelled the water, because they drifted in that general direction.

At the change in motion, Jake looked around. His gaze settled on Clair as though he'd just come back from some faraway place, and she wondered if he'd been thinking of her, of them? She hoped so.

"By those trees." He reined over and she gratefully followed.

The shade was heaven-sent and cool on her skin. The creek wasn't much more than a trickle, moving steadily along over the rock-strewn bed, making the rocks glisten rainbow bright.

"Want help?" Jake said, and she jumped, having been unaware he was there beside her.

"No. I can manage." But her saddle-weary body refused to move and, taking her by the waist, he lifted her from the saddle.

At his touch, at the sudden closeness of his body, everything changed. Her anger faded and was replaced by a much stronger emotion. He must have felt it, too, because he held her suspended in midair above him for a heartbeat, no more. Her hands rested in a familiar way on his broad shoulders, and their gazes met and held. Neither spoke. And then slowly, almost without breathing, he settled her on the ground. His hands lingered at her waist, hers on his shoulders.

"Clair, I..." he began as a sudden heat sparked in his eyes.

Her hand touched his cheek, lightly, feeling the day's growth of beard there. His face was so handsome, so grim. She said the only thing she could say. "I never lied about loving you."

His gaze searched her face and she let him look, willing him to believe her. She hoped that he would say he understood why she hadn't told him about Texas, something, anything...

Suddenly, though, his expression turned hard. His eyes went flat as stone, and he let his hands fall away as he stepped back more fully into the sunlight.

The constant gùrgle of the stream was the only sound—that and her breathing.

Jake snatched off his hat and slapped it hard against his thigh, then took a couple of long strides away from her. She waited, and when he turned back, he said, "Just tell me it isn't true."

Clair steeled herself to tell him the truth—the terrible truth that would destroy all hope. "I shot him, if that's what you're asking. I'd do it again."

Jake slammed his eyes shut and his head lolled back as he struggled to accept her damning confession. If only she'd said she was innocent, it had been a mistake, she wasn't the one.

"If I hadn't, he would have...raped me."

Jake's head came around sharply. "What?" He closed in on her and took her shoulders in his hard grip. His fingers pressed deep into her flesh through the white cotton of her shirtwaist. "What are you talking about?"

"Rape," she repeated, wedging her hands up against his chest.

"Is this another story, another lie? Clair, so help me..."

She shook her head violently, her hair flinging back

and forth as she moved. "He came into...my room. I ordered him out."

Jake's face was very close, his black eyes riveted to hers.

Clair continued, "He said he would go, but then he didn't. Instead he grabbed me and..." She swallowed hard. "He threw me...on the bed."

Wary, Jake listened to each word, watched her closely. "Then what?"

Clair shoved the hair away from her face. Anger suddenly overtook all other emotions—anger at her ordeal and most of all anger at Jake's doubt. "How much detail do you want!" Breathing fast, she said, "He climbed on top of me, sitting on my legs. He held me down with one hand and with the other he pulled up my skirt and—"

Jake shook her. "Are you telling me the truth or are you making this up to...to..."

"There's no reason for me to make this up," Clair exploded. "If you weren't so stubborn you'd see I'm telling you the truth. I managed to get his gun and it went off." A tear slipped down her cheek.

"You're telling me a sheriff, a man sworn to protect people, tried to rape you?"

The thought of another man, any man, raping a woman was abhorrent to Jake. The thought of a man, any man, touching Clair sent rage rushing through him like a flash of gunpowder.

"Dammit, it's true." Clair pressed, swiped the tears back with the heels of her hands, leaving red marks on her pale cheeks.

Jake wanted her story to be true. But could he believe her? Emotions, sullen and hurt, had ruled him from the time he'd found her gone.

Her words, her story, rolled and tumbled in his brain like a tangle of briars. He paced away, staring out into the shadows and the setting sun beyond.

He couldn't think. He'd hardly slept since she'd left, hardly eaten, hardly done anything but curse her for going and himself for following. But that, he'd convinced himself, was duty, not love. Yes, duty.

He couldn't think about the rest—about telling her that he loved her, about her telling him she shared his feeling. He rubbed his face with the flat of his hand as though to rub the cobwebs from his brain.

He knew she was there, close, watching, waiting for him to say something, knew she wanted him to say he forgave her, believed her.

"Is this story as true as you telling me that you loved me?" He said it like an accusation. "You left me, with nothing but that goddamned note."

"I left because I didn't want you to—"

"Find out the truth," he finished for her.

"Exactly," she said.

"Exactly."

"No. No!" Realizing he'd misunderstood, she reached for him. He backed clear.

"Stop it, Clair." He rolled his head around, trying to ease the tension in his neck.

"I meant what I said," Clair insisted. "I do love you, and I wouldn't have left except—"

"Except you got tired of the game, of seeing just how long you could pretend to be someone else, pretend to love me."

She moved in close, so close he had to look down into her upturned face, so close that he could almost kiss her lush lips. His hands actually trembled with wanting to touch her. He didn't.

"Oh, Jake, it doesn't have to be like this."

"What would you have me do? Turn my back on my duty? Let you go?"

"We could go..." Clair's voice trailed off.

His gaze held hers and he was instantly reminded of the woman who'd intrigued him so from that first meeting, the woman who'd never backed down from him in challenge or in love.

That steady, blue-eyed stare held all he'd come to care for. The barest stirring of warmth pulsed along familiar nerve endings. Unsure, Jake retreated to the part of himself that he trusted completely—the lawman. "No, Clair, I couldn't."

Chapter Fourteen

Three days later they boarded the train in Cheyenne. Since their discussion, Jake had been polite to Clair but distant. He bought first-class tickets.

"Why?" she asked, feeling hot tempered. "Do prisoners always get such treatment?"

"Because it's less crowded and you're less likely to cause any trouble. Lunch?" He'd bought several ham sandwiches at a counter in the station and filled a canteen with water before they'd boarded.

Clair wasn't hungry. She was tired. Tired of traveling, tired of fighting him, mostly tired of trying to make him believe her.

Too exhausted, too morose to care, she leaned against the window of the train, her hand a cushion between her face and the cold, hard glass. She watched the grassland move past, watched the clouds glide across the sun, watched hope slip away. Grassland turned to mountains as the train moved relentlessly south toward Denver.

Every once in a while she glanced over at Jake, who sat, eyes closed, in the seat opposite. His arms were draped casually across his chest, pulling the blue cotton of his shirt tight on his shoulders. The black wool of his trousers seemed to blend and disappear into the black linen of her skirt. It was as though she couldn't tell where one ended and the other began. It was the way she had felt about the two of them, but Jake had built a wall between them, one she couldn't scale.

They made several unscheduled stops through the night and the next day to take on passengers or off-load freight for local ranchers. Jake always offered her food and water.

"No, thank you," she said each time. It was hard to have an appetite on the way to being tried for murder.

By the next evening she was feeling light-headed, probably from the lack of food, or the lack of sleep.

Whatever it was, her stomach rolled and pitched like a flat-bottom boat on a stormy lake. Her head pounded and her mouth tasted as though something furry had crawled in there and died. She shifted awkwardly in the seat, first this way then that, in a futile effort to get comfortable.

"Are you all right?" Jake asked, his hand touching her lightly on the sleeve. "What's wrong?"

"Nothing," she lied, thinking everything was wrong.

A suspicious tingling stirred at the back of her throat. She swallowed hard and willed herself to relax, to be all right. She took a few sips of water. Yes, there, she was fine.

"Come on, Clair," he said, unwrapping a sandwich and holding it up to her. "Or is this a hunger strike?"

Her temper flared and she flounced around to him. "Fine. You want me to eat, I'll eat." But two bites of the salty ham and her stomach disagreed—violently.

Skirt flying, she raced for the door at the end of the car.

Jake was right behind her. One look at the misery on her face and he knew she wasn't faking. "Take it easy, honey," he said, holding her fevered head in his hand while she clutched the iron railing and hung her head over the steps. She retched and coughed for the next five minutes.

Weak and shaking, she managed to straighten up. "Sorry." Perspiration beaded on her forehead and her neck.

He pulled his bandanna free of his neck and dabbed gently at her face. "You going to be okay?" he asked, his eyes all soft, his voice quiet.

"I think so."

"Will you be all right until we get to Denver? We can get a doctor there if you need one." He handed her the bandanna, which she took with a confirming nod.

"Come on, then."

Arm around her waist, he helped her back to their seats. People stared but she didn't care, and evidently neither did he.

"I'm sorry," she managed to say as he settled her gently on the pressed velvet. She adjusted her skirt around her legs.

"It's not your fault," he countered, brushing the hair back from her face in a way that was heartbreakingly tender. "What can I do?"

Clair wanted to say, "Forgive me. Love me again." But she didn't. "Just let me rest a little."

"All right, honey."

He coaxed her to take small sips of water, holding the canteen until she obeyed his gentle order. She liked the way he was concerned, liked having him close.

Instead of sitting opposite, this time Jake settled in next to her. But any hope that he was softening disappeared, as Jake went back to his pensive silence. His expression, which moments ago had been so kind and compassionate, became shuttered again, keeping her out. Yet she couldn't help wondering if he realized he'd called her honey. Perhaps it was merely a thoughtless slip, perhaps it was more.

Resolutely she, too, pulled back into her own private world. One hand instinctively on her stomach, she shifted, trying to find a more comfortable position. She rested her forehead once more against the glass, finding the coolness soothing.

Her eyes had just fluttered closed when she felt his hand on her sleeve and she looked around. Without a word he pulled her into the curve of his shoulder.

She went gladly, her hand resting in a familiar way on his chest, taking solace in the steady rise and fall of his breathing.

Some time later, shivers prickled along her skin and she began to shake.

"Cold?" he asked before she could complain.

"Yes." She snuggled closer, pulling her knees up under the fullness of her skirt. She sandwiched her hands between their bodies, feeling the outline of his ribs against her knuckles.

"Let me get a blanket," he offered, and made to move.

"No." She looked up at him. "Don't leave."

His grip around her shoulders tightened and he

didn't leave, though eventually she released him for the few seconds it took to get his jacket from the rack over their heads.

Nestled against him, snug in the folds of his wool jacket, she drifted in and out of sleep, lulled by the rhythm of the wheels and the beating of his heart.

The ache behind her eyes never backed off and the movement of the train made the rolling of her stomach worse. Lord, she was miserable. But every time she woke he had little to say other than to ask if she felt better or worse.

By evening Jake was still holding her against him, though his shoulder and arm were long since numb. He flinched, trying to flex tingling muscles, and she murmured her complaint. "It's all right," he soothed. "Go back to sleep."

In his mind Jake was calculating distance, counting each turn of the wheel—or so it felt. In less than an hour they'd reach Denver. After that it would be stage south, then east to Texas. In a few days, a week maybe, they'd be there.

And what? You gonna turn her in? Just hand her over to some law dog and walk away, pretend you never loved her.

"How much longer?" Clair murmured, as though reading his thoughts. She lifted her head away from him long enough to glance out the window.

"I don't know," he hedged, not liking the reality of the situation. He raked one hand through his hair, then rubbed his face in a futile effort to wipe the fatigue away. "Go back to sleep, honey."

She snuggled against him. He was glad she was sleeping. It was the best thing for her, he told himself.

He was worried about her, and having her sleep on his shoulder felt good, too good.

As she slept he couldn't help noticing the way her mouth drew up in a pout, the way her hair fell lightly over her brow, the way her lashes formed shadows on her cheeks.

Beautiful Clair, he thought, remembering another time he'd watched her sleep. A familiar lightness moved through him.

Abruptly he sucked in a deep breath and let it out slowly as though to still the yearning. She wasn't to be trusted. She wasn't to be believed and yet, looking at her sleeping so peacefully, it was nearly impossible not to believe her, not to surrender to the enchantment that was Clair Travers.

When they got off the train in Denver, Jake could see Clair was too weak to go on. The dark smudges under her eyes and the paleness of her complexion were enough to confirm that fact. He got them a room on the second floor of the Continental Hotel, one of Denver's best.

Jake was signing the register when Clair smiled up at him. "Thank you."

"You're welcome," he answered, steeling himself against the sudden longing her smile stirred in him. Here he was on the way to return her to Texas to stand trial for murder, and all he could think about was wanting her. "I'll take you to the—"

"Jake—"

Jake managed to catch her an instant before she sagged to the floor.

"Which room?" he demanded of the startled desk clerk.

"Number three, top of the stairs," the narrow-faced man replied. With Clair in his arms, Jake took the stairs two at a time, the desk clerk in hot pursuit waving a brass key in the air.

Jake stepped aside long enough for the man to open the door, then stormed inside. "Get the doctor!"

"Yes, sir!" the clerk replied, wringing his hands.

Jake put her gently on the bed and began undoing the tiny buttons of her blouse. He needed to get her undressed and tucked into bed. This was all his fault.

The clerk hovered near the doorway. "Is she...dead?"

Jake spared him a heated glance. "Hell, no! But you'll be, if you don't get that doctor!"

The clerk retreated faster than a rabbit with his tail on fire.

Jake fetched water from the pitcher on the bureau and from a towel made cold compresses for her head. He undressed her down to her camisole and pantalets, all the while nervously checking her forehead for a temperature, changing the cold compresses every few minutes. She didn't seem hot, and he took that to be a good sign, at least.

"Honey?" He settled on the edge of the bed, her hand held lightly in his. "Clair?"

She looked so young, so beautiful, her hair spilling over the white pillowcase and across the top of her shoulder. She seemed so fragile, so vulnerable.

Looking at her now, remembering her over these past couple of weeks, it was impossible to believe that she was capable of killing anyone. She'd said self-defense and he believed her. He'd *always* believed her. He'd just been too damned angry, too damned hurt to tell her.

"Honey? Can you hear me?"

He went to fetch a fresh compress.

"Jake?"

She saw his back as he stood at the bureau, and when he turned at the sound of her voice, Clair was struck again with the power of him. Jake stood tall and straight, his burgundy shirt pulled tight over his broad shoulders. His faded denim trousers molded to his legs.

His dark eyes reflected his worry.

"What happened?" She tried to sit up, but he was there in an instant, forcing her down with a gentle touch.

"You fainted."

"I've never fainted in my life," she countered, and tried to sit up again, but a sudden dizzy wave stopped that notion in a hurry.

She slumped back down once more. "Uh, maybe you're right."

He brought her water to drink and held compresses on her head, and after a few minutes he did help her stand long enough to get her safely in between the sheets. The doctor, Sam Bell, arrived none too soon, according to Jake, who hovered like an avenging angel, dark and fierce, watching every move, while the doctor examined Clair and pronounced her well but exhausted.

"I'd prescribe rest," he told a grim Jake. "You need to take better care of your wife."

"I will," Jake confirmed, not bothering to correct the doctor's mistake. He hadn't taken good care of her, hadn't done a great many things he should have done, all because he was to busy being a son of a bitch.

Jake paid the doctor, assured him that he would indeed be looking after her, and the doctor left. Jake slipped back into the room quietly in case she was asleep. She wasn't.

He went to her bedside and fussed with straightening the covers, tucking the white sheet up around her shoulders. "Okay, now I'm going downstairs and see if I can't get you something to eat."

"I don't really—"

"I know, but it's doctor's orders," Jake countered in a soft but firm tone. "Now, you stay put. No trying to get up. Promise?"

She nodded. "Promise."

He returned a short time later with a plate of scrambled eggs and a glass of milk. Pulling up the only chair in the room, he insisted on feeding her.

"Jake, to the best of my knowledge I'm not a cripple, you know. I can do this for myself."

"I know," he agreed, holding up another forkful of scrambled eggs anyway.

His concern touched her and, not wanting to spoil the moment, she said, "Okay," and let him finish feeding her. She did insist on holding her own glass, however.

"My mother always gave us scrambled eggs when we were sick. Sometimes chicken soup," he offered as explanation that this was necessary. He watched her while she drank every last drop of the milk. "How's that feeling?"

"Fine." She handed him back the glass. "I've never fainted before." She smoothed the bedcovers, the brightly colored quilt rough against her fingers.

"Evidently you did, though. *Now* you need to get

some sleep,'' he softly commanded through a smile that was warm as sunshine. She felt calm for the first time in days. His gentleness, his concern soothed her raw nerves and quieted fears.

Clair snuggled lower in the bed and slept peacefully, content in the knowledge that they were together the way she'd always wanted.

When she woke, he was seated by the window, looking out into the black night sky. A kerosene lamp on the table next to the bed provided light, the flame flickering, making shadows on the white plaster walls.

Silently Clair studied him, this man that she'd fallen in love with.

She'd tried not to love him, but she'd been helpless against him and the feelings of desire that curled inside her with his every look, every smile.

She'd known that once he knew the truth, he'd have no choice but to take her back. She'd seen him do his job, seen him bring in a man dead, seen him face down drunken cowboys. Other men might have taken the safe road, but not Jake.

So it was obvious to her that for one to win, to survive, the other would have to lose all.

Was she afraid? More than words could say. But there was a sense of the inevitable about the whole thing that made it bearable. The fact that Jake was the one taking her in and not some stranger—well, that, too, seemed to somehow make her fate endurable.

She watched him for several minutes, and then he turned as if he'd realized she was awake and watching him. His smile was immediate, and devastating to her trembling nerves.

"Hello," she managed, as though she was waking up from some beautiful dream, as though her fears and regret didn't threaten to consume her. "What time is it?"

"Late," he replied, and crossed to the bed.

He stared down at her, and Clair remembered another time when he'd come to her bed in the room over the saloon.

"Are you hungry?"

She sighed. "No. Not now."

"Are you feeling all right, though? Would you like the doctor again? I could—"

"All things considered, I'm fine."

"You scared me, you know." He was cast in shadow, his face lost to her.

"I'm sorry," she said.

Without warning, he reached toward her and lightly stroked her cheek. She turned in to his palm, needing the warmth. Jake sank onto the edge of the bed, the springs protesting the added weight. His hand covered her smaller one. "Ah, Clair, *I'm* the one who's sorry." He kissed her fingers at the knuckles, the lamplight revealing his face, his eyes haunted. "I've been a real son of a bitch. I was too hurt, too angry, and I wanted to punish you. It was wrong. *I* was wrong. Can you ever forgive me?"

Joy bloomed in her like a fragile flower. Her grip tightened on his, their fingers interlacing. "Oh, Jake, why didn't you tell me before? It's been awful thinking that you hated me for..."

"I tried," he told her honestly. "But when I came back to town and you were gone..." He brushed a nonexistent lock of hair back from her face. "I could never hate you, Clair. Never."

Tears threatened. "Jake, if only you'd said something. We could have talked. I tried to tell you."

"I know, honey." He kissed the knuckles of her hand, sending delicious shivers skipping over her skin. "I wanted to talk to you. I should have, but the truth is…"

"What?"

"The truth is I was afraid." A startling admission for a man who spent his life facing down fear. "I lost you once and I was afraid that if I believed you again, if you lied to me again…" He released her hand and twisted away, raking his fingers back through his hair in an agitated gesture. "Loving you happened so fast. I never knew one person could be so much a part of another."

Tears slipped silently down her cheeks. It was impossible for her to be strong any longer. "Oh, Jake, what are we going to do?"

She rolled onto her side, not wanting him to see her like this. She did, after all, have some pride.

Jake didn't hesitate before turning her toward him and lifting her into his arms. Her face nestled in the curve of his neck, her hands rested lightly on his shoulders. It was all so familiar, so good.

Jake felt her body tremble and shudder as she cried, felt the wetness of her tears soak through his cotton shirt and dampen his skin beneath. And he realized, perhaps for the first time, the full extent of the terror she must have been feeling for days now. No wonder she was ill.

"It's all right, honey," he crooned to her, his hand stroking her hair, trying with the simple gesture to make up for all he'd done, trying harder to avoid her question, because he didn't have an answer.

She sobbed and he kept on holding her, tightly, needing to feel her body against his, needing to touch her. Lord, how he'd missed her these past days.

When her crying quieted, with her face still buried against his neck, her hands still gripping his shoulders, she said, "I'm glad you told me." He kissed the top of her head in response. "No matter what happens later."

"I love you, Clair. That's all I know, all I want to know."

He looked longingly into her face, taking in her exquisite blue eyes, her delicate cheeks, the sensuous curve of her mouth, and he was as certain of her truthfulness as he was of his next breath.

His expression turned seductive. "I've missed you." His voice dropped to a husky timbre. "I've missed loving you." His fingers glided through her hair, sending the few remaining pins flying, then stopped.

"I've missed you, too," she said, stroking the side of his face and hair. "I've missed you so much."

As his dark heated eyes locked on hers, he untied the silk ribbons on her camisole, then slid the loose material off her shoulders. His gaze drifted down to her breasts, the nipples hardening as though they'd been touched—which she wished they had.

"I'm sorry, Clair. Sorry for ever doubting you." His breathing had visibly altered.

She reached to take his face in her hands. "Oh, Jake, I was so afraid. I didn't know what to do. I wanted to tell you everything. That morning when you said you loved me, I wanted to tell you, but I didn't know how."

"It's all right, honey. It's over and done. I'll never

leave you, and you, sweet Clair, must promise never to leave me again."

"I promise," she murmured in a voice low and husky and rich with invitation. She kissed his face, his cheeks, his brows. When her lips touched his, this time it was with all the power of two lovers reunited, lovers clinging fiercely to each other and to life, as though they both knew life would end in the next heartbeat. Perhaps it would.

His arms curved around her, one at her waist, the other around her shoulders, and she was locked in his embrace, a willing prisoner this time. He pulled her against him, pushing her hair back one second, the next hugging her closer, tighter, his desire escalating faster than his temper ever had.

Jake refused to think about tomorrow, about the hopelessness of their situation. There was only now, this minute. She was his woman and he wanted her more than he wanted his next breath. And so he made love to her with all the tenderness he possessed, willing her to know, to understand and to forgive.

And when she was ready, he glided into her, feeling her heated core wrap deliciously around him. She began to move even before he did.

It was heaven.

It was home.

Clair made love to him. He was all she wanted and he was here. The past was the past. Now was all that mattered.

Jake was all that mattered.

Much later, after they'd made love, after he'd brought her to lush climax, they lay together on the bed, Clair tucked securely in the curve of his shoulder, the patchwork quilt draped lightly over their bodies.

Content and confident for the first time in days, Clair said, "How would you feel about living in New Orleans? I know a lovely street where we could get a place." Her hand lovingly caressed his bare hip.

"New Orleans?" he repeated, his voice sounding half-awake.

"Uh-huh," she murmured, still lost in her passion-induced haze. Fueled by that newfound confidence, she'd decided that they would simply go away from all their trouble, start over together. She would...

Abruptly he twisted away from her and sat up. She braced up on her elbows, staring at the broad expanse of his bare back. When she touched him he stood and stalked away from her.

"Jake?"

"We can't go to New Orleans." He pushed back the white lace curtain with the side of his hand and a patch of silver moonlight fell over her naked body and his.

"Somewhere else, then? California, perhaps?" she murmured, the first icy-cold prickles of reality snaking up her spine.

There by the window, he turned. His body cast in shadow so that he was only a silhouette, he said, "There's only one place we can go."

"Where?" she managed to ask, her earlier fear returning.

"Texas."

Chapter Fifteen

"Oh, no." She sat straight up in the bed, the sheet falling around her hips, the cool night air sending a shiver over the bare flesh of her breasts. "I thought you understood. I thought that when you made love to me that you...that we could..."

"We have no choice."

Clair shook her head in denial. "No. Don't you see, they'll never believe me."

He stalked back to her. "I don't want to spend the rest of my life, *our* life, watching every stranger's face, worried that he'll be the one who recognizes you, remembers you. What kind of a future is that?"

She knew then that the battle was lost, knew he'd made up his mind, but she played against the odds, hoping against futile hope. "But we'll be far away, and in time all those posters will disappear."

"How long will that take? A year, two, five? This is murder you're charged with, and while I believe you're innocent—" he reached to touch her and she shrank back "—I know we have to face this to put it behind us." His tone was flat, emotionless. His gaze held hers across the small distance that separated them. It might as well have been a million miles.

Clair fell back against the walnut headboard. "Oh, Jake."

"You'll see. The law works. Trust me."

"Have it your own way." She pulled the covers tight under her chin, hanging on with both fists. "This time you're wrong, Jake."

The trip to Texas was the longest, or perhaps the shortest, of her life, she wasn't sure. In her mind, she had thought that the night she'd run from this town was the worst time of her life. She was wrong. Having Jake make love to her, then tell her he was taking her back to Texas, knowing what he knew...

Nothing would ever be worse than this.

They made changes from one stage to another. After a while they all seemed the same to her. Reality blurred and numbly she went along. She felt as though she was in a dream of some sort, as though this was happening to someone else, not her.

They arrived in Mule Shoe about two on Tuesday afternoon. The stage was two hours late due to some wheel problems.

Jake helped her step down onto the sidewalk in front of the office. "Wait here," he instructed, then went to claim their gear from the driver. With a quick stop in the office he arranged storage for a few hours until they found a hotel or rooming house.

As he came out of the office, Clair was there, standing proud and straight, looking for all the world like the most beautiful woman in the world—in his world, at least.

It struck him then that she was alone, all alone in this town except for him.

The afternoon was warm, downright hot. Perspiration beaded on his neck and on his forehead under his hat. Since he was from Wyoming, anything above eighty degrees seemed hot to him.

"Hi," he said, coming to stand beside her. She was wearing her blue traveling suit, the one with the high neck and long sleeves. Up close, she looked pale and nervous. He was feeling nervous himself. Still, he forced a confident expression that wasn't quite a smile and, taking her arm, said, "We'll go down to the marshal's office and take care of...things—get that over with first."

She nodded but didn't speak as they started on the brief walk toward the other end of town.

Mule Shoe was pretty much the same as she remembered. The stage stop was at one end of the street that stretched out about half a mile on the Texas prairie. Bilson's Mercantile, she noted, was in the process of getting a new coat of blue paint, but the saloons, all five of them, looked as they had all those months ago, a hodgepodge of false fronts and two-story clapboards in various stages of disrepair, including peeling paint and rusting roofs.

As they walked past Russell's Restaurant, the sweet smell of fresh bread wafted out the open front doors. Clair remembered taking most of her meals there that week, a lifetime ago. Across the street was Meyer's Hotel, where she wished like crazy now she'd stayed instead of taking a room over the saloon. If she had, that terrible night would never have happened.

They walked along in silence, the only sound her heels on the wooden sidewalk and Jake's boots thudding in counterpoint. It wasn't far now, only a few steps—she knew that too well. Fear coiled knot-hard in her stomach. She wouldn't panic. She wouldn't.

Perhaps they'd walk in and, through some miracle, someone would say it had all been a mistake, that they knew the truth and she was forgiven. It was a futile hope, but still, she felt better holding on to hope than giving in to the stark terror that circled in the shadows of her mind.

Her fingers—her whole body—were ice-cold. With strength of will, she kept walking, putting one foot in front of the other, her skirt skimming the dusty sidewalk. Jake matched her step for step. His hand on her elbow was not reassuring as much as imprisoning.

Life seemed normal. No one paid her any mind. There was a part of her that was screaming at her to run, before it was too late, just turn and run while no one cared. Leave Jake. Leave everything and run!

She didn't. On some rational level, one that she hated, she knew Jake was right—turning herself in was the best thing to do. He was right about living in fear. She'd done that for months, always looking over her shoulder, always wary of every man who approached her.

She would tell the truth, the whole story, leaving nothing out. Surely someone else in this town had heard something, seen something, knew something about the marshal that would help her.

If there was such a person and she could find them…

She glanced over at Jake walking stiffly beside her. He hadn't said a word since they'd started walking. For a moment she wondered if he was having second thoughts, perhaps reconsidering her story, his belief in her.

No, she told herself sharply. First things first. She needed to prove self-defense, to prove herself innocent of murder.

Ultimately, it came down to her being alone in her room with Marshal Atkins. He had made sexual advances. She had refused. He'd attacked her and she, in her struggle, had shot him.

She'd seen no one, except the deputy, Hilliard, who'd appeared at her door like an apparition from hell. He'd taken one look at Atkins on the floor and, like an angel instead of one of Satan's own, he'd let her go.

He was the one man who knew for certain that she was guilty, that she'd fired that shot. He would not be a help, except to the prosecution—unless perhaps he'd left town. Now, there was something she hadn't thought of. Perhaps Hilliard had left after his boss was shot. Perhaps the new marshal had hired his own deputies. If Hilliard was gone, then there'd be no one to testify against her. Hope flared and she actually felt a ghost of a smile brush her lips.

They paused outside the door of the marshal's office. Jake turned her around to face him, his hands gripping her shoulders tightly as he bent at the knees to look her directly in the eyes. "I'm going to be right beside you. No one will hurt you."

She nodded and gave him an uncertain smile. Her blue eyes were bleak and grim, and seeing her like this tore at him.

You'd better be right, McConnell, he told himself. The alternative was too frightening to consider.

Taking her hand in his, he shoved the door open and walked in, Clair beside him.

The office was large, square and reasonably neat. The walls were thick adobe and the floor was worn pine plank, blackened from age and use. Two windows on either side of the door provided light.

The marshal's lean, wiry frame was stretched out in the chair, feet propped on the corner of the desk, eyes closed, a magazine lying on his chest. He looked for all the world as though he was asleep. His greasy blond hair fell over his brow and partly covered one eye. Clair's stomach fell as she came face-to-face with Buck Hilliard.

Obviously the town had promoted Buck when Atkins died. Buck Hilliard, the one man she never wanted to see again in her life. Her fingers instinctively tightened on Jake's hand; she was relieved when he responded in kind, though a quick look told her his gaze was focused on Hilliard.

"You the marshal?" Jake asked, his voice strong and firm.

Hilliard's eyes sprang open, his feet hit the floor and he stood all in one motion, magazine held in his hand. "Who the hell are you?" he snapped, wiping the sleep from his face and raking his hair back.

Clair's gaze was drawn to the two cells clearly visible behind him, and she shuddered. Any second he was going to come around that battered excuse for a desk, grab her and toss her into one of the cells. Locked up. Trapped.

Her childhood fear merged with her ever-present terror.

She grabbed Jake's arm for support. "Jake, I can't..." She tried to back away, but he held her firmly in place as he spoke. "I'm Sheriff McConnell of Carbon County, Wyoming," he said in a voice hard and commanding. "This is—"

Buck Hilliard tossed down the *Saturday Evening Post*, and it slid over the top of the desk and fluttered to the floor. "Clair Travers," he said on a suddenly exhaled breath, his blue eyes wide with surprise. "Son of a bitch!"

For a full five seconds Buck just stood there. It couldn't be her. It was. What the hell was she doing back here?

The man's words registered in Buck's mind. "Sheriff?" he muttered. "You said you're a Wyoming sheriff?" He was trying to get his brain to work, but it was still fogged with sleep and the bottle of whiskey he'd consumed last night.

"Yes," the man said. "Jake McConnell."

He took the two in. He was law, all right, but she wasn't in handcuffs. In fact, they were holding hands awful intimate like. He didn't like the look of this.

"From where?" Buck was stalling for time. What the hell was going on? What was some county sheriff doing bringing in a prisoner? That was a deputy's job, sure enough, unless the man was worried he wouldn't get his reward.

"From Carbon County, Wyoming," the man replied, annoyance clear in his tone and his expression.

Trying to look relaxed, Buck sank onto the edge of the oak desk, his moist hands, resting lightly on his thighs.

"Nice country up your way. I was there once years ago. Me and a bunch of the boys was doing some buffalo huntin' when the price of hides was good. Ever do any?"

"No," McConnell said in a superior way that rankled Buck's temper. "I don't hunt for sport...or money."

Arrogant son of a bitch, Buck thought, but didn't say. The man looked hard as winter and Buck saw no reason to piss him off. He just wanted to get on with the business and send him on his way. Yeah, send him on his way.

He forced a smile and said, "So, how'd you catch her?" He went around behind his desk and pulled open a drawer with the cell keys in it, the brass clinking as the keys fell together.

"I didn't catch her," McConnell said. "Miss Travers turned herself in."

Buck's head came up sharply. "No kidding." He slammed the drawer shut. "I never would've figured on that." *I never figured on seeing her again*, he thought, but didn't say.

"I didn't catch your name," McConnell was saying. He thumbed his hat back from his face.

"What? Oh, Buck Hilliard." He offered his hand, and McConnell actually looked at it as if he thought it was dirty or something. Buck's temper moved up a notch.

"So," Buck said, schooling his expression and his temper, "you'll be wanting to collect your reward. I can tell you we're glad to have her back, what with her shooting poor old Bert like she did."

He moved in closer. All he wanted was to put her in a cell and send this north country sheriff back to where he came from. Buck was the law in this town, and he didn't like anyone who might challenge his authority.

"So, you turned yourself in," Buck said to Clair,

stopping just two feet in front of her. "Won't do you a damned bit of good, sweetheart." He shot McConnell a smug glance. "She tell you she murdered our sheriff?"

"She told me he tried to rape her," McConnell countered.

Hell! Buck faltered for a second. Judging by the look in this man's eyes, he believed her. Now, that was dangerous. Real dangerous.

Buck's gaze shot to her, then back to the sheriff. "Well, you know how her kind are. Bert was just a fine man. Ask anyone. She gunned him down in cold blood."

Clair had had about all of this she could take. "Bert Atkins was a lying snake who tried to rape me and—"

Buck laughed, a harsh sound that held absolutely no warmth. "She gunned Bert down, all right. I saw her."

"You saw her?" Jake asked matter-of-factly.

Buck nodded, his blond hair falling onto his face. He raked it back. "Sure did."

Jake took a half step in Buck's direction. "Why didn't you arrest her?"

"What?" Buck stilled. His mind went blank and he started fumbling with the cell keys he held in his hand. "Why, I did...I mean, I tried. I was so...upset by seeing Bert laying there, well, she just got away from me, is all. Lucky you brung her back."

McConnell stared at him in a way that was making him nervous. "Like I said. I didn't bring her back. I'm just along for the ride, a guarantee that everything is going to be fair, if you know what I mean."

Yeah, Buck knew what he meant. He meant he was going to hang around and be a pain in the ass.

"Well, look, there's reward money." He went back to his desk and fumbled around in a drawer, searching for one of those damned reward posters he'd had printed up. "Let me get her locked up and I'll walk on over to the bank with you." Buck plastered a smile back on his face and gave up looking for the poster.

"I don't want the reward."

"What?" Buck couldn't believe his ears. Wasn't no woman worth turning down five hundred dollars for, he thought. "You sure? I mean, they have the money over at the bank."

"I'm sure."

Buck's gaze settled on Clair, on the way the two of them were still holding hands. She must give the man a hell of a good roll in the hay. His own lust stirred as he thought of having her locked up here day and night for a while. Since she seemed to like lawmen, well...

"Have it your own way." He shrugged, then turned to her. "Well, come on, sweetheart, there's a nice cell all ready and waiting for you."

"No cell," McConnell said, and Buck stopped dead in his tracks.

"What?"

"I said no cell."

Buck bristled at the order. He didn't like taking orders from anyone. "Look, mister—"

"Sheriff," Jake countered.

"Look, you," Buck returned, squaring off in front of Jake. "The law says she gets locked up and then there's gonna be a trial."

The two men glared at one another. Buck looked

away first and hated McConnell for making him give way.

"What the hell do you want?" Buck snapped. "You can't come into my town and my jail and start telling me the law. I know the law, and she's going to jail."

"I know the law, too," Jake countered. "She's entitled to bail."

"That's for a judge to decide, not me or you," Buck snarled. "Now, turn her over." He came around the desk and grabbed for her, his hand stopped in midmotion by the sheriff. McConnell's grip was bone-bending hard on Buck's hand, and he flinched as he twisted free.

"Don't touch her," Jake warned.

"Like hell. You done your job, but this ain't your jurisdiction." Buck puffed up a bit. "In fact, you ain't got no say at all in Texas."

Jake never flinched. His free hand drifted slowly but conspicuously to his gun. "You want to test my authority?"

Buck didn't answer.

"Where's the judge?"

"Ain't no judge, not until day after tomorrow." Buck took perverse pleasure in the telling. He was smart enough to sidestep clear of the man as he spoke. "He's due in on the circuit, so leave her to me and—"

"No." McConnell turned away. Taking the woman by the arm, he started for the door.

"You ain't bringing in a wanted murderer, then waltzing outta here again," Buck threatened. Who the hell did he think he was?

Jake never faltered. "It appears that's exactly what I'm doing."

Buck moved back and shoved the desk drawer closed with a bang, but didn't say a word.

"We'll be at the hotel. When the judge gets in, let me know." He opened the door and sunlight flooded the room. "We'll see about setting bail."

"Ain't no bail for murderers," Buck sneered. "Only jail...if they're lucky." Looking directly at Clair, and in a voice rich in resentment, he added, "You shoulda never let him bring you back, sweetheart."

Outside in the sunlight, Jake continued to hold Clair's hand. He looked at her then for the first time since they'd walked into the marshal's office. He'd been busy keeping an eye on this Hilliard. Jake knew scum when he saw it. He didn't trust the man alone with Clair locked in a cell. No way in hell.

Clair was cold, bone-numbing cold, and her knees were shaking so hard she wasn't certain how much longer she was going to be able to stand. She was eternally grateful that Jake had taken her out of there. But for how long?

"Maybe you should have let him lock me up," she told him, her voice small and fragile. "Sooner or later I will—"

Jake looped his arm around her shoulders and started them in the direction of the hotel across the street. He spoke as they walked. "Honey, do you think I'd leave you with that bastard? Not on your life." No, sir. He'd meant it when he'd said they were going to prove self-defense, going to get her off. He wasn't handing Clair over to anyone.

Clair was in a state of disbelief. She'd steeled herself against the inevitable and then Jake had simply turned everything around. Even so, fear sat like a rock in her chest. She was having a hard time thinking, focusing.

Jake checked them in to the hotel and, after sending someone to get their luggage from the stage station, got them settled in their room.

Clair sagged down on the edge of the double bed, its patchwork quilt a rainbow of bright colors in the afternoon light coming through the white lace window curtain. "What now?"

Jake looked at her, shaking his head slightly as he did. He sat down beside her, hooking his hat on the walnut post of the footboard. "Now we get some food, then you get some rest. I'm going to see if I can find a lawyer in this town." He made to stand. She stopped him with a touch on his sleeve.

"If you can't?"

"Then I'll wire around and bring one in." He had some money with him, not much. He could wire his bank in Rawlins for more. Since he was single, his living expenses were small, and so he'd saved quite a bit over the years. He'd spend it all on her and beg, borrow or steal more, if that's what it took.

Hell, he was scared, but he was holding on to his belief in law and justice. If she'd convinced him of her innocence, then she would surely convince others. Jake McConnell was a hard sell, or so various fast-talking outlaws had told him over the years. He had good instincts and he'd learned years ago to trust them. And his instincts told him that Clair was telling the truth.

"All right, Jake," she said, head down, her hands smoothing out the creases in her lap.

Oh, Lord, it tore at him to see her this way. He wanted her to feel the same sureness, the same determination he felt. There were no words for him to say, and so he kissed her, a long, slow kiss, willing her to understand and believe in him and in the justice that had guided his life for so long.

They had a quiet lunch in the dining room of the hotel. Jake got the name of a lawyer from the desk clerk.

"I'd like to see the saloon where it happened," he said to Clair as they walked in the direction of the lawyer's office.

"There," she said, nodding toward a two-story clapboard building with faded white paint. A sign on the window proclaimed The Sleeping Bear, Free Lunch To All.

With Clair in tow, Jake pushed open the door to the saloon and walked inside. She let him lead her, and as she stood there in the entrance a sense of foreboding swept over her that was almost too much to stand. Everything looked the same, as though time had stood still.

The floor was littered with sawdust. The bar was the same, painted black and scarred across the front from the toes of too many boots. The same stern-faced bartender was stationed strategically near the end closest to the door.

Two cowboys were trying their luck bucking the tiger—a futile effort, she knew. No one ever won at faro. Sunlight filtered through dirty windows to illuminate the inside. The place smelled of stale beer and tobacco.

Conversation ceased as they stood in the doorway.

All eyes turned to her and Jake, and she couldn't help wondering who held their interest.

If Jake noticed he didn't show it. "Now explain to me exactly what happened," he instructed quietly, for her ears only.

Those present seemed to whisper a word or two, then, evidently losing interest, went back to whatever they'd been doing.

Not wanting to relive the ordeal, yet knowing that he was trying to help, Clair dragged in a steadying breath and started. "It was Saturday night and the place was full because it was also payday. I was seated about here—" she pointed to a table two feet away "—playing poker with three…no, four cowboys." She tried to picture that night in her mind.

"Do you know their names? Would they remember playing poker with you?" Jake's experience came to the fore.

Her brows drew down. "I don't know their names."

The table was empty and so they went there and sat down. Her skirt billowed around her legs and onto the floor, sawdust clinging to the linen.

Jake straddled his chair. His hand rested lightly on the curved wood. "Were they from a local ranch?"

Thoughtfully, she gave a slight shake of her head. "It was so busy that night. There was a lot of talk about a bank robbery a day's ride east in Harmony." She was thinking out loud. "One of the men mentioned the XJT was taking their money out of the bank here, just in case…so, yes, I guess at least some of them were local."

"Good. Okay." He gave her a smile. "So I can go out there and talk to them."

"Why? What for? I left them to go to my room."

"Yes, honey, I know, but they might have seen something you didn't. One of them might have seen the sheriff going up the stairs. Which way were you facing?" He thumbed his hat back and scanned the room.

"This way." She indicated the door.

"See? One of them might have seen the sheriff when you weren't looking," he said encouragingly.

Her hands splayed lightly across the table's gouged surface and she let her mind drift. She wanted there to be something, some piece of evidence that cleared her of murder, that showed what she'd done was self-defense, nothing more. In this part of the world, self-defense was excusable, murder wasn't.

So they sat there, Clair not knowing what exactly she'd expected to find or, for that matter, what Jake expected her to find. Perhaps nothing. Perhaps everything.

"Did you see the sheriff at all that day?" he asked, reaching across to touch her hand lightly as he spoke, drawing her back into the conversation.

"Yes. Yes, I saw him earlier."

"Was he here? Did anyone see you talking to him?"

The memories flitted at the edge of her mind like the flash of fireflies—here first, and then quickly gone, only to appear again in some other place, some other form.

"The sheriff was in that night. Early," she said, her eyes drifting closed in thought.

"Did you play cards with him?"

"No." She shifted in the chair. "He was at the bar, drinking. I remember because I looked up several times and saw him staring at me.'' Bile rose in her throat at the memory of his drunken leer.

"Did he say anything to you?"

"No. We'd argued earlier in the day and he—"

"Argued? Where?" Jake's tone was urgent.

"Here."

"Did anyone see you or hear the argument?"

"I don't…" She paused, trying to sift through the memories. "I remember I was coming downstairs." She glanced at the staircase near the back of the saloon. "I was hungry and was going to the restaurant to get an early dinner…so it must have been about four in the afternoon. He was there." She pointed to a table at the foot of the staircase.

Jake looked over. A couple of locals, men in brown suit jackets with ties loosened, sat at the indicated table. He could just imagine her hesitation, her fear, as she spotted this man waiting, blocking her path. Rage welled up in him, but he quickly tamped it down, needing to concentrate.

"All right, honey, then what did he say?"

That afternoon came to Clair as clear as day. "The usual things."

When she looked around, Jake was frowning. His fingers curled tightly around hers in the center of the table. "What *usual* things?"

She felt suddenly embarrassed of what she did or, more precisely, where she worked. She'd always taken rude remarks and explicit offers as part of the job, a part that she'd always turned down. Still, repeating them to Jake made her feel, well, ashamed.

"You know, remarks about being…" She shifted again, sliding her hand free of his. "Do I have to do this? Can't you use your imagination?"

"I don't think I'd better." He leaned in, gripping the edge of the table as he did, and waited.

Clair remembered every insulting crude word, every disgusting touch. She remembered how her stomach had rolled from the heavy scent of alcohol on his breath. She didn't want to repeat these things to Jake.

"Come on, honey," he encouraged.

"He took my hand," she began resolutely, leaving out the part about him rubbing her arm and fondling her breast; humiliated, she'd slapped his hand away and seen the deadly cold rage flash in his eyes. "He said I was a looker and that we...that he and I..." She swallowed and willed the frantic beating of her heart to still. The sound of men's voices filled in around her, and the scent of tobacco burned her nostrils.

Steadier, she continued. "He said this was his town and that if I wanted to stick around I ought to be willing to—" no way was she repeating the obscene words the sheriff had used "—be nice to him." She looked away, only half seeing the saloon, mostly feeling rage and disgust.

Jake was very still, very quiet. He knew or could guess what the bastard had suggested. That earlier rage threatened and he thought that it was a good thing the man was dead already, because if he weren't, Jake would be tempted to hunt him down. "I'm sorry, honey. But it wasn't your fault. Remember, you didn't do anything to be ashamed of."

Clair nodded. "I tried to move around him, but he stopped me with his hand on my...arm." No way was she telling Jake that the bastard had grabbed her around the waist, pushed her against a wall and leaned into her, grinding himself against her as though she was some whore. Oh, Lord, remembering was awful. "He said he'd be seeing me later."

"Then what?"

"I told him to stay the hell away from me. That I wasn't interested." A shiver of revulsion snaked down her back.

"That son of a bitch," Jake hissed, his imagination filling in all the gaps she'd so discreetly glossed over. He'd been in his share of saloons; he knew how men—some men—treated women as if they were property, some object without feelings.

Clair straightened, her sense of pride overcoming her lapse into embarrassment. "Look, this kind of thing happens. Men make mistakes." She shook her head. "I'm a gambler, a woman working in a saloon, and to some men that makes me a whore."

Jake took his hat off and slapped it hard on the scarred surface of the table. "Honey, let's get something clear, okay? You are not a whore, not before and not now. I never thought you were." He kept his eyes riveted on her, willing her to know that he meant what he said. "Even if you were, it wouldn't matter to me. Do you understand? It's you I want, Clair Travers."

Clair felt tears threaten at his words. He was being so nice and she was feeling so guilty and angry and about a hundred other emotions, all of which had to do with loving this exceptional man; all of which had to do with the very real possibility of losing him forever.

For a moment neither spoke.

"Can we go now?" she finally said.

"Honey?"

"Please."

"Okay."

Their chairs scraped the floor, leaving marks in the sawdust. Jake glanced around once more. It was up to him to make a case for her, he knew. He'd brought her here so that he—they—could have a future together. Now he had to put all that lawman training to work.

Standing, Clair moved in front of him, heading for the door. Jake was thinking out loud, looking around as he did. "If we could find someone who heard you argue, heard him *threaten* you, it would show that he intended to—" *Rape you*, he almost said, but couldn't bring himself to say or even think it. "It would show his intentions. That you didn't invite him to your room. That you are the victim here, and that makes it self-defense."

Clair stopped. "This is hopeless."

That's when Clair saw her.

The woman was seated at a table in the back, cast in shadow so that she wouldn't have been noticeable at all except for the sudden flash of sunlight on her gold dress when she moved. Clair remembered that dress, remembered the woman, a short, small-framed woman with hair redder than fire.

As though she was thumbing through a deck of cards, Clair saw images flash before her. A woman on the landing, their eyes meeting, the exchange of a greeting as the woman preceded Clair down the stairs. The woman poised at the end of the bar as Clair talked to the sheriff.

Clair's heart was pounding as she looked at Jake.

"She—" Clair nodded with her head "—she heard us."

The woman watched them warily as they closed in on her. She even made to leave, but Jake discreetly blocked her path and she sat down again.

Quietly Jake said, "We'd like a word with you."

Chapter Sixteen

Dammit. This wasn't supposed to happen. Buck Hilliard paced the length of the marshal's office, six short steps from the two cells in the back to the dirty front window. He paused long enough to see them going into The Sleeping Bear saloon.

He leaned in, shielding his eyes from the afternoon sun. What the hell were those two about? He straightened. He had a bad feeling, especially about that sheriff.

He thrust one hand through his hair, the greasy strands falling right back into his face in a way that annoyed the hell out of him. Not nearly so much as those two, though. He was angry, teeth-grinding angry. The damned stupid woman was supposed to be a million miles from here by now. Was she crazy coming back here? What did she hope to prove?

Ah, now, that gave him pause, and he ran over the events of that night in his mind. The early part he didn't remember too well, what with having consumed a considerable amount of whiskey. He did remember rounding up Lily, and the two of them heading up to her room for a tumble.

Yeah. He'd been well in the saddle, riding Lily hard the way she liked it, when a gunshot had bounced off the walls and sent him careening out of bed, his manhood limp as a Chinese noodle.

He'd been madder than hell and, stuffing himself into the trousers he'd bothered to take off, he'd grabbed up his gun and slammed out the door.

Four steps and she'd banged right into him. Well, hell, it didn't take a genius to figure what had happened.

Bert Atkins had tried to get it on with the wrong woman. Hell, Buck could have told him she wasn't no ordinary saloon type. He ought to know—he'd tried to corner her himself and got a knee in the crotch for his trouble.

He gritted his teeth at the memory of that encounter. Damn her. He knew her kind, too good to spread her legs for ordinary men...not too good to take their money, though. Nope, she didn't mind doing that, all right.

Well, Buck hadn't minded Atkins being dead. Matter of fact, he'd been right pleased, considering they'd had a run-in early in the day over the split of a little money they'd, well, sort of inherited, he thought with a cheeky grin.

But he'd grabbed the woman anyway and was half intending to haul her in for the shooting after the way she'd treated him. But that was when he'd got a better look.

The woman was struggling, ranting about self-defense and him letting her go. Trying to hold on to her was like trying to hold on to a damned tornado. Then out of the corner of his eye he'd seen Atkins's fingers move and he'd known the bastard wasn't dead.

A slow smile curved up his lips and he ambled over to his desk.

Yeah, he was too smart for Atkins, that was for damned sure. In a heartbeat, a perfect plan had flashed bright in his head. No sense wasting a perfectly good shooting.

Nope. He'd just let her go.

That smile of his got a touch bigger. In ten seconds he'd picked up the gun and finished the job. It had been easy.

There'd she'd been, running out the back door, men shouting and chasing her and Buck leading them. Perfect. Why, those dumb fools had been so taken with the way Buck organized a posse and all, they'd appointed him the new marshal right then and there.

Lord, it couldn't have been any more perfect if he'd planned it. Atkins dead and her taking the blame.

Perfect, until she'd shown up with that sheriff in tow.

His smile faded and he sank into his desk chair. Yeah, she could try to prove self-defense, but it wouldn't do her no good. Buck was smarter than her, smarter than that lawman she had drooling after her. Buck was smarter than old Bert.

He glanced around his office and rubbed the cuff of his shirt on the badge pinned conspicuously to his chest. He was the law in this town. People in this town believed pretty much anything he said, and he said she killed Atkins in cold blood.

Let her prove it wasn't true.

He glanced up in time to spot them coming out of

the saloon and heading down the street, probably to that smart-mouth eastern lawyer's office.

He followed them with his eyes until they disappeared from his line of vision. Yup, that's where they were headed, all right.

Buck lounged back, propped his feet on the desk and picked up his magazine.

See all the lawyers you want, lady. You're dead. You just don't know it yet.

The lawyer's name was Hartsell, Sam Hartsell, and he was from Baltimore, he told them. He had come to Texas a year ago with his family when the doctor had told him the dry air would help with the ache in his joints.

Sam was medium height with thinning gray hair and a round face that was well lined. He wore a three-piece suit of dark brown with a white shirt, and he fussed with straightening his tie as he spoke. He smiled and offered his hand immediately, then offered them chairs and even adjusted the shades to make sure the sun was out of Clair's face.

He had an easy way about him that Jake warmed to right away. This was no small thing, considering Jake had about as much use for lawyers as he had for coyotes—all scavengers, in his mind. Still, he needed one.

Introductions were made all around, and Sam settled into his chair behind the large walnut desk, where papers were stacked neatly in one corner and a kerosene lamp was perched on another.

Jake took in the office in one quick glance. The room was rectangular and neat. One wall was filled with oak bookcases jammed with law books. Light came in through the two windows on the north wall.

Clair sat nearest the window, Jake nearer the bookcases. Leaning forward, elbows on his knees, he said, "We're looking for someone willing to represent us."

"Well, that's my business," Sam replied, shifting to rest one elbow on the chair's arm. "I hope it's not divorce. You look like a very nice couple."

Jake straightened and made a small sound at the back of his throat that could have been a chuckle. "Thanks. No, it's not like that—it's more serious, I'm afraid. We need a lawyer for a murder trial." He hooked his hat on his knee and waited for the word to sink in. It took only about one second.

"Murder?" Sam's bushy eyebrows shot up in surprise. "Who's been murdered?"

Jake glanced at Clair, then said, "Do you remember when Marshal Atkins was shot?"

"Yes. Yes, I do. They said some wh— Excuse me, saloon girl…" He looked at Clair with new interest. "Sheriff McConnell, maybe you better tell me just who's accused and what you expect me to do."

"Miss Travers here is the accused and she needs representation." Jake met his gaze square on. "It was self-defense, Mr. Hartsell."

"Self-defense, huh?" he muttered in a tone that dripped skepticism.

"Yes. Self-defense. She's not saying she didn't shoot him. She is saying that he came to her room and tried to rape her."

Sam's gaze shot to Jake. "Rape? I thought women like—" Sam shifted in his chair, looking uncomfortable. "Look, I'm not so sure I'm the one to handle this case. I mean, it seems pretty clear that she, that you..." He started shuffling papers on his desk in a polite sort of dismissal. "Let me get you the name of a man in Langston. It's only about a day's trip south." He kept shuffling paper. "He's better at this than I am."

Jake wasn't having any of it. He needed a lawyer, but more than that he figured this was as good a place as any to start convincing people that Clair was innocent of murder. "Now, you listen to me—"

"Do you have a wife, Mr. Hartsell?" Clair spoke up for the first time, her voice soft and calm.

Jake paused.

Hartsell looked suspiciously at her. "Yes. Yes, I do."

"Have you been married a long time?" she asked.

"Nearly thirty years this October," he said proudly.

"You're a man who takes care of his wife—I can see that."

"Of course." Sam puffed up a bit, hooking his thumb in the pocket of his brown vest.

Clair stood and went to the window, lifting the shade a small bit with the tips of two fingers. She spoke as she looked out. "But what if you died today, Mr. Hartsell, what would your wife do to survive? How would she eat, pay for a place to sleep, buy clothes? There are very few choices in ways to earn a living. Cooking, cleaning, marrying the first man who asks, or perhaps selling her—"

"Miss Travers, you forget yourself!"

Clair dropped the shade and turned on him. "No, sir, you forget yourself. You forget what it's like for a woman alone." She closed on him. Bracing her arms on the edge of the desk, she leaned in. "I'm not a whore, Mr. Hartsell."

Sam looked startled, then embarrassed. "I never accused you—"

"Yes, Mr. Hartsell, you did. The minute you found out that I work in a saloon you assumed the worst. I'm a gambler. Nothing more—and even if I were, does that mean I deserve to be raped?"

Sam's cheeks mottled red with embarrassment. "Certainly not!"

"Well, Mr. Hartsell, that's what happened. I had already refused the marshal earlier in the day, and when I went back to my room that night he was there, drunk and waiting for me. When I tried to send him packing, he grabbed me and...and tore my clothes. We struggled and I got hold of his gun." She looked at him then, unwanted tears glistening in her eyes. "What would your wife have done under the same circumstances?"

"Why, Addie would give the man what for, I can tell you. She's a real scrapper—" Sam rubbed his chin thoughtfully, and a smile started in his eyes and then tugged on his lips. "Miss Travers, you're a persuasive speaker."

Clair straightened. "Does that mean you'll take the case?"

"It means I'll listen while you answer some more questions."

"Fair enough, Mr. Hartsell. Fair enough."

For the next hour and a half Sam asked and Clair and Jake answered, and when they were finished...

"Miss Travers, you have yourself a lawyer."

The trial started on Wednesday, a week after they had arrived. Court was held in the church. The pews were full—probably more than on any Sunday, Jake thought, shouldering his way in. He wore his badge and gun, so that people would see him giving his support to Clair.

Sam and Clair were there at a small table. Clair managed a weak smile as Jake gave her an affectionate pat on the shoulder.

"I stopped off to make sure Lily is coming over from the saloon," he told her as she angled her head around. "She is."

Clair had on a new dress they'd bought yesterday at the mercantile. It was light blue with tiny white stripes and complemented her eyes, he thought.

"You look lovely," he told her, his hand still resting lightly on her shoulder. Her golden hair was up, tiny wisps framing her delicate face.

"Thanks," she replied, her voice slightly weak and shaky. She looked pale as a winter ghost and he noticed she had a death grip on the arms of the chair.

"Sam." Jake shook his hand. Sam was decked out in his courtroom best, Jake supposed—a three-piece blue suit and white shirt. "You all set?"

Sam's expression was somber. "Ready as we'll ever be, I guess."

Jake would have liked a little more reassurance. He took his seat, wedging in between the arm of the pew and an overly plump white-haired woman who made no secret of resenting Jake's intrusion in what she considered her space. Too bad. No way was he going to be any farther from Clair than he had to be.

The judge's name was Frankle. Jake had met him a couple of days ago when he and Sam had gone to get him to waive bail. He'd agreed to let Clair stay out of jail on Jake's word that she'd be there for trial. Jake had been in a few courtrooms in his time and he sized the judge up as a fair man, which Sam confirmed. That was a good beginning, a good omen. He needed all the help he could get, from whatever source. Justice would prevail, he was sure.

Jury selection took less than three hours. It was a lottery of sorts—local townspeople's names in a hat, a few questions from each lawyer and the person was kept or dismissed. Jake didn't think he would have changed anyone.

The prosecutor, Bob Wendell, was tall and lanky with hardly enough meat on his bones to fill out his black striped suit. His hair was blond, almost white, his skin tan and, for all his thinness, he looked as if he spent more time outdoors than in a courtroom. He appeared too eager to get going. He had notes spread out in front of him on the table. His witnesses were lined up on the pew behind him like blackbirds on a wire, and Jake could see the man felt confident about his case.

Jake was worried—but that was only natural, he told himself for about the hundredth time. He didn't care how many witnesses Wendell had. He knew that it would come down to Clair and Hilliard.

Clair was smart and poised and telling the truth. Hilliard—Jake glanced around the room, spotting the man skulking in the back—was a devious bastard whom Jake hadn't liked from the beginning.

Besides, Clair had convinced Sam Hartsell of her truthfulness, and she would convince the men on this jury. If they needed more, they had Lily, who was willing to say she'd seen Clair send the marshal packing on that afternoon, which confirmed Clair's statement that she had not invited or encouraged Atkins.

Jake had also found some of the local cowboys willing to say that she played an honest game of poker, never made overtures to them and did not appear to have been drinking on the night of the shooting. He looked around and spotted them in the third row. They were slicked up like Saturday night for their day in court. Feeling better, he settled back against the hard wood of the pew.

"All right." The judge banged his gavel several times. "This court is in session. There'll be no talking except by the witnesses or I'll have everyone removed from this room. Is that understood?" He glared at the spectators, who quieted down immediately. Satisfied, he said, "Mr. Wendell, you can call your first witness."

"Call Ed Hodge."

The first day was spent listening to witnesses tell how they'd seen Clair playing cards, seen her talking to the sheriff on several occasions. They testified that she did indeed work in a saloon. There was testimony from several sources about the morals of women who worked in saloons. The minister categorized them as fallen angels, and the local temperance-league president, who was booed as she got on the stand, said that women gambling, liquor, saloons—the list went on for quite a while—were all an abomination.

Sam, Jake was glad to see, objected strenuously to all of this as hearsay and irrelevant, having nothing to do with the issue, but the judge allowed it, saying it spoke about character and motivation. Jake didn't like it, but he knew it was probably correct. The jury could figure it out.

Jake knew Hilliard's testimony was coming. He kept glancing over at the marshal, who was standing by one of the four windows that lined each side of the church. Hilliard was wearing a white shirt with black trousers, and his greasy blond hair was slicked back from his clean-shaven face. He had a smug look on his face, like a cat toying with a mouse.

That look made Jake nervous. Hilliard was up to something, but what? In the days since they'd arrived, Jake had spoken to the man a few times and disliked his attitude more with each conversation. Jake had tried to question the man, since he was the one who'd been there that night. But every time the questions got down to why he let Clair go and what happened after, the man seemed vague.

Jake's lawman instincts told him Hilliard was holding something back, maybe even lying. Why? As he waited through the long afternoon of endless superficial questions, an eerie sense of foreboding coiled tight in Jake's stomach.

Hilliard was the last to testify.

"So, Marshal," Wendell began, "tell us what happened on the night Marshal Atkins was murdered."

Jake bristled at the word but, since it was a murder trial, he could say nothing.

Hilliard seemed to be enjoying himself, settling comfortably in the chair, legs crossed casually at the knee. "Well, I heard the shot and, being the deputy marshal, of course I ran straightaway to see what was going on. 'Course, I never expected to find the marshal...murdered," he finished on a low, accusatory tone. "There he was, lying on the floor of her room. Right next to the bed."

There was general mumbling in the court. All eyes

in the courtroom turned to Clair, who faced the man defiantly, chin up, though inside she was shaking harder than a San Francisco earthquake.

The judge banged his gavel and everyone fell silent again, each seeming to hang on every word Hilliard spoke.

"Go on, Marshal," Wendell prompted.

"Well, when I got there, she—"

"You mean the defendant, Miss Travers?"

"Yeah, her. She was trying to run out of the room."

"Did she have a gun?" Wendell asked, standing near the jury.

"She sure did," Hilliard returned.

"How did she get away from you, Marshal?"

Hilliard shook his head as though embarrassed. "I'm ashamed to say I was so surprised by seeing my old friend dead, seeing his murdered body, blood running onto the floor…"

Several women in the courtroom groaned at Hilliard's blunt description.

"Yes. Yes," Wendell encouraged. "What then?"

"Well, she just ran right past me before I could think to stop her. By the time I took notice, the boys had come up from downstairs and was blocking the doorway, you know?"

"Yes, we understand." Wendell nodded, and Jake noticed that so did several of the men on the jury. Evidently they'd been in the saloon that night.

"What did you do next, Marshal?"

"Why, we got up a posse and took off after her, but it was night and she, well, she got around us. You know, her type can hide anywheres."

It all sounded plausible, sounded reasonable. It was

not quite a lie, but Jake knew it wasn't the truth, either. Clair had told him how Hilliard had caught her, how he'd *let* her go. It was possible Hilliard was trying to cover his incompetence. Now that, Jake could believe. It sure as hell wasn't kindness that had made the man let Clair go. There was something else going on here, but what?

Chapter Seventeen

The morning of the second day dawned cloudy. But the lack of sun didn't keep the heat down. If anything, it seemed hotter than the day before. The court was just as crowded. Didn't anybody in this town have anything else to do? Jake wondered.

He was tense. He and Clair had sat up most of the night talking. Jake had promised, reassured. Clair had said very little. She was scared. He knew it. Finally they'd gone to bed and he'd held her through the rest of the night, had felt her body tremble, and once in the darkness he'd thought she was crying, but she'd denied it when he asked. He kept telling himself and her that the law and justice would see the truthfulness of her story and she'd be exonerated. They'd be free.

She'd refused breakfast this morning. Jake had ordered food but hadn't had any stomach for it, either, so he'd settled for coffee, which was now swirling in his stomach like kerosene.

Side by side, he and Clair had walked to the court, not touching, not talking. Jake wondered for the first time what he would do if they lost, if he lost her. It was a concept too terrible to even consider.

The prosecution had rested yesterday after Hilliard's testimony. This morning Sam was ready to go. Last night, over dinner, he'd talked to Clair, asking her the questions he'd ask today, helping her form her answers to give the most information as briefly as possible. He said juries had notoriously short attention spans. He'd instructed her on speaking directly to the jury, on speaking quietly and slowly and keeping her expression serious—something she said she'd have no trouble doing.

Sam put two cowboys on the witness stand first, and they testified to Clair's honesty at cards, which the prosecution characterized as not being caught cheating. The same men said she'd been polite, reserved and had not in any way made overtures to them or anyone they knew. The prosecution characterized that as them simply not having enough money to buy her after she'd won all their cash at cards.

Jake's temper moved up with each snide remark. Muscles tensed and his hands naturally curled into fists. Who the hell did this Wendell think he was? No one talked about Clair like that. No one.

But he tried to keep his temper, knowing it wouldn't do Clair any good for him to lose it now. He told himself these were just courtroom tricks. Still, it was damned tough to sit and listen to someone slander the woman he loved.

Sam objected to the malicious statements. Wendell countered, and the two lawyers and the judge were suddenly in a verbal battle.

Jake leaned forward and touched Clair on the arm. "Okay?" The question was one of those foolish ones people asked when the answer was obviously the opposite. A blind man could see she wasn't okay. How could she be? She was shaking like a leaf and the look in her eyes was stark terror. Fear, like a predator, circled the edges of Jake's mind. If he lost her...

It was late morning when Sam said, "Call Miss Travers to the stand."

Jake couldn't have been prouder of Clair on the stand. She was self-composed and direct. She told them the marshal had been waiting uninvited in her room. He'd tried to rape her and they'd struggled. She'd gotten the gun and fired, then, frightened, she'd fled. She said she realized now that she should have stayed and told the truth then, but she'd been afraid.

When Wendell tried to shake her story, accusing her of everything including being a liar and a cheat, she remained calm as Sam had instructed. Too bad Jake hadn't listened more closely. When Wendell hinted broadly that Clair was a whore, well, for Jake that was it.

"You son of a bitch!" He was out of his chair and halfway across the courtroom intent on doing some serious bodily harm. Lucky for Wendell, some fast-thinking men restrained him.

Spectators surged to their feet. Men shouted for or against him—Jake couldn't tell, didn't care.

The judge banged his gavel and Wendell, visibly shaken, cowered near his table.

"You call her that again and no one will save you," Jake yelled, twisting to break free of the four men who held him.

"Sheriff, sit down!" the judge ordered.

His gaze flew to Clair, who was on her feet, one hand extended as though to reach him.

"Please, Jake..."

Jake quieted. He shook free of his captors and straightened his shirt. "I'm not letting him call her names," he fired back at the judge.

The judge surged to his feet. "Sheriff, I'm warning you."

Grudgingly, Jake nodded. The judge turned his fierce glare on Wendell. "No more name-calling, Mr. Wendell. Stick to the facts, or else you'll find yourself in contempt of court."

"Yes, Judge," a wide-eyed Wendell managed to say.

"All right," the judge admonished the room in general. "Everyone sit down!"

There was a general mumbling and grumbling as people settled back in the pews.

When the room was quiet, Sam turned to face the spectators. "I call Lily Jones." All eyes turned to the back of the courtroom and the woman standing just inside the door.

Jake swiveled around like everyone else. Lily looked like a frightened sparrow, dressed as she was in a faded brown dress that was too small for her slender frame. Of course, that red hair of hers set her in a class no sparrow was ever in.

Seated on the witness stand, she was clearly uncomfortable. She tugged at the high collar and squirmed inside the long sleeves. She looked at those present with a sort of blank-eyed stare that seemed both protective and aloof.

"Sure I remember her," she said to Sam's question.

"How do you remember her?" Sam moved up closer, stopping right beside the witness chair.

Lily angled around slightly to look at him. "She

come into town and set up gambling at the back table in The Sleeping Bear.''

"Where you work."

She stiffened. "Yeah. I work there. What of it?" She pushed at her upswept hair nervously.

"No offense, Miss Jones. No offense. Just trying to establish that you were in a position to see and know the defendant."

Lily eyed him suspiciously but remained silent.

Sam walked to his table and appeared to be searching for something among his papers. After about thirty seconds, he turned slowly. "Now, Miss Jones, do you remember the night in question?"

"What?"

"The night that Marshal Atkins was shot?"

"Ah, yeah, sure." Her blue eyes grew large before settling on Hilliard, who gave the barest of nods. Jake would have missed it if he hadn't been looking right at the man. What the hell was going on? Why would Lily need Hilliard's encouragement?

"Can you tell us what happened?"

"I was going into my room when I seen Atkins on the landing. I remember hoping he wasn't looking for me."

"Why's that, Miss Jones?"

She crossed her legs and every man there got a good view of black silk almost to the knee. "'Cause Atkins was a mean son of a bitch when he was drinkin'."

There were a couple of audible gasps from the women in the audience at her choice of words. Sam paused—to give the jury a moment to absorb this revelation, Jake knew. He wandered over and rummaged in his papers again.

"And was he drinking that night?" He was facing the audience, his back to Lily.

"Yeah." She tugged at her collar again. "I could smell it a mile away."

"Ah," Sam muttered, pausing again. "Did you see Marshal Atkins with Miss Travers in the afternoon?"

"Yeah."

"What did you see?"

"Well…" Jake saw the woman's gaze flick to Hilliard again. That niggling feeling of unease got a touch stronger in his gut.

Lily continued. "I seen her coming down the stairs and I seen the marshal…Atkins, not Buck," she amended strongly. "Atkins was sorta waiting for her."

"Can you describe what you mean?" Sam pressed.

"Well, you know, he was drinkin' and when she come along he sorta sidled up to her kinda friendly like."

"Could you hear what he said?"

"Oh, sure, he weren't making no secrets. He was telling her he wanted a piece."

Sam looked surprised. "Excuse me?"

"You know," Lily continued, casual as you please, "he wanted to get a poke, you know, to get in her—"

"Yes," Sam interrupted, "I think we all know what you mean."

There was some laughter from some of the men. Jake was not laughing.

"What did Miss Travers say?" Sam asked.

"Oh, she told him to go to hell." Lily beamed and gave a triumphant nod in Clair's direction.

"I see, so then is it fair to say they were not on friendly terms?"

"I guess you could say that."

"Then about later that night," Sam asked. "You said you heard the shot, is that right, Miss Jones?"

At the mention of the shot, Lily's whole demeanor changed, or at least Jake thought so. She'd been uncomfortable before, but now her brow drew down and she went very still. Her gaze kept flicking to Hilliard as though for support—or answers, perhaps? Was Hilliard paying her, bribing her to lie?

Jake didn't like the look of this. That fear he'd been holding at bay got a little closer.

"Yeah," Lily announced, "I heard them shots."

Sam was looking at Clair when she answered. As the words registered, he spared Jake a glance as if to see if he'd heard the same thing. He had.

Shots? More than one? That was the first he'd known of it. Clair had always told him that she fired once. Swiveling in her chair, Clair said, "But I—"

Jake stopped her with a shake of his head. He didn't want anything to distract Lily.

He and Sam exchanged another fleeting glance before Sam said, quite calmly, "I'm sorry, Miss Jones, I didn't hear what you said. Did you say you heard the shots?"

"Yeah." She scooted forward on the edge of the chair. "Me and Buck—Buck Hilliard, the new sheriff," she added proudly, and gave him a lovesick look that was so obvious no one could mistake it. The woman was grinning from ear to ear as though she'd just won the prize at the county fair. "Me and Buck was, well…we was sleeping." There was a snickering in the audience. Lily glared at those doing the chuckling. Buck, Jake noted, was grimacing like a man who was embarrassed. This was, after all, his town. He had to be elected here, and having your supporters laugh at you wasn't a good sign.

"You were saying, Miss Jones?" Sam asked.

"I, uh, the shot near to scared us both to dead. Buck was madder'n a bee-stung bear and he stormed outta the room to see what the devil was going on."

"And where were you?"

"I was still... I was lookin' for my wrapper."

More snickering.

"Well, I was, wasn't I, Buck?"

There was no reply from the scowling marshal.

"Go on, Miss Jones."

"So I heard Buck's voice talkin' to someone and then I started out the door to see what was happening."

"Did you see the defendant?"

"Who?"

"Miss Travers?" Sam gestured in Clair's direction.

Lily gave her a smile that revealed one broken front tooth. "Oh, sure, I seen her run down the hall and out the back door."

"I see," Sam muttered. "Now, you're sure about this?"

"Sure I'm sure."

"So then if you saw the woman running out the back door, when did you hear the second shot?"

"Why, a minute later I—" Lily went very still, then pale. Her gaze riveted on Buck Hilliard. She squirmed in the chair as though it was full of ants. "I, uh, I heard the second shot right after the first one, of course," she said, her tone daring him to deny her statement.

Damn.

McConnell, you're not doing your job.

He should have checked. He should have talked to more people, to those who were there.

Two damned shots. Why would there be two shots? Was Clair mistaken? Every time they'd talked she'd been adamant she'd fired once and that was by accident—the gun going off in the struggle. She'd said it had actually fallen from her hand, the kick had been so bad.

Then she'd run—right into Buck Hilliard, who'd let her go. Why?

Questions were ticking off in Jake's mind. He wasn't liking the answers he was getting.

Sam was finishing his questions. "Miss Jones, did you see anyone with a gun?"

"No."

"Did you see the defendant with a gun?"

"No."

"Thank you."

Jake was only half listening. A possibility was forming in his mind and he didn't like the picture.

Atkins was dead after two shots, that was for sure, but had he been dead after one? Jake had a bad feeling he hadn't.

If Atkins hadn't been dead and if Clair had fired only one shot, then only one person could have fired that second shot, the fatal shot.

Slowly he pivoted and looked right at Buck Hilliard. Buck's gaze settled on Jake. It was as though a silent understanding passed between them. Buck tore his gaze away and slipped quietly out the door.

With terrifying certainty Jake knew Buck Hilliard was a cold-blooded killer, and there wasn't a damned bit of evidence to prove it. None.

For the first time, Jake's faith in the law wavered.

Sam's summation was direct and to the point. He faced the jury, moving slowly along the line, making sure to catch each man's attention. He told them Clair was a gambler, not a murderer. She'd been defending herself—as any woman would do—against a drunken man who'd tried to force himself on her earlier in the day then had come to her room that night. There was some doubt, Sam said, about when the sheriff had died and by whose hand, since Clair had fired only one shot. Sam talked about justice and fairness and lack of evidence.

Then it was the prosecutor's turn. Wendell took a more blunt approach.

"Gentlemen. Clair Travers is a murderer. She has admitted to being in the room with the marshal, which has been verified by our present marshal, Buck Hilliard. She has admitted to shooting Marshal Atkins. The woman claims self-defense but, gentlemen, women have been scorning the advances of men, if in fact the marshal did make advances, for a long time without having to resort to murder. Did she scream for help? No. Did she try to run away? No. These are all the reactions of a genuinely terrified woman. But Miss Travers isn't an ordinary woman. She's a woman who works in saloons, earns her living gambling with men. Miss Travers is a woman who knows how to handle men better than any woman here. It's her stock-in-trade.

"No, gentlemen, Miss Travers deliberately murdered Marshal Atkins and, in the name of justice, I demand that you find her guilty as charged."

Jake watched the faces of the men on the jury. Most were schooled, but it appeared to him that a couple seemed to be nodding at Wendell's remarks.

He hoped it was only reflex. He feared it wasn't. Jake felt totally helpless and scared.

The jury was out only an hour.

Jake and Clair were in Sam Hartsell's office when the word came. Relief and worry merged in his gut. Clair sat silently by the window, seeming to look out on the street, though Jake had a strong suspicion she was only pretending. Lord knew he was only pretending when he said, "It's a good sign, honey. They know the evidence is clear that it was self-defense." He took her in his arms, holding her. She stood there lifelessly, limp. He felt her body tremble. Putting her slightly away from him, he looked into her eyes. "Honey, don't worry. It'll be all right." It was a prayer he'd been saying to himself ever since they'd left the courtroom.

"Well, we'd better go." Sam spoke up.

They made the short walk back to the court. The last few spectators were filing in, their expressions eager, as though something wonderful was about to happen, instead of it being a woman's life about to be decided upon.

Clair and Sam took their places at the little table. Jake settled in right behind them on the pew.

The judge entered. The jury filed in, feet scraping on the floor, chairs sliding as they got themselves seated. Jake looked at each man's face, trying to determine the outcome. It was impossible. They all looked cemetery somber.

The judge leaned forward, his hands clasped in front of him. "All right, Mr. Watts," the judge began, "you boys have a verdict?"

"Yup, we sure do," Watts replied, standing.

Jake leaned forward, elbows on his knees, straining, wishing for the verdict he so desperately wanted. Heart pounding in his chest, he held his breath. *Please.*

"Let's hear it, then," the judge ordered.

The room was suddenly silent, as though everyone was holding their breath in anticipation. Jake knew he was. He reached out a hand to Clair, touching her lightly on the top of her arm.

Watts stood and held up a piece of paper, which he read from. "We, the jury, find the woman, Clair Travers...guilty as charged."

"No," Clair said on a sharply expelled breath. She shook her head in denial of what had been said.

This couldn't be happening. This was wrong.

Guilty.

The word ricocheted in her brain like a gunshot. Panic consumed her.

Dear God, this has to be a mistake.

More frightened than she'd been that night, she swung around to look at Jake. Jake would help her. Jake wouldn't let this happen. One look at his stunned expression and she knew it was true. Her greatest fear was all too real.

Guilty.

She made a conscious effort to breathe.

A cold numbness settled in her, as though to still the fear, the stark terror, of what was to come.

There was general mumbling in the court as voices of affirmation and a few of disbelief could be heard. The judge banged his gavel. "Order! I want order in this court!"

People slowly stopped talking and the judge said, "Clair Travers."

At Sam's nudge, she stood. Her knees wobbled and threatened to fold under her. Sam grabbed her arm.

"You've been found guilty of murder and it's my duty to pronounce sentence. Do you have anything to say?"

"I've admitted that I shot Marshal Atkins, but I did so to protect myself. I did what any man or woman in this room would have done, under the same circumstances. I did the only thing I could without allowing myself to be raped. I make no apology for defending myself. It may have been the wrong thing, but I did it for the right reason."

There was silence in the room after she spoke.

"Very well, then, Miss Travers. For the murder of Marshal Atkins, I sentence you to twenty years in the prison in Galveston."

Clair sank into her chair. Twenty years. She felt as though a fog was enveloping her, blurring all she saw and heard.

Jake was on his feet, moving to her, prepared to fight, to kill if necessary to protect her.

Hand on his gun, he squared off against the entire room, as if that were possible. "No! No! This isn't right. What the hell kind of court is this? She's not the one you want. Can't you see that?"

The judge banged his gavel again. The court erupted in a ruckus. Jurors stood, and some glared back at Jake. One man said, "We ain't takin' no whore's word over a man like our marshal."

Jake grabbed Clair, pulling her into his arms. This was wrong. They were wrong. He wasn't letting her go.

The judge banged his gavel hard on the wooden desk. "Quiet! Order!"

Out of the corner of his eye Jake saw a leering Hilliard moving up, handcuffs obvious in his hands.

"Let's go, lady," he said when he got close

enough. To Jake he said, "You ain't so much now, are ya? Don't worry, I'll take *real* good care of her."

Fury and anger converged in Jake like two raging rivers and he hauled back and slammed his fist, bone-breaking hard, into Hilliard's smirking face.

Blood oozed down Hilliard's chin. Blood trickled out of the split on his lip. He touched the injury with his hand, then looked at the blood as though in disbelief. "Why, you whoring bastard!" Hilliard lunged for Jake, which was just fine with him. Jake landed another blow to the gut and Hilliard doubled over, dropping to one knee as he clutched his stomach.

"Stop it!" the judge hollered. He kept banging his gavel. "You men there, break that fight up!"

Men moved in, pushing Jake back, away from a sniveling Hilliard, who was curled up on the floor.

His rage only slightly eased, he went to Clair. He held her tight, her arms wedged up between them, her small fists pressing against his chest. "I'm sorry," he breathed as he kissed her. "Please, God, I'm so sorry."

The judge banged his gavel again. Men helped Hilliard to his feet.

"You and me ain't finished, McConnell," Hilliard snapped, still clutching his gut. "I'll see you later...after I see her."

Jake released Clair and in one motion spun around preparing to finish the job he'd started.

This time it was Sam, along with three other men, who stepped in between. Hands braced on Jake's straining shoulders, Sam said, "This isn't helping any, Jake. Stop it!"

The judge was on his feet, banging his gavel repeatedly. "You men stop this fighting. I won't have this in my court."

Hilliard glared at Jake with an ominously cold expression. He winced, touching his bruised and bloody face. "You'll be sorry, McConnell," he snarled, spitting blood on the floor.

Jake shielded Clair from Hilliard. To the judge he declared, "You're not putting her in that bastard's jail."

The judge looked mad enough to chew nails and spit tacks. Jake didn't care. "Sheriff, you're an officer of the law. I expect better than this from you." He glared at those closest. "I'm not putting Miss Travers in jail. There are no facilities there to accommodate a woman. She'll be locked in a room at the hotel until such time as the prison wagon can arrive. Since Marshal Hilliard seems...indisposed, Mr. Wendell and Mr. Hartsell, I'll expect you to see that Miss Travers is taken to the hotel, given a room and locked in."

"Yes, Your Honor," the men said almost in unison.

Jake still held on to her. "Clair? Honey?"

She looked up at him with tears glistening in her eyes. "We should have gone to New Orleans," she whispered, then stepped out of his embrace.

Helpless, all he could do was watch her walk away. All he could feel was the heart inside him shatter.

Chapter Eighteen

Jake was waiting in Sam Hartsell's office when the lawyer walked in a half hour later. Sam didn't speak, just hooked his hat on the peg by the door then went to his desk.

"How is she?" was the first thing Jake asked.

"She's okay. Mrs. Myers will be keeping an eye on her. She's a good woman, so you don't have to worry there."

"This is all my fault." Jake dropped into the chair. "I was so damned sure that justice would prevail." He gave a bitter laugh. "So much for right." He plucked the badge off his white shirt and revolved the smooth metal around and around in his fingers. "I've spent my adult life thinking that where there was law there was justice, fairness. Now I know it's all just words."

Disgusted, he tossed the badge down on the desk top, the metal clinking against the edge of the lamp. He was through. Today he'd seen what the law was really all about, and he didn't like it, not one bit.

Slowly lifting his gaze to Sam, he said, "How could those idiots believe Hilliard over Clair?"

"Local boy," Sam replied, rummaging in first one desk drawer then another, until he finally found the papers he was looking for. "I'll be filing an appeal right away." He pushed the drawer closed, the wood making a scraping sound as it moved.

Jake paced away to the window, looking out toward the hotel. She was there, alone, frightened, facing twenty years... My God, twenty years.

Agitated, he closed on Sam. "How long will it take to get a hearing?"

Sam was already filling out the official-looking documents. "Could be months." The sad look in his eyes, the thin line of his mouth, said much more than his words.

"In the meantime?" Jake queried, knowing the answer as he asked the question.

Sam shook his head sadly.

"Can we keep her here until then?" Jake asked, hoping against hope.

Again Hartsell shook his head.

"I'm not letting her go to some hellhole." He'd never seen a Texas prison, but if it was even remotely like that stone fortress in Rawlins, it was a nightmare.

"Calm down," Hartsell coaxed.

"The hell I will. I got her into this mess. Me. I'm the one who said, 'Sure, honey, let's go back and clear your name. Justice will see the right.'" He slammed his fist against the wall, the pain shooting lightning-quick up his arm to his shoulder. He didn't care—about the wall or his arm. "Where the hell is justice? You and I both know she's telling the truth. You heard what Lily said about two shots. You know who fired that second shot. You know the only reason to fire a second shot is if the first one wasn't fatal."

"But we can't prove it."

"Ah, the hell with it." Jake slammed out of the office.

He went to the hotel to see Clair. Actually, he demanded to see Clair. His demand was met with a staunch denial, backed up by Mr. Myers, wielding a shotgun.

It wasn't the first time he'd looked down the barrel of a weapon, so he hardly flinched. He offered a bribe—all the money he had, which was about a hundred dollars. The Myerses refused. *Great,* he thought, *finally I find some straight-thinking people in this damned town.*

At last Jake gave up.

Clair, can you forgive me?

Could he forgive himself?

He stormed out of the hotel and headed for the nearest saloon, which just happened to be The Sleeping Bear. The place was nearly full. The crowd had probably come over from the trial, he thought churlishly.

He ordered a drink, grabbed up the bottle and sat at a table in the corner. He was in a bitch of a mood and if anyone thought to say anything to him they wisely refrained from doing so.

He tossed back two drinks in quick succession, the liquor burning the back of his throat but doing little to take the edge off his rage. Yes, Jake was angry, damned angry. Mostly at himself.

The sound of a woman's laugh caught his attention and he glanced around to see Hilliard looking smug and cozy with a blonde at the table near the stairs.

Son of a bitch. Sitting there having a good time while Clair was locked up, waiting to go to prison.

The law might have been followed today, but there'd sure as hell been no justice. Well, the law be damned. Jake McConnell was going see justice done this day!

His hand went instinctively to the gun tied to his leg, his fingers curling around the well-worn handle.

He didn't even remember standing.

He'd taken only one step when a familiar voice and a touch on the arm stopped him. "Sheriff, I wanna talk to you." He didn't have to look to know it was Lily's high-pitched voice.

"Not now," Jake said, his gaze fixed on the target of all that rage, who sat not twenty feet away, swilling whiskey and whispering in the blonde's ear.

Lily's grip on his arm tightened, and he was forced to spare her a glance. He was momentarily surprised to see that she was sporting on her cheek a couple of fresh bruises that hadn't been there yesterday in the courtroom. "But I wanna tell you about that night."

"Did he do this?" He knew the answer. It was pretty obvious that Buck had moved on and Lily had gotten in the way.

"Yeah." She spat out the word, cringing and touching her lips with the tips of two fingers. Anger flashed white-hot in her eyes as she stared past him to the object of their discussion. If looks could kill, Hilliard would have been coyote food, which was pretty much what Jake had in mind anyway.

She dragged out a chair and sat down, her hand still on Jake's arm. With the slightest pressure, she pulled Jake down to the chair beside her.

Jake poured her a drink and she winced when the